WILLIAM EASTLAKE was born in New York, spent his early life in the Delaware River country, then moved to California. He served time in the Army and after the war attended the Alliance Francaise in Paris. On his return to this country he moved to the American Southwest where he continues to live today.

Among William Eastlake's other novels are *Castle Keep, The Bamboo Bed, Dancers in the Scalp House,* and a book of travels entitled *Jack Armstrong in Tangier.*

GO IN BEAUTY

A CLASSIC NOVEL OF THE AMERICAN SOUTHWEST

BY

WILLIAM EASTLAKE

SEVEN WOLVES PUBLISHING

LC Card Number 91-066227

ISBN 0-9627387-3-5

Published by Frank Gargani/Seven Wolves Publishing, Fall, 1991

Cover illustration by Jo Anderson
Cover design by Charles Benefiel

FOR MARTHA AND MARILYN

GO IN BEAUTY

1

Once upon a time there was time. The land here in the Southwest had evolved slowly and there was time and there were great spaces. Now a man on horseback from atop a bold mesa looked out over the violent spectrum of the Indian Country—into a gaudy infinity where all the colors of the world exploded, soundlessly.

"There's not much time," he said.

The young man was confiding things to no one beneath a single buzzard witness sailing in patterned concentric rounds without tracings in the hard, perfect New Mexico blue, way up. Now the young man swung the horse and walked it slowly along a ledge that looked down on the geological southern end of the Rocky Mountains above an unknown wash called the Rio Salado. The Rockies finished in a flaring red Morrison formation set off by a dwindling stripe of white gypsum. The long, giant, heroic Rockies died here in a crumpled flag motion where few people knew.

Closer to the young man but still blued by the distance was the trading post. The post appeared to be set down in the middle of nowhere and surrounded by no one but it was the exact center and capital of the world for the Navahos

1

who called themselves The People and shaped domed houses named hogans that matched the feel and color of the country. The post was big and sprawling and built of enormous logs chinked with adobe and it lay between two mushroom-shaped and bright-colored mesas in the dry heart of the Indian country. Nearby was a low, native-type house made of petrified wood which the young man's ancestors had built. The spread of the buildings was cut off from the outside world, or from what one Indian named Quicker-Than-You called "the violent pretense of reality," by the quiet long mountains and the weird huddled mesas and the blue deep arroyos and total indifference.

Below at the post, the exact center and capital of the world for The People, two Indians crouched at the massive stone root of the petrified-wood house where it made its way into the ground.

"This crack—" Tom-Dick-and-Harry said, tracing it with his brown finger.

"They can fix it," Rabbit Stockings said.

"No," Tom-Dick-and-Harry said, both Indians still crouching outside under the log overhang and beneath the high voices within. He traced the crack again with his brown finger close to the red earth where the stone root entered the ground. "No," Tom-Dick-and-Harry said again. "And perhaps even The People cannot stop something coming apart and beginning here at the center of the world."

Still above and at the edge of the gay and loud-striped mesa, the rider allowed the horse to move up over a beginning sharp and purple butte away from the post and everything below.

The horseman, Alexander Bowman, ran the trading post

with his brother George and his brother George had recently got a beautiful wife. The trading post had been with the Bowman family almost one hundred years. It had passed down through many generations, and when the Indians first saw the new white woman they thought it would get nicely through another. The Indians did not sense anything wrong in the fact that there was only one wife; neither did George Bowman, whose wife she was. George Bowman, like his brother Alexander, was tall, lank, high cheek-boned and black haired, which would have made them look perfect and banal if all these qualities had not been exaggerated. Alexander was older than his brother George and it was he who got his education first, leaving the post with George, and then, of course, George went and got his. And now that George had got a wife the Indians reckoned that it would not be long before Alexander went and got his. That's what George thought too.

But Alexander did not think this. Alexander was a writer and he thought many strange things. But Alexander did not call it thinking, he called it knowing. He knew that George's wife was not happy in the Navaho country. He knew she had been to Paris and when she saw one of the Indians' sand paintings she did not think of The People, she thought of Picasso. He knew she had been to Vassar and when one of the Navaho People talked to her she did not listen to what he said but wondered what went on in his subconscious. Still, she was beautiful and she was not the only one who felt hemmed in by the mesas.

Alexander felt hemmed in by the mesas himself. He was hemmed in by the mesas, the blue mountains and by circumstances. He felt that George's wife had a great deal of

3

understanding along with her great deal of beauty. Together Alexander and Perrette could be with the whole world. Together they could see and feel everything a writer must see and feel, and a writer who is going to be any kind of a writer must see and feel everything.

Alexander Bowman was as certain that he knew this as he was certain that George's wife, Perrette, was in love with him, Alexander. Love was a word that was used loosely and no one seemed to know the meaning of the word but that was one of the discoveries he might make as a writer. But Perrette used the word anyway and with her it meant that now the word "writer" sounded more romantic than the word "trader" had sounded seven months ago. It meant that Paris and Rome and Cap-d'Ail would be exciting to see again and that the romantic idea of living in nowhere with the Indians had worn off. The word love also evidently meant to her that Alexander should play the beautiful joke on his brother of running off with his wife.

No, Alexander thought, a man couldn't rightly do that. Alexander pushed the stick, prodded it into the jaws and sprang the trap. It was a big Victor trap and it went off with a loud clack. The trap had been concealed on a narrow path on the mesa where the big cats had been moving down. A man could just walk out on the whole business, Alexander thought, but then she will leave him anyway. Alexander pushed the big trap with his stick off the ledge so that it hung down on its heavy chain over the sandstone rock of the mesa. Alexander climbed up now over the sheer face to the wide ledge above where his horse waited. He picked up the reins and the horse followed.

Alexander had sprung four traps in the last hour and

picked up two saddle bags of poisoned meat the government had placed. The government policy at the moment was to make coyotes and big cats extinct because the ranchers complained. When the animals that these animals preyed on increased to overrunning proportions, then the farmers would complain and the government would make these animals extinct.

Alexander had spent the morning making traps and poisoned meat extinct. Let nature take care of keeping a population in balance. Once you destroy that balance you would be overrun with something which you have to make extinct too. Eventually everything would be extinct. Alexander already missed the howls of the coyotes that he had grown up with. Nothing else much had changed in the mesa country. The government trapper had come in silently with poisoned meat and taken away the coyote, that was about all that had changed. They were beautiful animals, and clean, he thought, and part of the country and they belonged. With their noises and their swift running and their shadows in the moon, they belonged. But she does not belong, he told himself. With her beauty even, she does not belong.

He had reached a wide basin in the yellow sandstone that was strewn about with concretions, pieces of bowl-shaped soft stone that had once formed around hard objects and were now freed by erosion. They made good ashtrays. There were giant hunks of petrified wood too, and he sat down on one of these. The wood had weathered out of the rocks above and had gotten down to this basin. Soon a loud flood would push it over the cliff and it was at this point below this cliff that they had gathered most of the petrified wood for the house. And it was on this basin, where all the eroded-out

5

objects were scattered neatly about on the surface of the smooth floor, and plainly visible, that he had always searched for fossils. If all those millions of tons of wood had fossilized why had no animals? A good question, a scientist named Cope who had horse wandered from his expedition, based at Gallina, had told old Bowman in 1869. Keep looking.

The Bowmans had looked ever since. Cope would have been proud of their tenacity. Cope, who had discovered the first fossil horse on the same venture, would or should strike off a medal for persistence. And Darwin had written of similar rocks when they tumbled in flood in South America. "The thousands and thousands of stones which, striking against each other made one dull uniform sound, were all hurrying in one direction. The ocean is their eternity and each note of that wild music spoke of one more step toward their destiny." Alexander had memorized that and thought about it each time it rained rocks off the cliff. It would be nice to be able to write as exactly as that.

He had come to this basin which looked out over the wide Indian Country to write ever since he was a boy. It was just at the ponderosa line in back of the basin, in creative revery over a stroke of genius (which he tore up in the clear revealing light of another day), that he had tumbled into a mine shaft, an abortive project that the courageous Conquistadores in the name of God and at the price of fifty heathen Indians, had sunk in vain. Alexander had spent three days there until George had got him out.

Alexander pulled on the reins of the horse now from his seat on the petrified palm trunk. The palm trunk was an exactly preserved anachronism from the days before the land pushed up when this dry, empty country was dense and lush

and steaming, hanging with monkeys, primordial and rife. His horse, Fireboy, standing awkward in front of him, had picked up some cactus burs on the dry slope and complained by whinnying as Alexander pulled them out.

"No, this isn't a very nice thing to do to a brother, is it?" Alexander repeated to the horse. "Run off with his wife? No. I don't think anybody woud give us a medal for that. I'll tell you what we'll do. Let's just write it out of us, write a story about it and let it go at that. Let's not spoil everything; let's anchor ourselves here; let's make this place our eternity, not make any wild music toward any destiny with any ocean. Let's just write about it." And then he made a low throat noise when he thought of Perrette and decided after all it wasn't, like a stock Western movie, a matter you could be philosophical about with a horse. Perrette was very real and—well, Perrette was very real. There wasn't anything about Perrette that could be anchored by scenery or a horse. But with a brother, that's different, he thought. That could be very rough.

He got up now and mounted the horse and watched carefully all the gentle color of the distant folding hills.

That's right, he thought. Try to get away from George and Perrette for a while and back to the plans for the novel. A person can always lose himself in a good novel. His book would be about the mountain men working their way south from Bent's Fort and their meeting and joining Carleton's army from California. The idleness and boredom of the army with no South to fight in New Mexico. Their fighting and exterminating the Indians in Carleton's need for glory. The gradual degeneration of the mountain men that makes them finally accept Colonel Carleton's plan to place the remaining

Indians in a concentration camp called Bosque Redondo, where most died.

And Kit Carson would be the hero. It was not a bad plan for the novel. He knew the country well enough and the descendants of those involved including reds and whites. But what was he trying to prove? Maybe that evil is a permanent thing in any country among any group of people, even the nicest. Once there was nowhere a more generous and understanding man than Kit Carson. Maybe he was trying to prove that heroes must exist in the long periods of boredom because in the period of hysteria all heroes are victims. And words like "evil" and "good" must be avoided because they are abstract and do not exist. A gradual twisting process exists, that bends men into animals.

But the novel would have a strong surface movement of the bang-bang of the cowboys and Indians, then if somehow the writer could get this across there was—there should be—there must be put in an even greater, bigger, but quieter bang-bang beneath all this, an attempt to keep the beast human. But that would take some writer. To avoid being pretentious, to avoid making a speech, to keep the entertainment there and the reader always there would take some writing.

The buzzard witness, now borne on an updraft, laid his slow circles cleanly against the flat blue, higher and higher, as the horse dropped off the ledge and began the steep climb down and Alexander's mind got back to George and Perrette.

This dependency, this hero worship, George had for him, wasn't it bad for George? Wouldn't it be best for him to shock George out of it? Everything was always getting back to George and Perrette. George he knew in his youth had

made a short catalogue in writing of everything he had wanted in a wife. It had begun with the usual platitudes digested in every digest and consisted of all those rationalities that ignore the deep and undying need for everyone to know his true individual self which is so different from another it frightens us. Perrette must have made a mental catalogue too, that was now breaking up on these mesas of reality. And what about his own? All he knew was that he had a loyalty to George and the Indian Country and his forefathers and particularly to George, and that was all breaking up now too and all he could do each day was fight it and watch the inevitable destruction of something valuable grow into a bigger destruction. Why not finish it now—go off with her now, before it, the inevitable end, got even more tragic?

Alexander had arrived at the corral now and he slung the saddle in the corner and started to say why the hell not. When he got to the bridle and slung that in the corner instead of hanging it properly as was his custom he did say, "Why the hell not?" But he dismissed the thought now and finally hung up the saddle and the bridle properly.

"That's better," Rabbit Stockings said.

"What's better?" Alexander said.

"That you don't take it out on things."

"Oh," Alexander Bowman said, and he walked out into the hard light of the corral and got on the top rung and sat there where he could see her. He could see too the long spell of emptiness covered by the one gray of the chico, chamise and sage that hid the arroyos from this height, but the desert growth did not hide the mountains that circled round it, did not hide the occasional Indian pony nor the adobe and log post nor the petrified-wood house. He could also see the

9

Indian hogans way out there in the distance and the three Indians driving out a sheep. But mostly he could see her.

Perrette Bowman was painting on a picture. She had studied in Paris under Lhote and she was painting it the way he had said. She was organizing it the way he said and using the colors he said and she had set herself up a still life of apples and pineapples and roses the way he had said. She had had George bring her the apples and pineapples and roses especially from Gallup. It was the kind of a still life Lhote would have liked. As a matter of fact the painting was a weak Lhote. Next she wanted to paint three dead fish all in a row alongside three lively baseballs. Alexander would be going to Albuquerque tomorrow and he would get them for her although it would be nice to go and pick out the three dead fish personally because there are Braque fish and Matisse fish and the kind you eat. Alexander would get the kind you eat although he would certainly do a better job of selecting fish with a feeling than his brother, her husband George.

"His brother, my husband, George." She repeated this feebly out loud, glancing over her still life but not seeing the Indian Country all around. Yes, she would definitely go to town tomorrow with Alexander when he went to the wholesale ring to buy cattle. And what was Alexander doing wasting his time buying cattle when he should be writing? There was no one in the whole world who had his talent. There was not too much here to write about. Nothing ever happened. The country was blank and unexciting, it was part of that long stretch of land between Hollywood and New York, or better, between Carmel and Paris. It separated Texas from California so their incredibilities did not interfere with each other. It was that endless nothingness beneath the clouds when you

are going to Los Angeles. Still, at one time it had been an exciting idea. The country as it had been described by the Santa Fe writers was romantic and awe-inspiring with picturesque and spiritual Indians and sunsets with poetry, described by Lawrence, where a woman could find herself. To be taken here by George when she had met him in New Haven had been her dream, and now her dream, she thought, touching her brush into one of Lhote's roses, had not turned into a nightmare. No. It had turned into a long, quiet bore. And it was not George's fault. Nothing would ever be George's fault. George was dedicated to the Indians and what could be more noble, more altruistic, more—how could she put it?—more depressing, than to be dedicated to the Indians? She admired him and respected him but she did not see him now as he came over a salt mound on his horse Ute. She was mixing some exciting things on her pallette.

George Bowman was trying to bring the horse into a walk. He had been recovering some breachy steers that had wandered into Apache country and he had told his wife he could not wait till morning to get them. They were branded fine but the Apaches did not seem to mind the brand when they ate. He had left Rabbit Stockings and Quicker-Than-You in charge of the post so he had not thought about that much on the way back—things could not be in worse hands. He had thought some about the salt blocks that were stolen, the wool that must be bought and the tuberculosis among the Indians that refused to yield to government statistics. He had thought, too, about the dream of cheap feed, the illusion of weight when the Indians rolled their wool in sand before they traded it to him expensively, the low price of beef on

11

the hoof, beautiful horses, fat cows, heavy sheep, and he wondered aloud that the country had changed none since his grandfather's time in 1863. Alexander would put all this beauty into words, all the beauty of the land, the mesas, the mountains and the pure sky and his white wife. Perhaps Alexander could put into words, and make acceptable by arranging the words properly, the fact that a Navaho, a man in Indian Country is, within, the same man as in any country. No, Alexander could not write that well. No one could ever write well enough to make truth acceptable to some people. But Alexander would write well enough to be number one and if the Indian Country ever fell to the advancing ravages that civilization called progress it would all be set down. The shock of a simple naked country would be set down. The shock of a simple naked country shot quietly in the morning with poles of purple light bending through the cliffs, and in the evening the same light shattering the whole world in spectrum violence would be set down. The Indians would be set down. Everything would be set down. George hoped he himself would not be set down but he hoped that Alexander would take an interest in Perrette. He wanted Perrette to be happy. George pulled up his horse on the top of the mesa. From here he could see Perrette painting and Alexander watching her. Good, he thought. Everything is going well.

"Lousy. Things have been going lousy." Rabbit Stockings grabbed the bridle as George Bowman got off for the gates. The Indian was dressed in yellow-and-black tall boots and blue jeans and he moved easily as he caught the horse.

"They haven't spoken to each other all day," Rabbit Stockings said as he brought the horse through the gate.

12

George Bowman dropped the hoop on the gate and followed toward the barn.

"I'll get the saddle," Rabbit Stockings said.

George Bowman broke away and walked over to the corral and sat on the top rail next to his brother Alexander.

"I got those steers," he said.

"Apache country?"

"Yes," George Bowman said.

"Fence cut?"

"Hard to tell."

"It was cut all right."

"I got the steers."

"Those people got nice habits."

"It's a custom," George Bowman said.

"Those people got nice customs."

"My Indian spy tells me you two haven't talked all day."

The two brothers from their high perch on the rail were staring out over the head of George's easel-crouching wife, their eyes not focusing on anything, just taking all the big emptiness in.

"Your Indian spy is right." Alexander removed a pack of Camels from his shirt pocket, pounded one out and lit it deliberately and talked into the smoke.

"I hoped you two would get along fine," George Bowman said. "You got a lot in common."

Alexander watched the tip of his cigarette carefully. "Yes," he said. "Yes."

"Painting and writing and everything."

"Yes."

"How is the writing going?"

"Fine. Fine."

"I put those Angus steers over in the Largo pasture. They're not putting on weight."

"Angus don't do well in this country. We should stick with Herefords."

"It was an experiment."

"And was she an experiment?"

George now too took out a cigarette and lit it from Alexander's cigarette that was handed to him.

"You think we should stick with Indians?" He handed the cigarette back.

"I don't think she is doing too well here, George."

"Not if she gets the cold treatment," George said.

Alexander took one foot off the rail. George now, too, swung one foot over the rail so he faced his brother.

"If you'll talk to her about the things that excite and interest her—she's concerned about your work, Alex, as I am—we can be three happy Indians."

There was a silence as both brothers studied the railing.

"By God," George said finally in recognition. "I've got it. You think I don't trust you. You think complicated like a writer. You'll do fine. But this is real and you're my brother."

Alexander got down off the fence. "You're my brother," he said to himself as he walked alone to the post. As he lifted the latch he said aloud, "Three happy Indians."

2

Inside the post Quicker-Than-You, an intelligent and delicate-faced Indian, was explaining the medicine man's business to the medicine man to whom the trader's father had given the extra name of Paracelsus. The medicine man, who was taller than any other Indian, was resplendent in sheep-suede trousers and a dark velvet jacket; white seashells circled his neck twice and silver coins circled his waist once.

Quicker-Than-You was behind the counter but as he talked he pointed out the inadequacies of the medicine man's medicine to the medicine man with the aid of his finger.

"We cannot accept your word that a man is going to steal something and that this will cause an endless drought."

Alexander leaned against the gun rack and listened.

"Tell him he's crazy," Alexander said.

"Tell him yourself," Quicker-Than-You said. "You speak Navaho as well as the People."

"I can be as stubborn about speaking the Navaho that I know as he can be about speaking the English that he knows."

Quicker-Than-You turned to the medicine man.

"He says he can be as stubborn about speaking The

15

People's language as you can be about speaking the foreign language."

"It is no ordinary theft," the medicine man said, slowly in The People's language. "The theft that will cause the great drying up will be no ordinary theft of things."

"Tell him he's crazy," Alexander said quickly in Navaho, ignoring the medicine man.

Alexander turned and went into the back room where the hides were kept and sat on a pile of hides in the dim airless room and looked out the slot window at his brother who still sat on the fence.

"Those Indians," he thought, rubbing his face, "they know too much. He calls it medicine but he knows too much."

He felt and then heard the door open and she came in and sat down beside him on the pile of hides.

"The medicine man knows," Alexander said, still watching out the window.

"How could he know?" she said quietly, her voice meeting the dim quiet of the room.

"That's why he's the medicine man," Alexander said.

"Will he talk?"

"No. He won't talk. Even after it's over he won't talk, but now they will know that he always knew and they will think him some medicine man when it's over."

"When is it going to be over?" Her voice was still gentle.

"Never," Alexander said, watching his brother through the slit window. "Maybe never."

"But when are we going to leave?" Her voice was still gentle and smooth.

"Maybe never," Alexander Bowman said. "The medicine man predicts a drying up of everything."

16

"And if we don't there will be a drying up of everything."

"Yes, yes," Alexander said. "All the medicine is bad."

"Listen," she said. "There is no medicine. This is the twentieth century and people do what we have to do because we are still animals no matter what century. Nice animals."

"Nice animals." Alexander caressed her arm that now lay across him. "Nice animals. Nice brother. Three happy Indians. It's a circle with no medicine."

"Three happy Indians. He likes to say that. He is a wonderful person. We must not hurt him, Alex. How can we do it without hurting him?"

"Call it off," Alexander Bowman said.

"Can you call it off?"

"No."

"We can no more call off love than we can call off our own hands or feet." Perrette was silent against the incredible silence of the big hide room. "Quickly," she said. "We must do it quickly."

"Quickly," Alexander said, watching his brother. "The medicine is to do it quickly, to hit Albuquerque and keep right on going."

"Yes, quickly, quickly," she said. "Quickly."

"But the medicine man said the land would dry up."

"We are in the twentieth century."

"But the Indians are not in the twentieth century. I do not know what century they are in but it is not this one. I only spent four years away from here at that university myself. Anyway the medicine man has never been wrong. He never says too much but when he talks he has never been wrong. That's why he's the medicine man."

Then she said, not listening, "We must move quickly."

17

"Quickly, quickly," he agreed, turning toward her alive beauty, her warmth now. "Tomorrow. Quickly."

They rose now as George dropped off the fence and came toward them. She went outside to collect her easel and Alexander went into the post. He thought "quickly, quickly, quickly" as he saw his brother through the leather of the harness he dragged toward the counter. Now he saw the medicine man standing alone with a quiet dignity amid the babble of the Indians and he thought, that's why he's the medicine man. But he forced this out of his mind and went back to the phrase "quickly, quickly, quickly."

Rabbit Stockings, who was one of the Indians left in charge of the post, was standing straight in the attitude he assumed when he was going to make a report to the trader George Bowman.

"That mission Indian, Tom-Dick-and-Harry, has been hanging around here all day. Every time a white rancher comes in he makes fun of him by singing one of their songs like 'I'm Dreaming of a White Christmas.'"

"They don't know they're being made fun of," Quicker-Than-You said.

"Just the same he shouldn't do it when they're our guests," Rabbit Stockings said.

"He thinks the whites are too vulnerable," Quicker-Than-You said.

"Yes, if that means the whites are silly. Yes," Rabbit Stockings said. "But maybe we believe things that seem odd to them too."

"Maybe we do," George Bowman said, not thinking.

"I don't think so," Quicker-Than-You said. "The whites don't think much. They got a lot of important things to do."

"They got books as far as you can see," Rabbit Stockings said.

"Did you ever read one?" Quicker-Than-You tried on four turquoise rings for size.

"No," Rabbit Stockings said. "I can't. I would if I could."

"But you can't." Quicker-Than-You did not like any of the rings. Now he tried the necklaces. "I can and did but I don't now. I tell you, let Tom-Dick-and-Harry have his fun."

"Do you think we should allow Tom-Dick-and-Harry to make fun of the whites' beliefs, Sansi?" Rabbit Stockings asked.

"No," George Bowman said.

"You think they're too vulnerable to be fair game," Quicker-Than-You said.

"Yes," George Bowman said.

"Be that as it may," Quicker-Than-You said, trying the turquoise rings again, "and I am in partial agreement with you, be that as it may, they ask for it." Quicker-Than-You held the ring at arm's distance to see it.

"Let's get on with the rest of the business," George Bowman said.

"Okay. Number two," Rabbit Stockings said. "Quicker-Than-You read all your and Alexander's mail and threw it all away."

"I saved a few relevant pieces," Quicker-Than-You said.

"That's nice," George Bowman said.

"I saved a bill for three dollars and seventy-five cents you owe the University of Oklahoma Press and another from Albuquerque Grain and Feed for seven hundred and thirty-two dollars."

"That's nice," George Bowman said.

"I saved two rejection slips that came for Alexander and that I don't think he should see until later when he's finished his writing."

"Considerate of you," George Bowman said.

Quicker-Than-You put all the pieces of jewelry back in the case.

"Alexander's writing damn well about us Indians. Of course some would think his Indians are atypical, but all Indians are atypical. People are atypical."

"What does atypical mean?" George Bowman asked and Rabbit Stockings agreed with the question with his eyes.

"You know what it means. It's Alexander's pose not to know what it means. He's the writer."

"Yes. But could I coax the rest of my mail out of you?"

"There's that usual letter from that girl you met at college. I burned it."

"Thank you," George Bowman said. "Like our great President you are indispensable."

"I function," Quicker-Than-You said.

"With my mail you function beautifully." George placed his hands broadly on the counter. "The next time I leave the post I am going to tie you up."

"I quit," Quicker-Than-You said.

"You're always quitting," George said.

"And you're always hiring me back. You come to the hogan. I don't come here."

"Okay, so I don't tie anybody up. By God, I hope I didn't hurt your feelings about a tiny thing like plundering my mail and running my life."

"Everyone can see there's an equity on your side," Quicker-Than-You said.

"Thank you. You're noble," George Bowman said. "By God, I hope I didn't hurt your little Navaho feelings."

"Without further facetiousness or racial prejudice on your part," Quicker-Than-You said, "I'd like to consider the incident closed."

"Thank you," George Bowman said. "By God, I'm lucky today."

Rabbit Stockings, who spoke a great deal of the foreign language, English, heard almost nothing of this except the last words of Sansi's, that he was lucky today—words with which, after what the medicine man had said, he could not agree.

"Okay. Number three. The medicine man has made a prediction. The prediction is that something important and valuable is going to be stolen. We better lock up double tonight."

"Valuable things can't be locked up," Quicker-Than-You said.

"That's Indian talk," George Bowman said. "Let's get back to white man's talk. We will lock up everything double tonight. The medicine man has never been wrong. He has an excellent grapevine of information."

"Now the second part of the prediction. After the theft there will be an endless drought."

"If we cope with the theft we won't have to cope with the drought. Lock up everything double tonight," George Bowman said, moving off to where there was something waiting to eat.

"Go in beauty," Quicker-Than-You called after him in Navaho.

The house Indian had set three places at the plank table.

Perrette sat in the middle in a costume that was fresh and chic and certainly the thing on the Riviera but odd in the Indian Country. She sat in the middle, her rope-soled espadrilles perched on the top rung of the chair, her bright, billowing peasant skirt covering the whole chair so that she might have been sitting on a studio floor in Cannes. The two brothers sat on either end of the table with their wide-brimmed Stetsons set alongside them.

"Three happy Indians," George Bowman said, looking into his pinto bean soup as he spooned it.

Alexander and Perrette looked up from their pinto bean soup and over at each other.

"How goes the writing?" George asked, still concerned with the soup.

"Okay."

"How many pages this morning?"

"Five and a half."

"Not bad. Is it good?"

"I've read worse."

"Prejudiced?"

"Yes."

"All us Indians are prejudiced," George said, still involved with the soup. "Even Quicker-Than-You likes it. He doesn't like much."

"Why don't you go in and pick up those cattle tomorrow, George?" Alexander said.

George looked up from his soup abruptly.

"That's been arranged. You're going in with Perrette. It will be difficult to drive all the way to Albuquerque and back without speaking to each other."

"Yes," Alexander said. He had not started his soup and neither had Perrette.

"I've got to bury those two TB victims at Star Lake, then they can burn down the hogans. It's all been arranged," George said eating.

"Yes," Perrette said. "The white man has an obligation to the Indian. He can learn from the Indians as well as steal from the Indians. The white man has got to work with the Indians instead of for the Indians. That has been the Bowmans for three generations now, ever since the white man came and it has been a happy life. It's all been arranged," Perrette said in a rote tone as though repeating something.

"But Alex will put that into believable language," George said. "He'll get a lot of fine books out of the country. But look, you two Indians haven't started to eat."

Alex and Perrette both looked down at their soup and then, as though at a signal and together, they began to eat.

"That's better," George said.

They all went through the soup and the salad without saying anything but when they got to the beef that the Indian woman brought George said: "The medicine man said something big was going to be stolen."

"Paracelsus is crazy," Alexander said.

"Then he said there'd be a big drought."

"He can have crazy ideas," Alexander said.

"He doesn't say much but he's generally right. That's why he's the medicine man."

"Then lock everything up double."

"That's what I figured," George said.

"I'd rather you went to Albuquerque tomorrow, George."

"Listen, it's all been arranged," George said.

"Everything is arranged," Perrette repeated.

"And if the medicine man has it from the grapevine that there will be a theft it's better that you two are gone and I am here."

"Perfect," Alexander said. "You think your arrangements will work against the medicine."

"I'll be trying," George said.

"I believe that," Alex said.

"I'll lock everything up double."

"But you say the medicine man is always right."

"Well, I'll be trying," George said.

"You are trying all right," Alex agreed.

Outside, after lunch, there were three horses saddled waiting for them.

"I'm not going," George said.

"But we're all going," Perrette said. "We planned yesterday to check that new gate we paid for."

"That was before I had to ride all morning looking for those cows. I'll stay here and get in some target practice with the Indians."

Alexander and Perrette swung onto the horses and made toward the cross fence, four strands anchored to cedar posts, that swept along the arroyo before it ran over the mesa. Alexander rode in advance on Fireboy and Perrette followed closely on a paint she had named Abstract. As they swung away from the arroyo and began to climb the mesa Perrette pulled Abstract even with Fireboy. They rode now in absolute silence through the diminishing chico and sage and beginning grama up the gentle slope that began the climb to the quiet mesa.

"Of course," Alexander said finally, "I must tell George."

"After it's done," Perrette said.

They eased the horses through the last of the cactus and grama and among a scattering of piñon, still climbing.

"The Indians," Alexander said, "call this hill The Long Blue Mesa. It's sacred. On top of it they gather stones for medicine." Alexander rubbed the neck of his horse. "But I must tell George."

"After it's done," Perrette said.

Alexander turned his head. "I think we're being followed," he said. "I heard something back there."

"Nerves," Perrette said.

The trail became nothing now as they climbed up through the loose rock, the horses feeling their way carefully.

"What medicine do they collect medicine for on this mesa?"

"Marrying Way, Shooting Way, Prostitution Way. Which one interests you?" Alexander said.

"Let's try the last one," Perrette said.

"Well, there's a disagreement," Alexander said. "The Jesuit school at Window Rock is generally a good authority but one priest writes in his book that the ceremonies are to discourage and another says in his book that they are to encourage prostitution."

"And how do you vote?" Perrette said.

"I vote to turn around and see who's following us."

"Nerves," Perrette said.

Now they came up to a round platform of rock and stopped their horses.

"Down there," Perrette said, pointing to the base of a distant, gay-colored cliff. "The road. We could reach it in one

hour, follow it into Cuba, take the bus to Albuquerque. Now."

"Now," Alexander repeated, "we'll get behind this overhang and find out who's following."

Alexander dismounted and he led both horses back of the concealing rock and they waited.

"No one," Perrette said, still atop her horse. "No one."

"Quiet," Alexander said.

"No one, Lover," Perrette said.

"Listen."

"No one."

"Listen."

"The wind."

The almost noiseless, moving horse came around the cliff now, ridden by the medicine man. He pulled up alongside them.

"You just happened to be out for a ride," Alexander said, annoyed. "You weren't following us."

"I was following you," the medicine man said.

"Thanks," Alexander said. "Dangerous country. We need your protection."

"I wasn't protecting you," the medicine man said.

"Forget it," Alexander said, and he slid onto his horse and swung it around. "Let's get home."

At the post between the two mesas they had the targets set up and the Indians were sitting one hundred yards away while one of them was standing shooting the seven shots that their Marlin or Winchester lever-action carbines held. They each had brought, or found at the post, a one-pound coffee can and at the end of the shoot the one with the most holes

in his can was the winner. They preferred the Hills Brothers cans because they were red but today most had settled for the blue Maxwell House cans because that's all the post had got.

"Shoot this cigarette out of my mouth, Gee," Alexander said toward George.

Perrette, the medicine man and Alexander had dismounted at the corral and walked over to the shooting. It was George's turn to shoot and Alexander had lit a cigarette and walked over to the target.

"Go ahead and try it, Gee. Shoot the cigarette out of my mouth."

George had already begun to raise the gun on the coffee can that Alexander stood in front of, but now he lowered it.

"No," he said. "It's silly. It was all right when we were kids, but now it's silly."

"Very silly," Perrette agreed.

Alexander tossed away the cigarette and walked toward the house. The others went back to watching the shooting. Soon Alexander came out of the petrified-wood house with a gun. All the others were watching the shooting. George had lit a cigarette and was watching the shooting carefully.

Now there was a shot that did not come from the gun of the Indian who was shooting at the coffee can and George's cigarette exploded.

Alexander lowered the gun and placed it against the house, then he walked to the target and lit a cigarette.

"Go ahead and try it, Gee. Shoot the cigarette out of my mouth."

George's face was all white as he raised the gun quickly

27

and then began to squeeze off the trigger carefully. The gun went off as Perrette hit it. "No!" she called as she hit the gun and the gun went off.

All of the Indians watched Alexander when the gun went off. The cigarette had not been touched. They could all see the cigarette and now they could all see the stream of blood that was very red against the white kerchief Alexander wore. Alexander went down on one knee.

Perrette got to him first.

"You damn damn fool," she said, taking his head in her arms. "Did you have to give him the chance? Did you have to ask him whether—?"

The others came up now and George examined Alexander's chin. The medicine man was the only Indian who was not concerned.

"It's just a crease," George said. "It will bleed a little but it will be all right. Have the doctor take a look at it when you take the semi into Albuquerque tomorrow."

Early the next morning Alexander and Perrette were in the cab of the great semi-truck and trailer. They were waiting for the Indians to finish putting the stake body on the trailer. They had taken the stake body off the trailer to haul sand from the Puerco Wash and now they were putting the stakes on again for the cattle Alexander was going to bring back. The medicine man, Paracelsus, was watching everything, standing alone on a dry hill above them. George Bowman was leaning against the cab directing the Indians and talking to his brother.

"Don't bid against the packers, Alex, and don't go over twenty-three cents on anything. And don't bid against Cass.

He stopped his bidding the last time I bought a bunch."

"And no Angus," Alexander said.

"That's right."

"They don't do well in this country."

"I thought we were going to forget that."

"Okay," Alexander said and he started up the engine and looked over at Perrette.

When the engine started the medicine man walked down the hill and stood in front of the truck. The stakes were all in place now and Alexander touched the horn. The medicine man did not move.

"Nashda, nashda, nashda!" Alexander hollered to the medicine man and then he hollered in English, "Out of the way!"

The medicine man still did not move. Alex raced the engine and sat on the horn. No luck. George went up and grabbed Paracelsus by the shoulder.

"Can't you see it's my brother?" he said low and in Navaho. No luck. Alexander raced the engine and hit the horn again. It was an air horn and it echoed big through the canyons and across the mesas, but there was still no luck. Tom-Dick-and-Harry came up and grabbed the other shoulder and together with George they pulled him along but the medicine man did not help with his feet so he was an awkward burden and his head hit the gate post causing a small trickle of blood, but he was quiet now and out of the way.

Alexander put the truck in gear and George jumped on the side of the cab.

"He's okay," George said. "These medicine men get a crazy streak once in a while. It's an occupational disease. I guess he figured you were the one that was going to steal something."

"Yes," Alexander said, racing the engine.

"I'll have the government doctor check him when he comes through."

"Yes," Alexander said, and he began to move the giant truck forward.

"And don't worry. I'll lock everything double. Enjoy yourselves. It will be raining when you get back."

The great truck was moving along good now and George had to drop off quickly. Alexander raced her into second gear as soon as he could. It will be raining when you get back, Alex thought as he double-clutched the giant and eased her into high. That was the nicest thing anyone could say in the Indian Country. But Quicker-Than-You had not come out to say his usual "Go in beauty." No one at all had told them to go in beauty. Alexander tramped down hard now on the gas as they hit the long straight stretches of sand road that dropped away from Indian Country.

"We're off," Perrette said toward him.

"Yes," Alexander said aloud and he said to himself as he checked the air and fuel gauge with his eye, "But not in beauty."

When George dropped off the truck he walked through all the silent Indians until he got hold of the medicine man and then, arm in arm, he led him into the back room away from everyone and sat him comfortably on the hides. Then he got out some cotton and dabbed at the slight cut.

"The white man's world is built on faith and confidence and understanding," George said.

It seemed that Paracelsus would still say nothing out of a stolid, implacable expression that could go through infinities

saying nothing, but then he said finally in a voice that was deep and grating, and at last in foreign English: "But supposing that the white man does not understand himself. I think that's what's happening here."

George stopped dabbing at the cut and sat down alongside the medicine man. He needed to sit down.

As the huge semi rocked along through the Indian Country Alexander took one more good last look. It was, he thought, what you are supposed to see when you are dying. Everything that has been of you for such a long time is going by you fast before the book is closed. Now he was, he thought, having the privilege of putting the final chapter first. As they hit a switchback he could see the petrified-log house each generation of Bowmans had worked on to make right for Indian Country. He could see the horses too that each generation of horses had worked on to make right for the terrain and altitude of the Indian Country, and all the outbuildings and the hogans the Indians had made right for the Indian Country, and ahead and all around were the cliffs, sage and rock and wide mesas the world had made right for Indian Country. The only thing that had gone wrong was himself. He felt the big weight of the enormous truck and trailer hurtle forward through the pass and knew that somewhere, somehow, something had happened that made him wrong for Indian Country. Anyway now it was true and when it was no longer true, when he, like the petrified logs his ancestors had sweated over and like the horses the stallions had plunged and sweated over and the hogans and the cliffs, when he too was made right for Indian Country then he could return—return.

His leg reached forward to touch the air brake and met hers

31

and then his eyes met hers and the great truck plunged on below the gay and loud-colored cliffs at greater speed, shot on big and lumbering and fast through the weird and simple Indian Country, dim and fading now with his memories of childhood, and the immemorial rocks rising enormous that had witnessed the first coming of the white man and would be there to see the last—all of the great dumb land, all of Indian Country, witnessing now this small chapter.

"Quickly," she said.

Now the big red truck and trailer wound down the long hill going much too fast as it entered the Pueblo country with the Navaho country well behind them and Perrette said, "Keep to the left. It will take us around Albuquerque."

"Yes," Alexander said. "Yes," and he gave it more gas as they approached the big curve.

"What are you trying to do?" she said. "Commit suicide? We'll never make that curve."

"We'll see," Alexander said and he hung on the wheel and gave her all the gas she would take. Perrette had her arms around him now as the big truck and trailer tried to make the curve. It began to rock and it tried to go over to the left and then it tried to go over on its right side, the whole rig, truck and trailer tried to jack-knife into the arroyo as Alexander pulled it out on the straightaway. But the wheels held and they were running level now and Alex laid his foot off the accelerator to take it down from eighty miles an hour.

"We made it," she said.

"Yes," Alexander said. "Maybe They want to see how far we can go. I guess it will be some trip."

He straightened out the big rig now and kept her at a constant speed with his eye on the long road ahead.

"No one told us to go in beauty."

"Quickly," she said.

Later that night on the long flat stretch between Albuquerque and El Paso the big outfit pulled up in front of a motel and Perrette and Alexander got out.

Inside the motel room after the fat proprietor had left them finally alone with the Gideon Bible and the Sears, Roebuck rancho décor Alexander began to fumble with his necktie.

"Let me help you, you damn genius," Perrette said, and she removed the necktie deftly and began to unbutton his shirt.

"Quickly," she said.

3

In Mazatlán, Mexico, Alexander wrote his novel quickly and
the publishers rejected it quickly. It occurred to him then
that they had set up wayside stations in the middle of conti-
nents to anticipate and return all those objects that looked
dangerously like manuscripts for it seemed that he was getting
the book back before he sent it. However, by persistence or
confusion of his name with another's, there at last arrived a
note borne to their room by Perrette saying that if all the
characters were changed somewhat and the locale, say (we do
not want to presume), were switched to Bombay where the
editor witnessed a similar scene—well, who knows. they
might be able to use it.

With this encouragement Alexander mailed it out again
to another and another and another, and finally (as a friend,
an unrealized author turned bitter, remarked), in error or
through mistaken identity or drunkenness in the publisher's
office—it was accepted.

"There," Perrette said, looking up from her easel. "It's
easy."

The book was about Alexander's early childhood among
the Indians and at the post. About his grandfather who had,

in the Civil War and in the territory of New Mexico, volunteered to defend the Union, decency, the blacks from the wisdom of Southern gentlemen. About his grandfather who was forced instead to fight, or better, slaughter, the Navaho Indians and concentrate the women and children at Fort Sumner where most died. About his grandfather who finally sickened, quit, resigned, "tendered his resignation in, got shut of murdering Indians at water holes, concentrating the women and children. I, who innocently, unconsciously, youthfully, volunteered to defend the Union, the blacks, decency, from the wisdom of Southern gentlemen, quit and took to trading with the Indians, just traveling around trading, without a gun, among the brutal, warlike savages who must be killed or concentrated in a camp." (It is our opinion at the office that this is propaganda, the personal prejudice of the author, that no believable . . .)

It was about his grandfather who, when he quit the Northern army, worked his way into the Cuba country and founded a post, began to build it of the petrified wood of the Eocene cliff, of his being caught by Kit Carson, the hero. No, maybe it wasn't Kit Carson who was the hero. Carson was a mountain man doing a job he didn't understand. Maybe Colonel Carleton, Carson's commander who was supposed to be fighting the Civil War, was the hero, he who gave orders like this: "I have been informed that there is a spring called Ojo de Cibola about fifteen miles west of Limitar where the Navahos drive their cattle. A cautious, wary commander, hiding his men and moving about at night might kill a good many Indians at this point."

It was about his grandfather who refused to exterminate the Indians, to whom, when he "tendered his resignation in"

35

Carson said, "We'll have to draft you as a private."

"If you can find me," Bowman had said.

It was about his grandfather whom Carson found three months later building his petrified-wood house. Carson, after thinking a while, but still sitting atop his horse, said, "But, well, I guess you killed your share of Indians."

"More," Bowman said.

"But we will have to concentrate or exterminate these Indians who are helping you build this house. Orders."

"Orders?" Bowman said.

"Yes," Carson said and he got down off the horse. "Unless you and me can think of something different about your Indians we'll have to take them in."

"They live in a petrified-wood house," Bowman said.

"Well," Carson said, kicking the petrified-wood foundation and then getting on the horse and riding off. "Then they can't be real Indians."

The petrified-wood house became just another rock, another outcropping of the land in the Indian Country where not Indians or whites, but human beings could—

"Yes," Perrette had said over his shoulder. "It stood there as a rock, a bulwark, a testament that people can get along together in the Indian Country, that they don't have to kill and steal from each other."

"Maybe that was it," Alexander said.

"And then there was your father, but did I ever tell you—" Perrette was staring out over the town of Mazatlán. "Did I ever tell you about my father?"

"He had a lot of money," Alexander said.

"Has," Perrette said. "And you should accept some of it."

"I didn't marry your father," Alexander said.

"Oh, Daddy wouldn't mind giving us a stack of it," she said. "It's just a game. Did I tell you that Daddy was a Socialist? One night in 1919 when he was eighteen he was beaten up by the Communists. He didn't mind that, it kind of made him proud, but two weeks later, and for his politics again, he was jailed by the New York police. When he got out he said he wasn't going to be serious anymore, he was going to play games. He said he was going to play the American game of making money. Oh, occasionally now he'll give twenty or thirty thousand to some do-gooder cause but his heart is not in it now and he always goes back to the game of making money."

"Where are the old ennobling dreams? But I didn't marry your father," Alexander said. "I married you. What effect did your father have on you?"

"I don't know," Perrette said. "Except he was very strict. He said he didn't want me getting any silly ideas or ways he had when he was young. If I was a boy I guess he would have sent me to military academy. I was a girl so he sent me to a convent school. Which was all right," Perrette said, "except that I had his blood in me, his bone, and when I looked at those walls I said, When I bust out of here watch me go."

"Watch me get back to the rewrite on this novel," Alexander said. "This part is about my father."

"Go," she said.

And it was about his father and not about his mother, who died young having George—not too uncommon in the Indian Country with doctors two hundred miles away—mothers dying. It was about his father, who was away a good deal of the time trading with the Indians. So the two boys grew up kind of like wild Indians. That is, they played with the Indian

kids but the Indians had a hogan, a family, so it was more like wild animals. But wild animals have a cave and a family too, so it was more like—

"Oh God, you've made your point!"

And mostly the book was about the two brothers. With his father gone trading with the Navahos, with everyone gone except the Indians, George, the youngest, fastened onto Alexander. When all the Indian kids would begin to circle the post on their ponies, getting ready to attack the whites, it was Alexander who organized the defense, barricaded the doors and windows with George following him around goggle-eyed and taking orders. It was Alexander who saved the day in George's boy eyes, saved the candy and kept them from getting chucked in the pond, till their father got back. And when they were ambushed by the Indian kids in the back country George always had Alexander. It was the big brother, Alexander, who bluffed the Indian boys by charging them with a big noise and then retreating fast before the Indians knew what it was, Alexander who got them quickly home, losing the horse's tracks in streams and dead-ending the Indians up box canyons. It was Alexander who always won. George always had Alexander.

Of course the proper names were left out and something else was left out too. Alexander had spent three days at the bottom of a mine shaft. It was the most important thing that had happened to Alexander. That was left out. Perhaps it was because he was not absolutely certain of how it ended. Diamond Jack was one of the very few who knew absolutely how it ended but he was not around when Alexander wrote the book.

This Jack had come early to the Cuba country when it was all open range, no fences, when you could run your cattle anywhere. Somewhere, way back there someplace, someone had stolen, or maybe borrowed, a cow. That victim then had to steal or borrow one to live. When they stole Jack's, Jack went right on getting even for years. They called him a rustler. Diamond Jack was a good friend to the Bowmans but they had fine cattle and Jack did not object to stealing them if they were conveniently around. Jack was conveniently around when the mine episode ended but he was not conveniently around when Alexander wrote the book. Perrette was conveniently around and she said, "You got in everything, didn't you?"

"Almost everything," Alexander said.

"You did not get in the part that George must have hated you, must have been jealous."

"Jealous?" Alexander said. "About what?"

"Sibling rivalry. Freud."

"Vassar," Alexander said.

"Well, his resentment of your taking over, dominating?"

"I don't think so," Alexander said, thinking. "George is a very gentle man."

"But underneath all that," Perrette said, "I felt something else, some kind of resignation, bitterness."

"Yes, I know what you mean," Alexander said. "I have sensed it too, but it was never that—jealousy. Would he alone, among all those people, have rescued me from the mine shaft? Would—?"

"You didn't put the mine shaft incident in the book," Perrette said.

"Because I'm not certain of all the facts," Alexander said. "If it were all known it might make a book in itself. But this book is finished."

And when it was published a film company recognized the book's success, bought it for fifty thousand dollars, and ended with an excellent picture. Better than the book, Alexander thought.

From Mazatlán they went to the Varadero Beach in Cuba, close enough to the name sound of his own little town in New Mexico to make him feel less dispossessed. The second book, still about Indian Country, was judged better than the first. The film company, alerted and awake now, paid a small fortune and really ruined this one with a perfect director and four million dollars. Alexander never saw this one but everyone else had to suffer it, as well as the TV version. But the book was in hard covers and Alexander was made.

"Not only made," Perrette said, "but I was right."

Perrette, who had begun life with ambition and wealth and the finest of convent schools and who finished at Vassar, had to be right. She was much too clever in her attested-to cleverness at Vassar to marry, finally, after one admitted mistake, anything but a genius. For an excellent reason she had never told anyone that she had attended, for one year, a public school in Tacoma. It was, she knew, because she had hated everyone there, all those "qui n'étaient pas de son monde," all those who had never appreciated her cleverness in the least. Now she would get even, now that she was the wife of a genius. In her life now the public school never existed. The convent schools that had marked her indelibly must be allowed to exist and Vassar would be allowed to exist too. Vassar approved depth.

Now they would leave the Varadero Beach. Now they would go to Europe. Soon Alexander must write about some-else than Indian Country. Soon there would be nothing more to write about Indian Country. One day it would be written out—so they went to Europe.

Everything that happened those long years in Europe seemed later to be only a searing powder flash of light, a series of brief hallucinations quickly caught and never allowed to be forgotten, sudden pictures of a brittle expatriate world survived sometimes by those with a real and hard and unprotected past. There was in Perrette's past nothing to protect her future. She was born into that kind of middle-class wealth that demands a greater outward show and inward certainty of nothingness called sophistication than Perrette or any human might mentally survive. There was no rock of family, and, beginning with her convent education, there was no rock of love. There was discipline for the sake of discipline, Latin for the sake of Latin, religion for the sake of religion, which so easily evolves into Marx for the sake of Marx, Bohemianism for the sake of Bohemianism, art for art's sake, but never love for any human sake at all. There was never that human kind of love, for that love is a normal, wretched thing, achieved without discipline, wealth, cleverness or kinds of sophistication at all. That kind of love, Perrette thought, is a many suburbaned thing.

"Yes," Perrette said aloud now from her deck chair on the Ile de France. "But it suddenly could become the thing. It could become chic."

"What?" Alexander said staring, watching a man named Bentley disappear.

"Nothing," Perrette said. "What did that man want?"

"Moral support," Alexander said. "He has plans for an avant-garde magazine in Europe. *The Joiner* or *The Booster*, he can't make up his mind. I half promised him something and he threatened to look us up. I figured you knew him. Ezra Pound is considering him and Ernest Hemingway has already knocked him down."

"I know no Charles Bentley," Perrette said.

"Tea?" the deck steward said, balancing his world against the north sea.

"No, thank you very much," Perrette said.

Bentley came back now threatening to let them in on the ground floor of the magazine. Bentley ran to tweeds and a heavy pipe and an Ivy League face and manner that would have been more at home, Alexander thought, in the Oak Room of Merrill Lynch Etcetera than under some gable on the Left Bank, more at home with the solidity of Continental Can and Miami Copper at 25 bid, 27 asked than with the airy instability of *Zero, transition, Tomorrow* or the name that Bentley had now finally decided upon—*The Joiner*.

"The name has a wholesome, contemptuous feel about it," Bentley announced to the Atlantic and his two captives bound in blankets as he paced in front of them on the leaning deck.

"Splendid," Perrette said from somewhere deep among her weight of blankets, sun goggles and books. "I think it's splendid."

Bentley did not know how to take this. He stopped his pacing and went over to the rail and looked down on the tourist class below, while he thought it over. Some of the tourist class have interesting heads, he thought.

"Don't bait him," Alexander said to Perrette from his

deck chair and from deep within the same mummy trappings that Perrette wore. "A writer has enough natural enemies without killing each other off. If we start a fight among ourselves on the wagon train we'll be a cinch for the Indians. An old frontiersman by the name of Bill Williams said that," Alexander said. "Don't insult Bentley. We may need him when the going gets rough."

"You've got it made," Perrette said.

"A writer is as successful as his last paragraph." Alexander said. "You might not like what some of the boys on the wagon train are up to but one day they might save your scalp. No one else is liable to."

"Old Bill Williams," Perrette said.

"He could have said it," Alexander said. "He said a lot of things like that that he didn't practice. The boys could always tell when there would be trouble because Old Bill would always disappear before an attack."

"A smart man," Perrette said.

"They found him one day," Alexander said, "standing at attention, his rifle standing straight alongside him, alone and frozen to death."

"But I wasn't baiting him," Perrette said. "I thought it was a good title for a magazine. I really did."

Bentley had at last decided that Perrette had not meant ill by her remark and he ceased examining the heads of the tourist passengers on the deck below and went back to pacing up and down in front of Perrette and Alexander.

"Let's say we price the magazine," Bentley said, "at one dollar a copy. I just picked that out of the air. Now let's say we sell, well, ten thousand copies. I picked that out of the air too. I have no idea what the circulation will be

but that's a theoretical ten thousand dollars per month."

"If you charged five dollars a copy," Perrette said, "you'd have a theoretical fifty thousand dollars a month."

"I see your point," Bentley said. "Well, let's say we charge fifty cents for the magazine and we cut the circulation down too."

"Yes," Perrette said. "Well, if you sold one copy each to your contributors you'd be taking in four dollars and a half a month. I'm afraid there's nothing theoretical about that."

Bentley went back to the rail, not because he was annoyed with Perrette or the low figures. He knew his break-even point on the magazine would be about five thousand copies and there must be some law that operates against your selling less than the break-even point. He did not go back to the rail to examine the heads of the tourist passengers either, but to examine the ocean, which he found intellectually stimulating.

"Lay off," Alexander said to Perrette. "Let him peddle his papers."

"He's mad," Perrette said.

"Anyone who has anything to do with writing is mad," Alexander said. "The editors, the publishers, all of us. If Bentley seems a little crazier than the rest of us it may be because he's younger."

"I have an intellectual spitball I'd like to try out," Bentley said, coming back. "I have a young genius in his teens and in my stable, a poet, Alfred Marlowe. He should get the credit for this."

"If we're going to give him all the credit," Perrette said, "who is he?"

"A very deep young man."

"If your deep young man's too deep for me what a very very deep young man your deep young man must be."

"Alfred's very aware of his limitations," Bentley said. "He realizes he's operating on the third layer of consciousness. That is, he's still being understood. He figures when he reaches the fifth layer he will break off contact and be on his own, then without the ropes of tradition holding him it will be an unrestricted search for the pure essences of poetry. Without those ropes holding him he figures he will catch it, or at least glimpse it down there someplace, which is sufficient for him."

"Supposing there is a cave-in? Perrette said.

"He has resources to withstand almost anything," Bentley said. "Intelligence, character, insight . . . He's a Texas Tech man."

"Resources?" Perrette said.

"I just told you."

"Money," Perrette said.

"Oil," Bentley said. "He was brought up in oil. But he's not happy. He's looking for new horizons. Truthfully, he's put some money in the magazine with no strings attached except, well—"

"Except he wants to run it," Perrette said.

"You could kind of say that," Bentley said.

"Unfortunately he apparently kind of said it," Perrette said. "But you go ahead. What's his idea for the magazine?"

"Yes. Well, the gimmick on the magazine is that there is no gimmick. All the stories are square. They all have a beginning, a middle and an ending, with all the commas and periods in the right places. They all have an up-beat

45

ending. The editorials will be written by a U.S. Congressman or a Member of Parliament. There will be no dirty words. And the thought for the day will be written by a Methodist minister. We will run editorials against modern art, close dancing, divers forms of fornication up to and including sexual intercourse where reproduction is not indicated. We will have editorials upholding and in praise of the Hawley-Smoot Tariff Act and Mrs. Smoot, George Horace Lorimer, the Republican Party, the Boy Scouts, the Epworth League, the American Legion, Carrie Jacobs Bond and the editors at Doubleday's."

"It's been done before," Perrette said. "When we were in school we got out a mimeographed thing like that."

Bentley stopped pacing.

"Why don't you get out a magazine," Perrette said, "in which all of the writing is a masterpiece, each one a classic, every story better than has ever been done before or will ever be done again, then set your price and the circulation will be enormous."

"Yes," Bentley said, but this time he did not go back to the rail but retreated down the passageway.

"Don't ever kill dreams, even silly dreams, weird dreams. People with shuttered minds will attack them soon enough," Alexander said, removing his dark glasses. "Do you know what I was thinking about while Bentley was talking? I was wondering how many head George would be running this year and I was wondering about George."

"Ole Hoss, you need a drink," Perrette said.

Below in a bar, camouflaged, it seemed, to appear a brothel, they had drinks. They talked about things that did not matter and then Alexander, after being quiet for a

few long moments, said, "Perhaps it would be nice to have some kids. Two boys, say."

Perrette thought it would be nice to have another Manhattan. Alexander finally had a Martini.

"What else would you like?" she said.

"To go back to Indian Country."

"There will be plenty of time for that," she said, "after you see the world. I don't want to go back to anywhere particularly. Vassar maybe? Home? At home we had a nice butler. At home Mommy and Daddy were always a little frightened of me. Daddy used to hide from me in the *Wall Street Journal* and Mommy hid from me by giving me presents."

"Tell me more," Alexander said.

"All right," she said. "I will tell you that when you run out of Indian Country material you don't have to worry. You can have a lot of experiences and write of them."

"Experiences?" Alexander said.

"Yes," Perrette said. "Waiter! Where's the waiter?"

They had some more drinks and then they went on top to their stateroom. The clerk at the steamship office had sold them the finest suite of rooms on the boat for mere money. All of the fixtures in the bathroom were silver except the bathtub faucets.

"These are gold," Perrette said, turning on the hot water, and it steamed heavy into the bedroom where Alexander was getting undressed.

"Everyone," Perrette said, "cannot travel like this. It's only writers, corrupt or lucky, a few millionaires and kings."

"I'll make a note of that," Alexander said. "And what am I, corrupt or lucky?"

"Now you are lucky," Perrette said.

A steward tapped on the door and Alexander threw on a robe against his lank and awkward nakedness and let in the steward with the bottle of champagne Perrette had ordered.

"Merci."

"De rien."

"Did it arrive?"

"It's arrived," Alexander said.

The steward had set the bottle of Mumms in a silver bucket on a teak tray between the twin beds and left.

"Ole Hoss, I reckon you ain't seen nothing like this before," Perrette called from the room that billowed with steam.

"Not rightly, ma'am," Alexander said, watching her.

"The champagne, I mean," Perrette said.

"Yes, ma'am," Alexander said.

"It ain't the homestead," she said.

"Not rightly, ma'am," Alexander said.

"I'm just a cowgirl myself," she said, coming into the room naked.

"I reckon," Alexander said.

"What do you think the critter would weigh, Ole Hoss?"

"One ten. One twenty. I wouldn't rightly know, ma'am."

Perrette put on a robe and sat on the bed.

"What are you going to write about in Europe, Ole Hoss?"

"I don't know. What am I going to write out of now?"

"New experiences, Ole Hoss."

"And why?"

"Money, Ole Hoss."

"That's all?"

"Art, Ole Hoss."

"That man has put up with a lot," Alex said.

"Well, he'll have to carry us too," Perrette said. "Let's drink to Art."

"That's all?"

"No. This," Perrette said and she sat on his lap and put her arm under his robe. "This," she said.

The ship made a bad list and the champagne, glasses, teak tray, silver and everything not nailed ended up in a silk-draped corner on top of Alexander and Perrette. There was a long silence as the big ship evened and until Perrette said weakly, "What's happening to us, Ole Hoss?"

4

All the time they were on the boat going over Bentley continued to appear and disappear suddenly. It seemed that all those lonely, long years in Europe he continued, as on the ship, to appear suddenly and with a look of bewilderment as though surprised to see them still alive.

Although he did not come when they were in Paris, Biarritz or Venice he came again when they were in Ischia and Alexander was half dead, blue-green and white as though he had been in the water four days. There were nurses working over him, kneading him, rolling him over like dough.

At the dock where Bentley landed from Naples there was still a lot of commotion, flags and color. Bentley learned soon that Alexander had swum from Capri to Ischia, an impossible swim that had probably never been done before, no one knew exactly.

Alexander and Perrette were living up in a castle that overlooked the town and the harbor. It had belonged to King Emmanual or some dispossessed royalty who must now settle for their picture on a sardine can. A big wedding cake of a castle, or château, glaring white over the small pink tile roofs of the town, a place that only an American can

afford, which is justice, Bentley thought, because no one else would take it for free.

There were two sets of marble stairs that climbed up in back of the town to the front entrance and when Bentley got to the top of one of these stairs a lackey in uniform let him in. There was Perrette, crouched over an easel, painting a picture in the middle of the entrance hall or place where the ancients took off their armor and helmets. It was that old. Perrette was painting Indians.

Bentley told her he had come for the story.

"Story?" she said, looking up puzzled from her easel.

"Yes," Bentley said. "Alexander tentatively promised me a story."

"Oh, I am sorry," she said. "Won't you follow me?"

Bentley followed her into a small, high, marble room with onyx columns, just off Alexander's bedroom.

"It's not much of a story," Perrette told Bentley leaning forward in one of those small gold chairs. "He swam from Capri to Ischia. You think that would impress his brother?"

"I guess so," Bentley said.

"Good," she said. "First it's climbing mountains, then hunting impossible animals in Africa, and now this. As a child he could always impress George, always win him over when he was mad by—"

"But this is not the story I came for," Bentley said.

"Oh," she said. "The money then. Well, we sent him part of the money. We sent him part of it to finish that petrified-wood house, or burn or throw away. It's Alexander's guilt, although he says the story was about George, partly about their childhood, so George should get part of it—but it was because of me. Yet I was twenty-one."

"But I came for part of the new novel. Fiction," Bentley said.

"Fiction?" she said.

"Yes," Bentley said and he named the magazine.

"Fiction," she said. "Then treat everything I said as fiction." She sat watching Bentley with her big open eyes, leaning perched forward on the small gold chair.

"What Alexander says is true," she said. "Soon, particularly now that he's not there, can't be there—soon there won't be anything more to write about Indian Country. What real experiences can you have when you live in this vacuum? You've got to make experiences, make things happen. So maybe it's for his books, maybe it's for his brother, I don't know." She went back in the small gold chair. "It's this awful business that happened today," she said. "We rowed alongside in a boat feeding him. When it got bad we tried to get him to quit but he's stubborn like a small boy, like all the Bowmans. Then they brought him out and up here all blue and almost dead, so is it any wonder that I am talking about things that should not be talked about? But unless they revive him soon I will go out of my head. I went out there to paint hoping that would get my mind off it. But you said you did not want an article but something to do with fiction."

"Yes," Bentley said and he named the magazine again.

"But that's not the same magazine."

"No. *The Joiner* went bust. We had a fight over the word 'exist' and Alfred ran out of patience before he ran out of genius. But we've got another backer now who still has both. His name is Wendwood Hopgood, Jr., and he likes the name *Nothing*."

"And he's probably awfully right," Perrette said. "Oh, you poor slob. I'll see if Alex is any better."

He was and she said Bentley could look in. Alexander looked very green. Bentley waited out in the onyx room until they called him, and this time everything was splendid. Alexander was sitting in the big chair in a smart robe with a drink but he looked very alert and interesting, as though he had just finished a book. He shook hands and he motioned Bentley into a velvet chair by a cathedral window that looked over the town.

"We had a sheep camp on the Largo," Alexander said finally. "You could see the snow on the Sangre de Cristos all the year around. I always get a place with a view if I can." He took a drink and then continued. "You wouldn't by any chance remember whether they black-topped that trail from Aztec to Dulce? I was just thinking about it."

"Dulce?" Bentley said.

"Yes. That's the Apache Indian headquarters. There was a lot of talk of surfacing it when I left."

"Dulce?"

"I'm sorry," Alexander said and he pulled a big gold-covered rope and the same flunkey who opened the door brought Bentley a drink.

"George would get a kick out of all these gold and marble halls. George was great for adobe floors, claimed it was hard as marble. The trick in adobe floors is light on the straw and heavy on the blood."

"Blood?"

"Sheep's blood. But you came about the story. Well, it's not much. People have swum from Capri to Ischia before,

53

but not in this century. You think George might get a kick out of it?"

"Who?"

"Yes," Alexander said. "Yes. Well, I see you have never been to Indian Country. Still it's not important. What story do you want?"

"A part of the novel you're working on," Bentley said.

"What magazine?"

Bentley told him and Alexander said, "Let's eat. You must be starving."

While they ate Alexander said, "I came out of the small magazines myself, so I help them when I can, if they want it. Anyway we feed everyone who comes to the post now. But we're not just knocking around the world, living in these marble tents. We have a plan."

"Listen to this," Perrette said.

"Yes," Alexander said. "When we make this swim, climb those mountains, hunt those animals in Africa, it's all experiences out of which a person can write. When the Indian Country gives out, when there's no longer a novel there, then I've got these experiences."

"Notebooks upon notebooks full of them," Perrette said. "The only thing he hasn't done against the day when he can't write about his own country is jumping from a plane without a chute."

"And it could be done too," Alexander said. "Those wings they strap to you—what do they call them?—batmen."

"Or fight a bull," Perrette said. "He hasn't done that yet."

"Another writer takes care of that and very well too," Alexander said.

"And there's one more experience we haven't thought of," Perrette said.

"Yes," Alexander said.

"Suicide," Perrette said.

Now fireworks began to burst around the castle, shot from the square below. Bentley did not know what the occasion was; it could have been that they were celebrating Alexander's swim. They would explode outside the window in red, green and purple streams of fire, spinning and hissing, stars exploding within stars, a pleasant nightmare in technicolor.

"Suicide," Alexander repeated. "I suppose," he said, "we commit suicide by living, by getting older."

"Yes," Perrette said. "But the whole thing can be cushioned with drink, which makes it a lot easier for me to wait while you're up there about to fall off a mountain or get run over by an elephant."

A big rocket exploded outside the château with a terrific noise. All the lights went out. Bentley waited around awhile drinking with them in the dark. When he left early in the morning the lights were still out and they were still sitting in the dark drinking, but the fireworks, the celebration, had ceased.

It was in Constantinople the next time Bentley saw Alexander and Perrette. They were staying in another one of those castles. This one was white too but it had a minaret, a tower. They were guests of the Emir, Alexander said—or Caliph. Bentley saw them on the Bosporus. They were driving a white carriage, huge, with gold wheels. That is, a big black Negro in costume, who must have belonged to

the friend, the Emir or the Caliph, was driving it. Four golden horses with black tails, purple plumes over their necks. Perrette and Alexander were sitting behind this costumed black on white cushions all dressed to kill with a small boy at their feet playing what might have been a dulcimer.

Bentley waved and hollered to them but they didn't hear. Maybe it was the noise of the dulcimer. Bentley expected any moment they would throw a gold coin. He followed them all the way to the castle, where there was a crowd, and again he expected them to throw gold coins. When they got to the castle someone belonging to the Emir or Caliph closed the big, wide, iron-grilled carriage gate in his face, and that was the end of that.

Bentley did not see them again until he had to take a temporary job as a correspondent and ran into them in Israel during the Arab war. They were all staying in the Hayarkin Hotel in Tel Aviv, where the correspondents were housed. Alexander was quite famous now and some magazine was paying him tons of money to write some opinions about the war. Bentley didn't feel good in Tel Aviv. He saw the war the way the Arabs saw it. Alexander? Well, the Israelis were losing at the time so he saw it the way they saw it. Finally he saw it so much that way that he disappeared.

Perrette would sit in front of his typewriter all day in the correspondent's room, the lobby of the Hayarkin, where they had the desks set up. Just sit there looking out at the ocean, past that wrecked ship that was always there. At four o'clock the Israeli information colonel would come in and tell what appeared to Bentley a pack of lies about the glorious victories of his heroic Israeli armies, then the colonel would pass

this out in mimeographed form and Perrette would take Alexander's and add it to the growing stack that already hid the ship if not the ocean. Then she bought a parrot, took to feeding it and teaching it to say something patriotic to please the colonel. It wasn't until later, not long before they discovered Alexander, that she began to bring a bottle.

They found Alexander in a hospital in Beersheba. He had joined up as a private and finally got hit badly; shrapnel. The hospital had overflowed so they had him in a captured Arab house. It had a dome ceiling, done in mosaic tile, no windows, just a door. Bentley drove Perrette down there in an old German jeep. Alexander was very bad. Bentley stayed there as long as he was still very bad. Perrette was with him three weeks. Alexander raved most of the time, turning over on the army cot, whispering into the dirt floor on one side and then turning over and talking to the dirt floor on the other.

"Go, George, and get help. Get the Indians. Get Father. Get a rope. Lower the rope and pull me out of the mine. I see a hole of light. It must be a mile above me. The side of the mine is slippery. I gain a few feet and sink back again. I have to go up a little way once more but until the daylight comes I dare not move. To keep my sanity I make up stories. Here at the bottom of the world I wait."

Bentley joined Perrette at the door of the arched hut.

"It's a symbol," Bentley said. "The mine is a word for everything outside of Indian Country."

"Symbol, no," Perrette said. "He really spent three days at the bottom of a real mine shaft, buried one hundred feet deep, lost. You don't know all the facts and maybe neither does he. All the facts," Perrette said. "There seemed to be

a feeling at the post among some of the Indians that the whole story never got out."

"But I got this out of his raving," Bentley said. "It was George who rescued him, brought him back to Indian Country, the world, life again."

"Maybe we don't know all the facts," Perrette said. "And neither does he."

"What were the facts?" Bentley said. "What are the facts about Alexander's entombment, his first burial, his being resurrected, snatched from certain death by his brother?"

"Plucked," Perrette said. "But I don't know. Ask George."

"Who's George?"

"His brother," Perrette said.

Alexander got well and they began to travel again and all those final years in Europe were images of those first sad desperate years in Europe. Their's was the way of expatriates, all those people who wander. But Alexander wrote another very successful Indian Country novel, his fourth, and had many new experiences against the day when the Indian Country material would be exhausted. And Perrette waited at the foot of the mountain or the edge of the jungle with her heart in her mouth, then drinking.

He finally had to write that book about his experiences, adventures, and it was silly. Maybe it was that his public had gotten to expect a great deal of him. Maybe it was as good as any adventure story but for him the verdict was that he was making up heroics. Sometimes a critic will wait a lifetime for a friend to write a book as bad as Alexander's. One of the nicest things they said was that "our boy has run out of gasoline."

Then Alexander and Perrette went back to Mazatlán

to get as close to Indian Country as they could get. In Mazatlán, as close, he figured, as his brother would let him.

The last time Bentley saw them in Europe, before they went back to Mazatlán, they had finally moved out of castles—marble hogans Alexander called them—discovered that you did not have to live in suburbia or a castle. There was something else. There were villas on the Mediterranean. It was in Cros-de-Cagnes and joined the hotel. It was very impressive. People thought he was renting half the hotel. Alexander would work in the morning, then in the afternoon they would hike up the stream to Cagnes-sur-Mer; they even had the courage sometimes to climb up the mountain to Haut-de-Cagnes. It took courage because it was full of rats—artists who lived like rats. The painters had burrowed into this old medieval fortress called Haut-de-Cagnes, built about the tenth century, lived there certainly without food, encouragement or even hope. Then Perrette and Alexander began buying their pictures.

"This one, that one and the one over there," Perrette would say. The outcasts would take their money in unbelief and haste as though expecting any second someone from the twentieth century would come and lock up Alexander and Perrette.

Going down the mountain they talked intimately so Bentley thought it best to lag behind, pretending an interest in the hovels. The steps were in tiers, about fifteen steps and then a platform. Bentley always stayed an echelon behind but he could still hear them. And then they drifted into a café halfway down the mountain. Bentley stopped at the bar while they went into the back room but he could still see and hear them. Alexander looked tired, empty, and

he rested his chin on the roll of canvases, looking over at Perrette, who was still young with that kind of youthfulness that will, someday, suddenly collapse under its own tricks.

"We've got to get home," she said.

"We're going," Alexander said.

"I mean home to the States," she said.

"And live in one of your father's marble tents on Long Island? I don't think so."

"Then I could try Indian Country again," she said. "George is here all the time with us anyway. And he may have forgotten or married or something by now."

"I've written him," Alexander said. "Nearly twenty or thirty times, and no answer." They had a drink. "I was thinking," he said, "the only thing that separates us from the rats, those people, is success."

"You look terrible," she said.

"I got the book off this morning," he said.

"Good," she said. "Then you won't have to write about Indian Country—ever. We can forget it."

"Yes," Alexander said.

"Jesus, you look terrible," Perrette said.

"The book can't help but be successful," Alexander said. "It's got everything—everything but Indian Country. I'm off the hook."

"Then let's celebrate," Perrette said. They touched glasses.

"To the future," Alexander said.

"My God, you look ill," Perrette said. "I'd better call a doctor."

"There's nothing wrong with me," Alexander said, grabbing her arm, "that any doctor, any white doctor, can treat. You remember a fool, an unscientific fool, on the reservation

called Paracelsus? He could help me," Alexander said. "And you remember a man called George Bowman, a brother, a husband? He could help me," Alexander said. "I've got to get home, the Indian Country, the ranch, something I know—interests me—I can write about, live about. And don't worry, George won't carry a grudge all his life. He'll come through when he's really needed. I was three long dying days at the bottom of an old mine shaft in the Largo country and George found me. George never let me down. We have got to have patience and hang on. George will—"

"You're hurting my arm," Perrette said.

"To the past, then," Alexander said, and he dropped her arm and raised his glass.

"Yes, to the past," Perrette said. "To those happy first four months when we thought we could find some kind of happiness in running away, to the first day I saw you, to the first night in Albuquerque, to our last night in Europe and our first night back in the States."

They got back to Mexico. That's as far as they got.

5

The Chevvy pickup made its way around the point of the dry mesa. The pickup was all blue and so was the sky. The rocks were orange here, further on they were yellow and jutted out over the trail so that soon the golden rock would form a roof over the blue pickup. There was a big splash of red in the back of the blue pickup because that was the color of the blankets the Pendleton people were showing this season in the checkerboard area. There were two Navaho women in the back of the truck facing each other. They were not saying anything but this was their custom. That they rode in the back and the men in the front was a custom too. The women were being driven from the post of George Bowman, the white trader, where they had had nothing but talk because they were without credit, back to their hogans which were without food, to put an edge on their knives. The long drought had given their hunger a splendid edge. This was becoming a custom too.

George Bowman and the husbands of the two Indians in the rear were going to drop the wives at a hogan to rig a pole and sharpen their knives to dress out a buck. The people in front were going to kill a buck. They had their guns hidden

under a blanket above the floor board. They were going hunting out of season. This wasn't a custom at all. But this hunger was becoming a custom and, among many other and more painful words, one Navaho found it a bore.

"I tell you, Sansi," Quicker-Than-You said to George Bowman, "it's becoming a big bore."

Once upon a time in the Indian Country there was rain but now the Indian Country had gone through fifteen years of drought. The great petrified-log house had been boarded up for fifteen years. Alexander Bowman had stolen George's wife fifteen years ago. To the Indians the drought made sense. It was brutal but it made sense. The medicine man in his prediction had been right. The medicine man was always right. George Bowman and Quicker-Than-You were certain that the theft of the wife had nothing to do with the drought (we are convinced after many consultations with many wise men that the drought is caused by insufficient rain). But the cruel drought continued as did the prestige of the medicine man, and the best of the Indian Country continued to blow away.

The Indians wanted George Bowman to write a letter to his brother, Alexander, to bring him back. They thought this might stop something. George was certain this would not stop the drought on the land.

George had an excellent reason for not writing his brother. All the Indians knew this but the drought continued and they tried. George believed, too, that he had a perfect excuse for never answering the letters he got from his brother, but the drought continued in his heart and he tried.

"Anybody but a human being could do it. It would be easy," the Indian next to the door said.

"What?" the Indian in the middle said.

"Forgive what we are doing today. My wife can't see it."

The two Navahos were wearing blue Levis, black-and-yellow boots, and each had a red cotton band around his forehead. George wore a leather jacket and a large and very worn Stetson. They wore the same thing in any season.

George said nothing but continued to watch the road. He was trying to drive the blue pickup and compose a letter in his mind.

"I tell you, Sansi," Quicker-Than-You kept up, "it's become an awful bloody bore." George still said nothing and the Navaho said, "I got that from a book, Sansi. Tell me, is that the way they talk at your Yale during the cocktail hour? That is, you can't possibly play football all the time even at your Yale. There must be a cocktail hour. Did you know that Sansi went to Yale? Alexander went to Yale too. It must be about fifteen years since he went away to be with the whole world. His last book was not so good. I wonder if he has reached the end of the world."

Rabbit Stockings was the other Indian in front of the blue pickup with the guns hidden and he said, "Shut up, Quicker-Than-You."

They arrived now at the hogans of the Navaho. George stopped the blue pickup and the wives who were riding in the back got off. They would erect a pole to hang the buck on and sharpen their knives and wait for the men to get back. The hogan was octagonal shaped and made of vertically placed cedar posts chinked with adobe. The roof was conical and of mud, laced underneath with piñon. There was a hole in the middle for the smoke to come out when they cooked but there was no smoke from any of the hogans.

There was a green-and-orange wagon parked outside the hogan with an enormous lever that was a hand brake and the big letters INDIANA written on its side. The trader's name appeared in smaller letters underneath. Between the gaudy wagon and the mud-colored hogan two skeletal paint horses refused to get off the trail for the blue pickup, just staring at it as it came up with their feral, stupid and beautiful eyes. Each of the paint horses had a ragged patch of white over his left eye, which gave them the appearance of having only two eyes between them. George was forced to go around the paint horses, knocking down the thick olive chamise brush, the pickup thumping heavily. The horses looked at each other as if they had won something.

They were on the trail tracks again now, their fenders brushing against the wide, heavy, head-high, olive-colored chico and chamise bushes and the rabbit brush that, from a distance, made the country all appear yellow.

"Tell us one of the stories your brother wrote about us Indians, Sansi," Rabbit Stockings said.

"I never read one."

They had to cross an arroyo now and there were two crossings, one a tender-looking bridge made of number five lumber, and a road that wound down the arroyo and up the other side for the heavier wagons. George tried it across the bridge and made it okay with the Indians not breathing.

"Didn't you tell us about the law of the brotherhood of man, Sansi?" Quicker-Than-You said. "Doesn't that apply to your own brother?"

"There are other laws too," George said.

"Like not stealing wives when the husband is around or not

hunting out of season," Quicker-Than-You said.

"I suppose so," George said and he swore at the Indian under his breath

The earth in the badlands all had wide cracks and was in waves. It was encrusted with alkali. Sometimes there was a big barranca where the scientists hunted and the government soil people looked and which the Navahos found difficult to cross.

"And our paintings aren't supposed to look like anything."

The driver didn't say anything.

"Check, Sansi?" Quicker-Than-You insisted.

"I said they need not look like something familiar."

"They have other laws, Sansi, like—"

"Shut up, Quicker-Than-You," Rabbit Stockings said.

The pickup was crawling in compound over a great mound that looked like a dome of salt and the land was without anything except the distant dry blue mesa as far as they could see.

"Okay, Sansi, I'm going to lay off it," Quicker-Than-You said. "I'm going to be a heap good tourist Indian. Tell me, Sansi, do you like my wife's pictures on the rugs she makes where the men's bodies are like a pencil? Are they unfamiliar enough?"

"I like them very much, very much," George said.

"Okay, Sansi, I believe that. You buy them even now when you can't sell them. But do you think my wife is beautiful?"

"Yes," George said.

"Okay, we better change the subject," Quicker-Than-You said. "And speaking of women, you know we Navahos haven't raided the Pueblo People for a little while now."

"Almost two hundred years," Rabbit Stockings said.

"I wonder if their women miss us," Quicker-Than-You said.

George had to shift down again to get over a bad place.

"Before the whites the Navaho could take what he wanted," Quicker-Than-You said slowly. "That went for the wives and the game too. Nothing was out of season."

George was hoping that the very-bright-indeed Indian would drop it for a while. He was trying to compose the letter.

The Navaho was still cricling in the attack and he came in now fast and under the cover of something else.

"You going to hit me with a writ, Sansi, on my wagon that isn't paid for?"

"No," George Bowman said. "Because it wouldn't do any good."

"That comedian from the used-car lot in Gallup hit me with a writ on my former Cadillac, Sansi. I tell you, Sansi, a Cadillac is not much of an automobile for this country."

"Especially when they hit you with a writ," George said.

Rabbit Stockings was not following anything. He always found Quicker-Than-You sharper than anything he had ever felt before. It cut him when he touched—understood him— which was not very often, but he could not put down Quicker-Than-You. Quicker-Than-You would not allow himself to be dropped. Quicker-Than-You had begun his campaign several days ago, when the hunger got bad, to go hunting out of season. Today he had succeeded.

Rabbit Stockings was not silent only because he found Quicker-Than-You too sharp but because Rabbit Stockings had nothing to say. Rabbit Stockings had just gone through a period when he had plenty to say; his wife had to have a kidney stone removed and the clan had had many sings for her to pull her through and Rabbit Stockings was very

popular. It was the biggest thing that had happened to his clan for two years. Even when the stone turned out to be much smaller than supposed, "and, of course, of no intrinsic value."

One thing you could credit to Quicker-Than-You was that he was not a professional Indian. They were passing two professional Indians. From this hill they could see the heart of Cuba city, which was worth about two professional Indians dressing as the Babbitts insisted they should dress and jumping the way the Babbitts insisted they should jump. Today the professional Indians walking toward Cuba were Tom-Dick-and-Harry and Silver Threads. The Indians in the pickup did not wave to them as they went by.

One credit you could *not* give to Quicker-Than-You, Rabbit Stockings thought, was that he knew when to keep his mouth shut.

"When the regular hunting season was on we were scared," Quicker-Than-You said. "I tell you, Sansi, I went through the war. It never bothered me very much, but I tell you, Sansi, when those shooting people from the city were here I was scared. What was the word they used, Sansi? Safari? What does it mean? Sansi says safari means they're trying to prove something."

"I did not," George said and shifted her into second, slowing her to go over a steel cattle guard.

"Well, say it now," Quicker-Than-You said.

"Okay, it's been a long time. Certainly I should write him, answer his letters."

"What?"

"Oh, all right," George Bowman said, looking over at

the Indian now. "I will say the safari people are trying to prove they've got more money than you."

"That's my boy," Quicker-Than-You said, clapping George Bowman on the knee.

"Speaking of writing, my wife's reading a book," Quicker-Than-You said. "What do you think, Sansi? You think that can be dangerous?"

They waited alongside the trail now for a wagonful of Navahos to pass.

"Sansi, it's called *The Power of Positive Drinking*, or *Thinking* I guess it is. I read parts of it. You know, Sansi, I think they're trying to fool us Indians."

"I think so too," George said, starting the car again. "But they're sincere." And then he wished he had said nothing.

"Everybody's sincere, Sansi. The game warden's sincere. Everybody's sincere, Sansi. We're sincere about killing a buck out of season. But we're hungry, Sansi."

"Half the world is hungry," George Bowman said.

"But the other half isn't as close to the deer as this half, Sansi."

"For an illiterate Indian you do all right," George said.

"I stayed out of Yale," Quicker-Than-You said. "That's more than a lot of the Indians who live this close to the mission did. I stayed out of Yale."

"But you can't live on that," Rabbit Stockings said. "You've got to accomplish something else. Your wife stayed out of Yale."

"True," Quicker-Than-You said. "But Sansi didn't."

"Okay," George said. "But can't you drop everything for a while?"

"Sure, sure," Quicker-Than-You said. "And I will accomplish something else today. I will kill that big buck. Five hundred yards, right between the eyes."

George Bowman winced.

They had passed through the great city of Cuba now and were going past the ranches of the white people. There were not many of them in these thousands of square miles of New Mexico and these were between the Navaho and the Apache Nations. Alexander, the writer, had called the white lands a buffer state. What Quicker-Than-You called them was not printable. Rabbit Stockings was patient and completely without heavy weapons to support his opinions so he was patient. Most of the other Indians were patient too.

They went by Red Feeder's place and Red Feeder with Cass Goodner and Whitey Johnson, all in identical wide black hats and sharp-pointed boots, were trying to pour a corralful of mixed white-faced and Brahma cattle up through a chute and into a huge semi-truck and trailer that would hold thirty-six. They wanted to get started back to the sale ring in Albuquerque, and the sharp-faced, city-dressed driver was swearing and trying to erect a center section in the semi to keep the cattle from going down in the hills above San Ysidro, but the cattle were pushing and he wasn't doing any good, and as they went by the people in the blue pick-up could hear the city man swearing.

They continued down the trail which had become a road now that went to Aztec and they began to count the gates. They would turn off at the third forest gate. The Indians had spotted the big buck some time ago and knew he ran with two does at a logged clearing near the center of the Cuba mesa. They had to get the trader in on it because he would

furnish the shells, now that they were without credit, and the pickup with a tarp to put the buck under, which would create no suspicion as they went by the ranger station in Cuba. They had nothing to worry about, the nearest game warden was one hundred miles away. The scheme was absolutely fool-proof.

"You have nothing to worry about but your thoughts, Sansi. And I tell you your thoughts are absolutely wrong." Quicker-Than-You counted the second gate and continued as he had been continuing for the last week. "It's not that I am bitter, Sansi. I am willing to let lost wars be lost wars and lost land remain forever lost. But remember, in this you're in the same position as the Navaho, Sansi. You are frightened as any non-institutionalized person would be to venture your head above ground while the city whites are banging away at each other during the hunting season to celebrate the next Du Pont Powder Company's dividend. You have seen the deer starving in the winter snows because of overpopulation since the wise policy of the Great White Father to kill off the big cats. You see the starving weak deer get killed every winter by the few remaining cats. I ask you, Sansi, are the mountain lions more privileged than us?"

"How many gates was that?" George Bowman asked.

"Two. We turn at the next one, Sansi."

"And if you keep it up," George said, "we will go back to the post."

"I'm not saying anything, Sansi. I apologize for being born."

They turned into the third forest gate now and Rabbit Stockings got out to pull the fence. There was a small clearing of logged country before they entered the forest. At the edge of this there was a Spanish family from La Ventana cording

firewood. The Indians, who did not have to get along with these people, called them Mexicans. The Anglo ranchers, who did, called them Spanish-Americans. Alexander had called them people. These people bent upright again and waved as the blue Chevvy pickup went by. The trader waved back. They had on red baseball caps.

The pickup entered the dark forest now and nobody said anything, even while they traveled for fifteen minutes and until George stopped the truck near an old abandoned mine shaft, and then they talked in whispers and signaled to each other with their arms.

This hunt had been carefully planned and they all knew very much what to do. They started off with Rabbit Stockings, who was probably better than anyone in the world at this sort of thing, leading, then came the trader followed quickly by Quicker-Than-You. They began to travel in a big circle in a direction that always kept the moving air coming into their faces, and up wind from the deer, and which would bring them soon to the point in the jut of the mesa where they would no longer walk in file but all make a half turn and sweep the mesa. The buck and the two does, if he still had them, could not outflank the hunters and double back, which is an old wisdom of theirs, because there was a sheer cliff on either side of this jut in the mesa. And soon the deer would have to make a break in the logged clearing the hunters were pushing them toward. This maneuver was a memorable startegy of the Navaho long before it was a classic strategy of the British Navy.

The hunters had made their simultaneous turn now and were combing the mesa. A big, gentle, wafer-soft snow began to come down as they made their turn but it did nothing to

their plans; if there was enough of it they could even use it for tracking. The great drought that had had the Navaho People down on one knee for a very long count might be breaking. On the way up George had noticed the fat gray cumulus building up to the cirrus and now, as the flat gentle flakes came into his face on a long downward curve, so individual, big and spaced apart that maybe you could count them, he was not surprised at all. He could still see the Navahos in a quiet white haze through the sparse piñon as the line moved forward.

The big dark gray buck with a white belly and great puzzled eyes beneath ten fine spreading points of antlers, who must easily go three hundred or more pounds, had his two does working a stretch of grama grass just above the logged clearing when the buck picked up the man smell. The buck felt toward the direction of the man smell with his square black nose that was shining wet, until he was certain there were three of them and that there was no hope of getting around their flank and coming in behind them. But he took several tentative but graceful and light, for his heaviness, quick steps toward the hunters to make certain he could not bring his does through them before he went with them toward the clearing he knew he must avoid.

The great buck with the large puzzled eyes who nuzzled the does now into movement had, in his wisdom and ten years of experience, gotten through eight hunting seasons, subtracting those years when he was illegal game. Now he had to get through an extra season. He had only last week finished weathering a month-long war which came each year at the same time when the man smell shot at everything that moved, including, not only each other, but, in some strange

rite, themselves (the great buck had watched from a crag with his two does a hunter stumble as he left his car and shoot himself, and as the pool of red spread, these three witnesses had fled into the Largo country, to return only three days ago to this part of the mesa on which he had, until now, been able to successfully maneuver and triumph).

Rabbit Stockings made an arm signal to the others that he had picked up the almost noiseless sound of the buck pushing his wide spread of antlers through the drought-dry ground suckers of the dwarf oak. The Navaho must have picked up other gentle sounds too because he pumped his left arm three times to indicate the number and then, with the same arm, made a great circle in the air to signify that the buck was moving in front toward the open clearing up ahead.

George signaled now to increase the pace, knowing they must press the deer and close the range—be able to take advantage of that moment's hesitation the deer would have before they broke across the clearing. The hunters clicked off their safeties. The deer would have to go any second now.

The does broke first, pushed out by the buck. They made their run fast and bounding. Then the buck came out but slowly as though to draw the fire on himself. He made an unnecessary turn and looked back straight at the trader, and George Bowman had never had an easier shot in his life. He raised the gun and squeezed off two shots. Rabbit Stockings on his right, who had an even easier shot, pounded off two more. The big buck turned, pivoted slowly again, his white tail flashing before he decided to bound off fast in the direction of the aspens where the does were already safe. They watched him go with no one firing. Quicker-Than-You had not fired at all.

They all converged on the trader now, but they said nothing until they had each lit up one of George's cigarettes. They all stood with the butt of their carbine alongside their left foot.

"Son of a bitch. I missed him twice," Rabbit Stockings said.

"I missed him twice," George Bowman said.

"I never got off a shot," Quicker-Than-You said. "I knew you boys had him."

"Son of a bitch. I missed him twice," Rabbit Stockings said.

When they finished their cigarettes it was beginning to snow very heavily and as they made their way back to the pickup they crossed the tracks of the buck where he had joined the does. They could tell by the size of the tracks he was as beautiful as they remembered.

"Too late to track," Rabbit Stockings said.

"Much too late," George said.

When they got back to the blue pickup it was already cased in white and George scraped the snow off the windshield before he started her up. He thought the snow would be heavy on the poles the Indian women had prepared.

There was a heater in the cab of the blue pickup and they were plenty warm going back. They did not hide their guns now; the Navahos kept them between their knees. They were short carbine twenty-inch lever-action Winchesters, pointing at the roof. George's big and old Clabrough-Martin, which had been the property of his father, was pointing at the floor. He had emptied it. All the guns were empty. When they got to the edge of the dark forest and came out into the light the Navahos waved to the people gathering wood. The Spaniards

75

looked up surprised but they waved back. One of them took off his red cap.

After they got through the forest gate there was a wagonful of Apaches pulled by two starving small Indian ponies, getting ready to camp for the night against the driving snow. The Navahos in the pickup waved to these people too. The wagonful of Apaches did not seem to know how to take it but they waved back. They were probably going to Zia for a sing. There must be, Rabbit Stockings thought, fourteen of those red Apaches piled in that green wagon being pulled by those two splashed-white and sorry horses.

At Red Feeder's the men had emptied the semi and were trying to load it again, properly this time. The men with wide black hats and pointed boots were waving at the mixed Brahma and white-faced cattle with sticks, and the sharp-faced city driver was on top of the red semi cursing and waving a stick too. None of them were waving at the Navahos in the pickup who were waving at them. The Navahos did not seem to mind.

In the heart of Cuba they stopped in front of Bart Montoya's New York City Bar and allowed the two professional Indians to get in the back of the pickup. Going out of town they waved to the small, thin, college-boy forest ranger in green uniform and Boy Scout hat sitting in the window of the ranger station reading a book of DeVoto's on the Wild West. He looked a long way from home. He wasn't waving to anyone.

Soon they were back in the checkerboard area and there wasn't any more waving. The snow was piling up on the north side of the hogans and there was no smoke from the holes in the dome-shaped roofs. All the chimneys were quiet. They

went by the petrified-log house that had been boarded up fifteen years now. This one was especially quiet.

When they got to Rabbit Stocking's hogan the snow was thick on the poles the women had erected to dress out the buck. George didn't stop; he kept right on going.

"Wait," Rabbit Stockings said. "I live here."

"I know," George said. "But first we must go to the post."

Inside the dark, great room of the adobe-and-log trading post George pumped up the Colemans and lit them and from underneath the bare shelves he managed to assemble two boxes of groceries.

"But," Rabbit Stockings said, "what are you going to eat?"

"I got plenty," George Bowman said.

Quicker-Than-You went around in back of the counter where he did not belong and then he stuck up his head and said, "There's nothing left but a case of beans."

"You cannot live on a case of beans," Rabbit Stockings said.

"I can live on a case of beans if an Indian can live on nothing," George said, and he lit up a cigarette and offered them each one which they did not accept.

"We can work up a credit at Johnson's," Quicker-Than-You said. "There's no need to rob you."

"Johnson's post is finding it impossible to carry their own Indians through this period. He absolutely could not carry you."

"I know," Rabbit Stockings said. "Our credit is worthless."

George was looking out the window toward the hogans and beyond these to the blue mesa. The snow had stopped. It wasn't much of a snow after all. It wouldn't do much good.

"After today we all maybe draw a little fresh credit," George

said finally and he pushed the boxes off on his friends and they left silently.

After they had left George took one of the cans of beans, the Coleman lantern and a pen and piece of paper into a small back room he used as a kitchen since he had boarded up the big house, and opened the can of beans.

Yes, George thought, when you had inherited all of the downs and ups of three generations, then maybe you could take one more bad year. Just one more year, he had been telling himself for fifteen years now, and now he told it to himself again. Just maybe one more year, he said. Just one more year finally adds up to eternity but I do not find eternity with The People too hard to take. Even with Quicker-Than-You. Perhaps it is only the Quicker-Than-Yous that make eternity bearable, he thought. Anyway you take it as it comes. George was feeling pretty good about the day's happenings. In the last fifteen years he had learned to be satisfied with being a small winner.

Yes, after today everyone deserves some credit, he said aloud slowly and to no one. Now he got down to the business of trying to write a letter to Alexander. He couldn't do any good so instead he would try to eat the beans. He was sick of beans.

After he finished the beans he got back to the letter again. "Dear Alex," he wrote. And then he wrote, "It has been a long time." And then he crossed this out and started again.

"Dear Alex: Today we went deer hunting but didn't get a deer but we talked about you. The country has changed a lot. It is getting drier all the time and they are beginning to drill for oil all over the place. Fortunately they have not found any and soon they may leave. There was a Malco engineer

here yesterday testing. He told me a foreign car club he belongs to intends to hold a rally here. As the Indians have just planted I will do my best to stop it. But I am writing around something, Alex. Backing into saying what I want to say to you—what I must say to you which is—"

George put the pen down and looked out the window. The snow wasn't falling any more. How, he thought, after fifteen years—? Then he thought, he's doing fine. Why should I bother. Forget. Then he said, against the window pane that was rough with ice, "Sure, why not? If it's impossible to write, to say all the things you must say, you can't say, then say this. George went back and picked up the pen.

"Tonight I am writing you for the first time in fifteen years. Why tonight? Because today we talked about you on the mesa where the old mine shaft is. You remember Rabbit Stockings and Quicker-Than-You? Well, today they talked about you on the mesa where the mine shaft is. Quicker-Than-You is always talking about you, reading your books and telling me about them. But today he made me realize that for twenty-five years, since we were boys, I have been avoiding that part of the mesa. I did not want to go up there but I went up there because the Indians were hungry. Fifteen years have passed since you and Perrette went away. Fifteen years of drought. The medicine man was right on all counts. Fifteen years of bad crops and not enough food for my Indians. Fifteen years of tearing up your letters. In fifteen years a man should forgive—forget."

George threw the pen down then took it up again and wrote: "I do not think I can do any real good for myself or the Indians until we settle this thing between us. I was thinking the best thing—" George scratched this part out. He

would get back to it later. "The Indians blame me for the drought. They say it would stop if you came home. They say you would come home if I wrote 'I for—' "

Now George picked up the letter. He walked across the small room and out into the great room of the post. It was dark and heavy with the cold in the big room and when he opened the front door even the night outside seemed bright. He tore the letter up now and allowed the pieces to flutter out of his hand in the cold wind. An Indian was huddled there someplace, against the wind, beneath the log overhang, watching the night and now the bits of white paper streaming past.

"Love letter?"

"Yes," George Bowman said.

6

Alexander had taken a room high in the hotel in Mazatlán so that he could look out over things and catch all the breeze there was.

The fifteen years that he had spent in Paris and Bombay and London and Nairobi and especially Paris and all the other splendid places that the expatriates go because they cannot go home, had, along with his inner longings, aged him on the outside more than fifteen years will. But on the inside it had been much more than this. It felt much closer to one hundred years since he had seen the country and people he loved because he knew and understood them. Now, after fifteen years, he knew that he must write about them again because everything else was written out of him. Certainly his last book proved that. Not as much as they said, he thought, but it certainly proved I have come to the end of something. But this is about as close as I can get to Indian Country now. Quicker-Than-You tells me in his seldom letters that I am responsible for the drought. I wonder if that medicine man holds me responsible for the Treaty of Versailles. I wonder if George will ever write.

As he thought these thoughts he was looking out over Mazatlán, Mexico, which rose sad across the gulf from the

tip of Baja California at a point on the Tropic of Cancer where the quiet desert ends and the poisoned jungles begin. It's on a flat, ocean-jutting peninsula, but along the land base rises a bald mountain. On its dome they had erected a radio mast and beneath this a wild red-and-yellow transmitting shack, now disintegrated. Once upon a time, and on a good day, and before something complicated had decomposed, the tower could send a signal almost to Tepic.

Today a herd of cattle grazes the dry brown grass of the dome. At some distance from the others stands an older seed bull; short ugly scars gouge his once brilliant flank, the horns are shattered and the eyes have begun to go dull. He is muscle-hurting and looking down at the town which he can't see sharply. Yet he would not have to see sharply to notice the sudden slab of ferro-concrete hotel that rises, alien, from among the aged red-tiled roofs at the deepest swing of the crescentric, eye-hurting white beach. Up on about the tenth floor, in a corner room, all of the windows are open but the curtains are catching no breeze.

Alexander, in a long-billed fishing cap and shorts, was sitting at the typewriter near the window but he was not looking at the machine that had been silent all morning, but looking up the dry, hot road that ran along the edge of the beach. The large modern, sanitary room in which he sat hung out over the sea and, from an angle way back in the room, it might have been the prow of a ship over the water; but even up here with the windows on both sides there was not any breeze at all. It was real Mazatlán weather. And right now he saw it all the hard way. But he had not seen Perrette. And now he looked through the heavy heat all the way up to the big rock at the end of the peninsula

that marked the end of the bay for the fishing ships. If she had gone to the post office she would be coming back soon. Alexander still hoped, after so many years of silence, that there might be that certain letter for him.

He could see the post office clearly through the heat and he could see the people walking on the streets but he could not see the Hawaiian red shirt splashed with gaudy yellow Perrette had worn. And Alfred was certain to be with her again. The Genius and the Child—he had been calling them that for several days now. And it had not started when the fishing went bad—it had started before that. He would have to give this some thought. He had been giving things like this much thought all morning and he felt like hell.

There was a knock on the door and the tall man leaning over the typewriter, looking thoughtfully out of the window, said: "Come in." The door opened but no one came in. A man stood at the open door dressed in a careful business suit, his white hair brushed immaculately over his forehead.

"I am from the Chamber of Commerce," the man said in pretty good English. "We did not discover until this morning that you were the famous American writer. We would have had a deputation at the airport if we had discovered it earlier."

Alexander, sitting at the typewriter said nothing, not even looking toward the clean man standing in the door.

"Now that we have discovered it," the man standing in the door said, "we are waiting on your pleasure. Is there something we can do for you?"

"Yes," Alexander said finally, not looking at the door, still looking out the window. "Go away."

"I have been chosen," the man standing in the door said, "to speak for the others, for the press. We did not want to bother you when we know you would be busy composing so they are all waiting downstairs and they nominated me as a party of one. Do you have something for the press?"

"No," Alexander said.

The well-pressed Mexican fidgeted at the doorway now, brushing his flat Indio face with his small delicate hand.

"Someone below said you might belong to the Kiwanis but I did not think so," the man said.

"Yes, I belong to the Kiwanis," Alexander said, "and I have a hole in my head."

"An Elk then?" the Mexican asked sympathetically.

"Tiger," Alexander said.

"We have quite a Rotary here," the business Mexican said, "of which I have the privilege to head, although I suppose you would not be interested in that."

"Fascinated," Alexander said.

The man at the doorway looked confused and searched for something different to say. "Your article on Mexico I enjoyed very much," he said finally. "It should bring tourists."

Alexander said nothing, still looking out of the window.

The booster was reassured, thinking he had gotten something going. "Your last book I could not follow," he said. "It seemed quite bitter. I thought that—"

"If you're going to give a talk we will sell tickets," Alexander said.

"But I must have something for the press," the man almost insisted.

"The press in this town must be quite an operation," Alexander said, not thinking about it.

84

"We have one paper," the Mexican said, "And then the man from the paper at Tepic is here. Soon, with a personage such as yourself, there should be someone from the big dailies of Mexico City."

"Do you have a pair of fieldglasses?" Alexander said at last, turning his face away from the window.

"Yes," the Mexican said. "There is a pair at the desk. They use them for spotting fish. I suppose you want to see if there are any fish breaking at the islands."

"Yes," Alexander said. "I want to spot some fish."

The Mexican closed the door quietly. Alexander did not move from his hunched position over the typewriter until the Mexican came back with his gentle knock. The door barely opened and the fieldglasses came in first.

"Thank you very much," Alexander said, taking them.

"I hope you see many fish running," the Mexican said.

"I hope I see some, but they will probably not be running."

"Still nothing for the press?" the Mexican said hopefully.

"Nothing for the press of Mazatlán, Tepic or even New York. Did you know," Alexander said, "that there is someone here from New York, a Mr. Alfred Marlowe, a famous young man from a famous literary publication? Few people have heard of the famous literary publication and only my wife has heard of Mr. Marlowe."

"I have not heard of a Mr. Marlowe being here," the Mexican said, confused, thinking.

"No one has," Alexander said. "But yet he is a big something. According to my wife he is a genius." Then Alexander knew that he had pushed it too far, but he noticed that the Mexican was not following it, wasn't putting anything together. But he thought he had better break it off before

he began putting it together. "You can go now," he said. "And thank you very much for the glasses."

"Perhaps you will have something to say later," the Mexican said, turning.

"Much later," Alexander said as the door closed. He went back to his seat at the window and hiked the glasses over the typewriter. He looked carefully and long at the horizon. There was nothing there but he was thinking about something else. Then he pointed the glasses down the oily road that wound out finally past the steep cliffs above the sea. He scanned the street along the hill that ran up to the beach road, focusing the big glasses. There was the gold and neon, once Spanish Colonial, now almost Hollywood, cathedral in front of the market place. The market place sprawling in back of it was big and dirty he knew, and yet how clean and orderly it looked from here. The federal school alongside the Plaza looked very hot in its red paint, and then there was the broken monument to Benito Juarez on the square in front of the cathedral. On each of the streets there was always one good building, usually placed conveniently in the middle, on which all the other buildings on the street could lean. On Angel Flores there was no good building on which they could lean so the angle on these buildings was a little frightening. There were very few people moving in the heat of this time of day and she was not one of them. Nowhere on any of the visible streets could he see her familiar gaudy clash of color.

Now he tried searching the outdoor cafés along the beach front at the foot of the hotels that only the Americans could afford. He tried the Corizo Café. There were only two elderly American women waiting over a lemonade for their husbands to return from fishing. He tried the front of the Utrillo Hotel

and as he did so he wondered if it was named after the painter. There was her splash of red and yellow in the middle of the café and she was sitting with someone else. He got a better focus.

He screwed the glasses until he removed her double image for she had never been a double image. Since the first few months after they had left together he had seen her quite clearly, when he wanted to see her at all. Watching her at this great distance reminded him that he had been watching her at a great distance for a long time now. This distance was surely not his fault and it was not her fault but each day there seemed to be more distance.

Still screwing the eye pieces she came abruptly into sharp picture now and he could see all the things that had not changed about her. She was still young, the fifteen years did not seem to have aged her a day. The hair still fell big and loose in a gentle swing to her shoulders and as she talked it vibrated and caught the sun. Her lips were full and not too short and her large light blue eyes must be very large and very blue down there in the sun and close to the water. Her heavy, firm, uptilted breasts jutted over the iron table with only the negative lines in the glasses outlining them. A wondering smile that was almost amazement flickered across her face now as she talked; he liked to call it youth and it flickered across her face now as she talked with eagerness across the small iron table to the man who was not himself. He shifted the glasses over to the man who was Alfred Marlowe, a rising poet, and young.

He had in his glasses now the man who was sitting across from his wife. In his book he might have begun to describe him in a first draft and then quit. The face, Alexander thought,

ran a little too closely to the face in the Boy Scout ads, nothing interestingly there with all its human contradiction, but something conceived in the high sterile clatter of a typewriter and the firm commercial arm of a firm commercial artist. He shifted his glasses slightly as the man moved—he could move and he could speak, the lips in the glasses revealed a cold whiteness of teeth as the man spoke—and as he speaks now he might even be saying something.

"You could look into it," the young man called Alfred said.

"I don't know what to do but I couldn't do that," she said.

"How do you know it won't work out?" The young man was thinking about something else. "Anyway you know what I mean."

"You mean you were thinking about your poetry. All right, if you want to think about your poetry then what shall we think about your poetry?"

"I don't think it matters a damn what we do," Alfred said slowly, and getting back to it. "He is going to punish himself no matter what we do."

Alfred had never seen Perrette's pretty face tense before, it seemed to give the face an illusion of insight.

Perrette crushed out a cigarette she had just lit but she was not watching the ceramic tray, just looking straight ahead.

"He doesn't work now," she said mechanically, as though telling something to herself. "He says there's nothing worth writing about."

Alfred thought he should not mix in anything at all, just wait for her to come out of it.

"All right," she said at last, removing another cigarette from the flat tin she had in front of her. "All right, Alfred," she

said, fixing on him as though trying to recall his face. "I don't think it's a bad title; you go ahead and use it. 'Sounds of Phallic Cymbals.' It isn't as bad as we said it was. It isn't too bad."

"It's bad enough," Alfred said. "I don't like it any more."

"'Sounds of Phallic Cymbals',", Perrette said as though considering it from every angle. Then she said definitely, "I wouldn't abandon the title, Alfred. It represents a whole morning's work."

"Thank you," Alfred said. "But as a matter of fact it's not a bad title. It's a satire on the sixteenth-century virelai ancien poetry. With a title like 'Sounds of Phallic Cymbals' my thought was to use the nada motif in a contemporary Dijon bistro setting in which the feeling is imposed of there being a brothel upstairs. Below the dialogue the poetry is a contradiction of the life process, a mere banal statement of the everyday questions and answers. Do you think Alexander could see it?"

"Well, I can't see it, Alfred. I'm sorry but I can't. You know since it's been going the way it's been going between Alex and me, I've been thinking that you and I—"

Alfred interrupted by taking one of her cigarettes. Alfred thought she had done a decent job in holding it in all these months since things had begun definitely to fall apart. But the fact that she could take it for so long without discussing it did not make Alfred feel any better now.

"I'm sorry. I didn't mean to say anything, Alfred. It just came out. I'm like Alex's Indian who did not want to retreat, his legs just moved toward the rear. Can I get you something, Alfred? You look faint. Should you be drinking those tequila cocktails in the sun, Alfred?"

"I'm all right," Alfred said. "I'm plenty all right."

"Very well, we'll discuss your poetry, Alfred," she said in a kind voice.

"Leave my poetry alone. I don't want to discuss my poetry," Alfred said.

"How about the weather then, Alfred?"

"All right. We'll get back to my poetry," Alfred said. "But I don't want any subjective reaction. I want you to relax and get our talk out of your mind so you will have a spontaneous objectivity. This is a little corny," Alfred said, "but are you ready?"

"I'm ready," Perrette said, trying to change her expression.

"Okay," Alfred said, slowly turning his head toward her. And then suddenly—" 'Sounds of Phallic Cymbals'!"

"Splendid, Alfred. I think it's absolutely splendid."

Above them in the room that jutted over the water like a stateroom Alexander in the long-billed fishing cap and holding the binoculars arched over the typewriter thought; and now she is telling him how much she does not love me any more and what a pity it is that all the books we have with us bore her. But I do not know what she is saying because I cannot read lips. Once I thought I could read lips pretty well but perhaps it was only my writer's imagination working. There was a rummy rancher near the reservation that I found very interesting. After he had drunk away his hair and his teeth and his cattle and his ability to walk he began to drink away his ability to talk and when it got very bad I used to think I could read his lips and I put what I imagined he said into some short stories. And what writer's imagination can I use on those two down there? It's that they're going

to kill me and run away with all the money or all the love, depending upon which lousy writer handles it. And what did I run away with when I ran away fifteen years ago? Perhaps that's what I should write about. But I can't. If I could then I would have nothing to worry about. If I could write it all down it would probably go like this. . . . Like what? No, you can't do it. Maybe it would go like it's going with those two down there. Maybe this is a repeat performance. Maybe it's a remake of the old film with different actors. People go on performing the same script. They get a new set of actors—faces anyway. I wonder if they'll change the lines much. I wonder if people are beginning to talk like the second- and third-rate writers who write imitation people; with all the television they've got going if people will begin to imitate imitations of man. All right, but if you tried to do it correctly how could you get those two down there on paper? In the rough draft Alfred would have to go down as an incredible idealist, big-blown with a plot to perfect the world, to perfect it all with love and art. And Perrette? Love and art too. Adolescent too. But in the meantime, while things are building, they must eat, not too well but very well enough. In the meantime, while things are building, they must starve to get the proletarian feel but then reject this as a capitalist myth. In the meantime, while things are opening out, they must love, honor and obey Jean-Paul Sartre, or some other substitute for God, assuming that they no longer had him, Alexander Bowman, as a substitute for God. How could he explain to those two down there that the challenge is to grow, that youth is for the young. Love is for all but youth is for the young. And now down there the young man must be talking about love and if he was, what was the attitude

toward love now? If he could read lips perhaps he could find out. He focused his glasses on their faces.

Below, the young man was watching the gaudy birds, three Mexican yellow heads and two beebees, on top of the sea wall side of the patio crawling stupidly around in circles. Inside the wall and seeming bright against the dull brick, a big awkward English-speaking, heavy-billed parrot with dirty white-blue wings, who kept looking down at Alfred and Perrette with yellow eyes, climbed the decomposed wall crookedly all the way almost to the top.

"Do you think," Alfred asked, "Do you think Alexander would consider a thing like this?"

"Why don't you ask him?" she said.

"The last time I showed him my work he said, it's not my pitch, Alfred. I can't help you. But then you must go ahead and make your play, you're entitled to make a mess of it, but I can't help you, Alfred. You're not fishing in my ocean. Jesus, does everybody have to swear in his key before he'll look at your stuff?"

"Why don't you do a story based on him, Alfred?" Perrette asked softly. "He might like that."

"Because at times I think he's a son of a bitch," Alfred said.

"Buenos días, caballeros y señoritas." The parrot had gained the top of the broken wall now and was strutting over the sharp, bottle-topped barricade. "Drink Carta Blanca. She's good for you all alone."

Alfred leaned over and took a cigarette out of the broad flat tin she had arranged in front of her breasts. She helped him by turning the box. "And so?"

"And so he's my SOB," Alfred said.

"That's sweet of you, Alfred."

"No, it isn't," Alfred said. "It's just that he's almost the best writer around."

"And that precludes—?"

"That precludes almost everything," Alfred said.

"You're sweet, Alfred. Look at the parrot, he's scolding us. I suppose that we should order something."

"Well, I won't order any of his beer."

"Tell me," Alfred said finally, looking up. "Couldn't we do something, you and I, that would open him out? This trip since we got to Mazatlán has turned into a parade of the dead. Couldn't we do something, you and I, something warm and generous? The last book was very bad but his next book will be a good book. We should do something to jolt him out of this."

"We probably will," she said.

"You want some more drink?" The waiter had intruded a dirty white shirt sleeve.

"No," Alfred said. The white arm hesitated and then remained. "No, no, no," Alfred repeated. "You said something, Perrette?"

"I see there's a man at our window." She was looking up at the hard UN façade of the hotel. "He has binoculars but he's probably only looking toward the Indian Country. Do you know, when I got up this morning he was staring out the window and he said: Out there beyond the border and hidden carefully by the horizon is the drought-ridden Indian Country." But Perrette seemed nervous. She closed her cigarette box and sat more erect. Alfred noticed her movement and got up.

"I've got to finish the poem. It's important that when you

start something you finish it while you're still in the mood."

"Very important," Perrette said, not looking up. "Very important that when you start something you finish it while you're still in the mood."

Alfred started to say something, decided against it and turned and left quickly.

The parrot repeated again by rote from high on the rotted wall, "Drink Carta Blanca beer. She's good for you all alone." Perrette looked out at the big, flat, empty ocean and up at the wide vacant sky, blue and without any clouds at all, but she did not look again toward their high window where her husband must be looking toward the Indian Country. She started to call the waiter but then she decided that what the parrot said was meaningless too.

"All right, bring me a Carta Blanca." Alexander said. Perrette looked up at Alexander as he sat down.

"I was looking out the window up there toward La Paz," Alexander said. "It can't be more than fifty miles. I think a person could swim it."

"Remember what happened in Ischia?" she said. "And remember why they didn't take you in the army."

"Bad heart," Alexander said. "But it's only fifty miles. I think it could be done. I was talking with an interesting wreck called Mimi Jimenez this morning. He's got an old harbor and pier that's going to ruin since they built the new wharf. He wants to sponsor the swim, furnish the boat and food, if we arrive at his place."

"Well, you have come to the final experience," she said.

"What's that?"

"Suicide," she said.

Perrette took out her pad and began sketching. "I don't

want to be throwing cold water on everything," she said, "but—but well, let's talk about something pleasant. Alfred was just here."

"I don't think anyone ever swam to La Paz. It could be interesting," Alexander said.

"Alfred," Perrette said, continuing to sketch, "has just written a new poem."

"Now the world can breathe again," Alex said. "What does he call it?"

"What difference does it make?" Perrette said, rubbing her forefinger now into the charcoal sketch she was making. "A title isn't important. It could still be a good poem. But," she said, taking up a new stick, "as a matter of fact he calls it 'Sounds of Phallic Cymbals.'"

"Splendid," Alexander said. "Still, it's one thing I suppose I won't have to take the blame for."

"Well, you could help him some," she said.

"He's never asked me."

"Well, you frighten him, Alex. You give him the impression—"

"That children should grow up."

"But he does admire you—your work. You know, Alex, I think he writes somewhat like you did when you were young."

"Oh," Alexander said. And then he said, "What are you sketching?"

"A picture of Alfred," she said and she held it up. "Do you like it?"

"Splendid," Alexander said. "I think it's—"

The waiter came up now with the beer and Alexander looked around the empty café and then out over the shimmering water to La Paz. The waiter left now. They both con-

tinued silent but the trained parrot knew it was time for the commercial and croaked, "Drink Carta Blanca beer. She's good for you all alone."

Alexander looked toward the horizon again now but not toward La Paz.

"That's right," he said to the parrot. "Indian Country, she's good for you all alone. I think there's a story up there that I might write and maybe George's writing it. It will start with 'Once upon a time' and will end with George's tearing it up. People destroy an awful lot."

7

All over the world people will see a sign, a portent in something big that happens to all of them. The day began now with a green sky and the sun rising orange and starting slow through the interstices of the log window. After the day was over an Indian said that this was the trouble the medicine man had predicted a long time ago. But that would have ignored these fifteen years of drought in the Indian Country since Alexander had stolen George's wife.

"Nothing can ignore the drought," George Bowman said. "It won't let you."

And whether he was speaking of the drought on the land or the drought in his heart was not important, for in both cases all that had been good for so many generations was drying up and blowing away and the homeless sand was moving in. But the Indians had cause to speculate and theorize and make big talk about this day. Nothing much like it had happened since they lost to the white man.

Now, fifteen years after the theft and the beginning of the drought and sixty-three years after they had lost to the white man, Kurt Heinitz, in absolute command of the third foreign car rally of the Southwest, watched the gaudy cars pull into the rendezvous place at La Ventana, ten miles below the

trading post at Tonatai, and he didn't approve of anything at all. Kurt Heinitz had begun his career with Rommel, achieved full command under Von Modell before he was switched to Guderian for the big push to Moscow. That the genius of Heinitz, Rommel and Guderian had failed was a monument to the insanity of a corporal trying to run things from Berlin. Heinitz had to remind himself occasionally that that was why he was playing with these toy bright cars that were streaming into La Ventana now, instead of doing something real, and he blamed it all on insanity in a politician.

But it was not insanity that annoyed him with the Van Esters and the Johnsons, the Jag and the Porsche that were closest to him now. It was plain stupidity which, along with naïveté, seemed to nail down Americans. Heinitz advanced toward the Johnsons.

The Johnsons in the canary-yellow-and-red Jaguar with blown-up fenders looked splendid in identical pink-and-white checked caps with purple poms, Red Ryder shirts, blue jeans and cowboy boots, and they were both worried about the same thing—Kurt Heinitz. Mrs. Johnson preferred to be known as Helen Hooyar and her husband as Lonesome Johnson. He had a TV show that went on when everybody went to bed. The Platter Parade King of the Southwest, Lonesome Johnson. Mrs. Johnson thought that her maiden name should not be allowed to die, that it kept her from being thought of as a housewife. She had records pressed in Albuquerque under the name of Helen Hooyar; her husband played them and she had a feeling they were beginning to catch on. Her husband was kind and never showed her the mail. She was kind and didn't tell him she was having an affair with his biggest account. Everyone was kind except Kurt Heinitz. Why

doesn't he pick on the Van Esters?

Heinitz hesitated between the two cars and walked toward the Van Esters. Mrs. Van Ester had a thin long face that never relaxed from that set, tight, holding-on-to-the-door-handle look—"Isn't this fun!"—that she achieved at that climactic, bone-shaking moment that passes for high speed in a noisy car. Raoul Van Ester had a round, cherubic face for a man who drove such a formidable machine. They were again accoutered in those identical checkered and pomponned caps that seemed to be the thing. They did not affect the cowboy get-up of the Lonesome Johnsons but ran to Tattersal vests and jodhpurs and King Alfonso boots, mail ordered from the Country Store in Aspen.

The Van Esters had a tape recorder with them in the car and were going to record cultural Indian chants and play these at the next Great Books meeting in their home town of Truth or Consequences. But right now they were afraid; they were afraid of Heinitz, who was coming up. They had turned up the speedometer in their car so they could compete for the Concours d'Elégance prize for cars with over sixty-thousand miles, and they were afraid of Heinitz.

Heinitz came over and touched the scooped door of the Porsche, gentle and relaxed. He wore a nondescript American suit on his long frame that made anything hang with a military assurance. He had emerged from a large, standard American car that was the color of dirt. When Heinitz selected a car he wanted to be inside when he was inside and outside when he was outside and no "Isn't this fun" foreign-car nonsense.

"Are you enjoying yourselves?" Heinitz said, quietly, looking down on the Van Esters' purple pompons.

"Swell! Exciting first pass," Mr. Van Ester said eagerly, his round face dancing up at Heinitz.

"Yes," Heinitz said slowly, hitting the door a quick bop with his palm and moving away.

"By God, I know when I'm being patronized, Skeets," Mrs. Van Ester said tightly toward her husband. "I'm not strictly Truth or Consequences. I grew up with a set in Santa Fe and I know when I'm being patronized, Skeets."

Mr. Van Ester clasped the purple wheel tightly, looking straight ahead out through the tinted windscreen and over the yellow bonnet.

"You're imagining things, Bullet," he said toward his wife. "We're out to have fun. Don't ruin everything by imagining things."

"Imagining things, Skeets? Swell! Exciting first pass! Jesus, must you grovel every time that Kraut shows? I mean, let's face it, Skeets, we're people."

Heinitz had placed his hands in back of him and walked up to the Johnsons' Jaguar as though he were thinking of something far away. The Johnsons seemed to scrunch a little closer to the gear shift on the floor and waited.

"I've been thinking," Heinitz said without any preliminaries to the Lonesome Johnsons, "how could the Van Esters have put sixty-thousand miles on their car in so short a time? I thought from the air scoop it was a '55. Still I could be wrong."

"I remember it was a '55," Lonesome Johnson said, excited. "November, '55. They drove it up to our house, nonchalant, as though they still had the Gordini, as though nothing had happened, said they wanted to borrow a Miracle Cloth, pretending that's what they came for, as though nothing had

happened. So I gave them the Miracle Cloth and pretended that's what they came for, as though nothing had happened. They got sore."

"Thank you," Heinitz said and thumped the car before moving away.

"Poor show, Loney," Helen Hooyar said without looking at her husband. "Did you have to squeal on those chaps? I think it was a very poor show."

"Those snobs," Lonesome Johnson said. "And don't forget we're interested in that thing ourselves. How do you pronounce it?"

"Concours d'Élégance," his wife said. "And all the more reason it was a poor show. We've all heard of a little noblesse oblige and it would be inverted snobbery to pretend we hadn't." Helen Hooyar removed something from her nose with her pinkie finger. "A bloody lousy show, Loney. Nothing resembling cricket at all."

"Bull," Lonesome Johnson said.

"That's what I mean by inverted snobbery, Loney. If you can't see it can't you feel it?"

Lonesome Johnson said one word preceded by "Oh." The word was short and obscene and the Navahocade moved off from an abrupt command by Heinitz and Helen Hooyar laid down her long cigarette holder on her Apache snake-skin bag and dabbed at her eyes with her handkerchief.

"It's Heinitz," she said. "There was nothing like this before Heinitz. He's making us into brutes."

The Navahocade was headed for an allotment or checkerboard area known as Tonatai. The Aspencade to Jemez had been brilliant under Heinitz' leadership and so had the Atomcade to Los Alamos. No one could organize like Heinitz.

And Heinitz enjoyed himself. It allowed him to keep his hand in. The club selected Tonatai because they said it was not just a big hole like Grand Canyon or Carlsbad where the tourists and tract dwellers came by the thousands to gawk and erect platitudes but a place made famous by the writer, Alexander Bowman. Another nice reason for having the Navahocade at Tonatai was that there were no roads.

Kurt Heinitz had two MGs working the point, scouting about two miles ahead. The MGs had army-surplus walkie-talkies installed and their tall whip antennas were in touch with Heinitz. Heinitz brought up the rear of the main body of cars and he was using two Siatas to cover the flank. When the MGs spotted any trouble or difficulty in the terrain they were to contact Heinitz.

Heinitz got a message now that the trail had ended at an arroyo and he answered back that he was coming forward on the double. The long string of garish and odd cars parted for Heinitz as he moved forward with his hand on the air horn. Some did not move quickly enough and Heinitz was forced to run them into the ditch, but there were no complaints. They realized that they had been quite stupid and were turning the Navahocade into a poor show.

When Heinitz arrived at the front his scouts were alongside their pink and chartreuse MGs looking vacantly into a thirty-by-thirty flood erosion, and making perfect targets, Heinitz thought absently. The wife in the pink MG, whose husband had a black eye patch, herself wore a pink snood and plaid-rimmed, very dark glasses which, along with her posture in the bucket seat, and despite the fact that she was straddling a case of Schweppes, gave her the appearance of a holy woman being patient at Benares. The wife in the chartreuse MG

had a chartreuse snood and a chartreuse alligator bag and very dark glasses trimmed in rhinestones and appeared out of the same litter except that she was suffering from a bad case of exposure and wished she had never left Tucumcari.

Heinitz assessed the situation immediately and sent the chartreuse to scout the left and the eyepatch to scout down the right bank and contact him when they discovered a crossing.

The sky over the Indian Country reminded him of no sky he had ever seen before, a sea of almost green shot with orange and long strokes of black. And what kind of people would live in this land that looked like the bottom of the ocean after the water had been removed?

Heinitz received a message now that chartreuse had made contact and Heinitz threw his car forward toward the scout. When Heinitz reached chartreuse an Indian was destroying a crude bridge across a low point in the arroyo and damned if chartreuse wasn't arguing with him. Heinitz grabbed a wrench with quickness of mind and hit the Indian across the skull just in time to save the Navahocade from an embarrassing wait.

The Indian had been trying to explain in Navaho that his farm on the other side was just planted to winter rye. He had also tried to explain to the Moving People in his small Spanish but the Moving People did not seem to speak any language at all. But fortunately Heinitz had arrived just in time to save the situation and Mr. Van Ester had wondered aloud where the hell the club would be without Heinitz and Mrs. Van Ester had said, "But a spanner, Skeets! It's not quite playing the game to hit one of their chaps on the head with a spanner." And then in a low voice that was more her own,

"We're not animals, Skeets." Mr. Van Ester seemed to think about this a minute before he said profoundly, "Biologically I suppose we are, Bullet. Yes, and by the bye, who's got the tonic?"

"I don't want to play any more," his wife said in a tired voice. "I don't want to play any more with all this rich man's junk. I hate quinine tonic and I hate jodhpurs and boots and I hate open foreign cars and I hate Heinitz and I feel sorry for that poor damn Indian who got hit with a wrench."

Her husband said, reaching down and chucking her under the chin, "We've got to carry on, old girl." And then, when he got no response but a sob, he grabbed the wheel and said in his own voice, "Jesus, I guess we have to go through with it now."

The Indian who had been hit with the wrench had fallen down into the bottom of the arroyo. There was a dead black-and-white feist dog at the bottom of the arroyo and the body of the Indian rolled until it almost touched the dead feist dog. The side of the arroyo was too steep for them to get to the Indian with succor so they fixed the bridge and watched while three Indians came down the arroyo with one other Indian leading a spare mount. They watched while the Indians hung the Indian who was hit on the spare mount, and one of the Indians who had not helped with the loading held the hit Indian on, leading both horses, as they went up the far bank and toward the log trading post and the great, boarded-up house they could all see in the distance. The Indians did not look at them once.

Felix Mount Royal, Lord Rundle and Rabbit Stockings had discovered the wounded Indian and with the help of

Tom-Dick-and-Harry, who was out chasing sheep with a spare mount, they lugged him up to the post of George Bowman, on into the back room heavy with the smell of sheep hides and brilliant with the blankets of their wives. George put some white man's medicine on the head of Coyotes-Love-Me and the Indian opened his soft dark eyes on the blankets that hung down too bright and turned his head until his soft eyes lighted on the hides that stank.

"Why really, he will be fine, he is better. Why really, everything will be all right." The Indians did not believe or disbelieve this that they told George Bowman but they wanted him to feel good about his religion, about his magic. The Indians always allowed him to try his magic first because, after all these years, they had grown to respect him and this was one of the ways they showed their appreciation. Sometimes it even did some good and they did not have to have a sing, did not have to use their own religion. For Coyotes-Love-Me they all knew that tonight they would have a chant. It was a terrible wallop. The white man's magic was not enough against the white man's blow; it would take serious medicine not only for the head of Coyotes-Love-Me but against the spirit of the man who had done it.

George Bowman motioned them all into the front room and sat down on a small Victorian stool covered with perfect velvet. There was something regal about it, sitting there surrounded by all the turquoise and silver jewelry The People had pawned against the flour and tobacco you could not see. It had an effect.

"Why really," George began in their own language, "why really, the jails of Gallup are full of The People who war

105

on the white man. I have some medicine to use against this man, this man and his spirit, if you will permit me."

"Why really, no," Lord Rundle said quickly, raising his fiery-jeweled hand to a brown face that was heavily dark-lined like a contour map beneath a red cotton band across his forehead. He was dressed in the Levis and boots of the others.

Some velvet-clad squaws came in now to watch the talk and sat on the floor sucking Pepsi and Royal Crown Colas.

"Why really, no," Lord Rundle repeated. "With this man we deal in our own custom."

There was a silence with George Bowman saying nothing, tipping a silver and turquoise pawn in front of him.

"Oh, but really, it is true," Felix Mount Royal said. "The Gallup jails are full of us."

Felix Mount Royal's squaw congratulated him with her eyes and switched her cold bottle of Royal Crown Cola to her other hand.

"Why really, maybe I will listen to your plans, Sansi," Lord Rundle said.

"Hokka-shai. Thank You," George said. "My plan is to make him lose face. That is complicated to explain but excellent for permanent cure if I have luck."

"May you have luck," Rabbit Stockings said.

All of the squaws banged their Pepsi and Royal Crown Colas on the floor in agreement and approval and to make a noise which they liked too.

Tom-Dick-and-Harry, a short, white-appearing Indian with bandy legs and a clean scar under his right eye, came in now from the back room and gave them permission to put the hurt Coyotes-Love-Me in his hogan as was his custom. It was not only that Tom-Dick-and-Harry was not convinced of the

truth of the Navaho belief that the bad spirits would return to haunt a hogan in which one of The People had died, it was also that he was certain that he had all the bad luck there was in this world right now and that no spirit could add much more to what was coming his way in the future.

All of the Indians helped carry out the body of the victim, with Tom-Dick-and-Harry leading the way and Rabbit Stockings bringing up the rear carrying a large economy-sized box of corn flakes and a pint of Sloane's liniment.

The squaws remained on the floor to finish their drinks. The squaws are not moved easily to excitement, which is probably good, George felt, because they carry the entire wealth of The People around their necks and waists in the form of coral, silver and turquoise jewelry of expensive and good taste and it costs nothing to giggle but with excitement you never know. They would pawn the jewelry with the trader when the winter was deep and win it back when they sold the sheep. The jewelry was shown off well against the billowing bright skirts of calico and velvet, cut in the manner of the American army officers' wives at the stockade of Fort Sumner where all The People were imprisoned from 1864 to 1868.

George Bowman put the velvet stool away on its shelf back of the counter where his father had kept it and took a piece of jewelry off the counter and put it back in the case, beneath the books of his father, *Ivanhoe*, *Burke's Peerage*, *The Lady of the Lake* and others his father had used to name the Indians away from some of the names that were too long for the ledger, like Son-of-the-Man-Who-Got-Kicked-in-the-Stomach-by-a-Deer-on-the-Other-Side-of-the-Mountain.

There was a Bible on the shelf too, a present from the

mission that had made a short and dull stand in the vicinity before it disappeared, to have immortality only in a sign which read: TRADITION IS THE ENEMY OF PROGRESS. When the sign was completed the missionary asked George to come and have a look and George had said that if the missionaries believed it the church would collapse in the morning. Nevertheless George was sorry when the mission folded. They brought food and clothing in winter. And if they were rude enough to insist their religion was superior to The People's religion, they knew not what they did.

But George was concerned now about the invasion of the Moving People. Maybe this too was some form of Progress. George was not a romantic who was opposed to the word but, although inevitable, he did not believe it could not be selective, and although Progress has many aspects, this would never be: the destruction of the rye and the winter wheat, the busting of The People on the head with wrenches. George had decided to make his stand here at the store. Later he might use The People but first he would meet the leader of the Moving People here alone.

When George had been tipped off to the invasion by an engineer from Albuquerque who had come up to check on the seismograph crews, George had told him to lay off because the Indians had most of the flat areas planted to rye and winter wheat that was beginning to show green in spite of the drought and it would be impossible to stay off it. The engineer said it was his duty to report possible scenic rally points to the club, and if Kurt Heinitz decided on this area there was nothing he could do, or anyone else for that matter. And if the trader and the population were going to be difficult and the terrain impossible, well, that was what

Heinitz was looking for—enjoyed. The engineer would get a brush on the back from Heinitz instead of a slap on the car and Heinitz did not give his favors lightly or often. He told George Bowman the date.

George had then gone into the vast back room to direct the sorting of the hides and think. When he had thought of something acceptable he wrote a message out on his father's desk and gave it to the sorter of the hides, Lord Acton, with instructions to ride full gallop to the trader at La Ventana. Then he drained the gasoline from his own Sears gravity-feed tank on stilts into his tractor and gave the last remaining two gallons to the medicine man, Paracelsus, to use for bright fires. He had busied the remaining interval of time until today with the organization of treating the Indians' sheep against blue-tongue. As he looked out the window now he saw the advance scouting pink and chartreuse MG's pull up. They circled the post three times, each time in a smaller circle until they finally stopped. One of the women got out and walked toward the post and the others remained behind to contact the main force over the walkie-talkie.

The woman in chartreuse with the huge chartreuse alligator bag walked up to the post and looked in the window, then she went to the door and opened it and looked in to see if what she had seen through the window was true. Then she closed the door and hollered to the others, "My god! The boy in here is a loveboat. He looks exactly like young Lincoln."

The others looked up from their sending equipment in surprise as she opened the door again and went in. She entered a room lined with silver and turquoise and food under a ceiling draped with saddles and boots, lanterns and harness, so that she had to move among them carefully until she reached the

counter laden with pawn. She pretended an interest in this but all the while she was staring at George Bowman, who was writing something, and working her way up the counter toward him, and now she was at the elbow of his heavy leather jacket.

"I don't like to be rude but did anyone ever tell you you looked exactly like young Lincoln?"

George put down his pen and looked at her carefully. "No, ma'am, they never did."

"No, but seriously, I don't say these things," she said. "You do look exactly like young Lincoln."

Helen Hooyar came in now and the lady in chartreuse said, "Don't you think he looks exactly like young Lincoln?"

Helen Hooyar was fiddling with the edge of one of the blankets and staring out at them between two saddles that hung down.

"By God, I think he looks like Alexander Bowman," Helen Hooyar said. "I never met Alexander Bowman but I've seen his pictures and he looks like Alexander Bowman. He's a real man, not one of these city creeps. Living out here alone develops the soul, and something else too. I bet I could write poetry if I lived out here. And that boarded-up beautiful petri-fied-log house—I bet there's a story there, an eternal mystery. I bet that's where Alexander Bowman wrote those books."

George went back to the sheep ledger.

Lonesome Johnson and Mr. Van Ester came in now and they noticed the squaws lined along the counter on the floor sipping their drinks with the decorum of any DAR chapter. Lonesome Johnson wandered down the shelves until he found a certain brand of soap. Putting this on his shoulder he walked up to the trader.

"Does this do anything to you?" he said. "Strike any bell at all? No? Twelve o'clock every night I merchandise this product. Still, way out here you're out of touch, kind of, with reality. You probably don't even have a TV set."

"No," George said.

"I certainly could use a character like you just to sit alongside me on the show and shill my pitch. You wouldn't consider it?" Lonesome Johnson said.

"No," George said.

"You know, you're right," Lonesome Johnson said and, turning to the others, "No, but he's right. My God, I wish I could live out here myself. The air! Notice the air," Lonesome Johnson said, taking a deep breath of sheep hides. "By God, this country makes a man of you. I might chuck everything some day and come out here and start again. I could paint pictures. If Alexander Bowman could write books here I could paint pictures."

Skeets Van Ester was looking through the window out at the mesa country. His wife wasn't playing any more. She was in the car reading T. S. Eliot. Soon she would wander to have a look at the latest thing in hogans.

"It's spectacular," Skeets Van Ester said, still staring through the window. "It's like something out of Cecil B. de Mille. It makes you feel close to God. Imagine what a man like Kurt Heinitz could do with a place like this. Why, he'd organize it into the greatest tourist spectacle in the world. All these beautiful possibilities wasting away for a man like Kurt Heinitz."

"Everybody outside." Kurt Heinitz was standing inside the door waiting for them to file out. They filed out.

Kurt Heinitz closed the door gently and walked quickly

toward George Bowman, pausing to examine a piece of jewelry on the way. "You have fine workmen," he said, putting the concha belt down. George didn't say anything. "I've come to apologize for that accident to one of your men." George still didn't say anything but he took the concha belt and put it under the counter before he went back to the sheep ledger.

"We want to be correct," Kurt Heinitz said. "We are not a mob. We are very well organized and I am the leader. We want to be correct if you will simply tell me what—"

"I think you had better go home," George said quickly, without looking up from his ledger.

"Before we can discuss that we will need some gasoline," Heinitz said.

"No gasoline," George said.

"Perhaps we can make a deal," Heinitz said quickly, picking up the edge of a blanket.

"No deal. No gasoline," George said.

"But I told them," Heinitz said, his voice loosening, dropping the edge of the blanket. "I told them when there was no gas in La Ventana that they need not go on to Cuba and waste their time. I told them there was gas here. I had it on good authority. If we had to walk out of here they would think me a fool."

George Bowman dropped his pen and looked at Kurt Heinitz for the first time.

"We will see what we can do to get you out of here. I gave the medicine man two gallons of fuel for bright magic. Maybe you can talk him out of it. It will take you to Cuba, where you can bring back enough to leave here."

"Good," Heinitz said, confidently. "I'm kind of a medicine

man myself. Have you ever seen my rockets over Alamogordo? That is, I'm a twentieth-century medicine man. Countries bid for me. Where is this other medicine man? I hope he speaks something recent."

"There's an interpreter outside the door. It has been arranged."

"Thank you very much," Heinitz said, turning.

"You have nothing to thank me for," George said.

"You Americans are all alike," Heinitz said, going out the door and smiling. "All alike."

George Bowman went back to his ledger with his pen but actually he wrote only one word in a clear hand and then he tapped the pen against his nose in thought before he reached down and crossed it out. He got up now and stared out the window. The odd cars of the Moving People looked strange against the hogans.

Tom-Dick-and-Harry was outside. He was a mission Indian and he spoke a little of everything. Tom-Dick-and-Harry was kind of a mess. He didn't fit in with the whites and now he didn't fit in with The People. Tom-Dick-and-Harry didn't believe anything any more. But he would be a good interpreter.

The medicine man that George's father had named Paracelsus was dressed like the other Indians except that the quality of his clothes was better, his hogan was bigger and his horses were fatter, just like most doctors on the outside except that the payoff was in sheep—but he had knives and herbs and such that go with the business. And besides all this the medicine man had sings, he was part of the religion, he treated the whole person. He had a lot of luck.

Was Heinitz going to get the gas? "Why really, of course,"

113

the medicine man told him, but first there were a few things he must do for a cure. Heinitz was desperate and willing and he tried to make some sand painting while the medicine man corrected him and the Moving People laughed. Now the medicine man explained the whole thing very carefully to Heinitz through Tom-Dick-and-Harry in one-syllable words. But Heinitz was still all thumbs and his Moving People laughed. He jumped on hot rocks while the Moving People laughed and he made signs to the sun while the Moving People laughed again.

But nobody laughed at the next medicine. Heinitz didn't have to do anything, The People took care of everything, and nobody laughed. No one laughed at all.

George Bowman was still busy with the sheep ledger when Rabbit Stockings came in and got some matches. George had some bad thoughts about the matches at first but then consoled himself with the guess that they were probably for Lady Blessington's pipe. She smoked a home-made mixture that was put together by Paracelsus which was marvelous except that it was non-combustible. Sometimes it took two boxes of the matches to get a good fire going. Lady Blessington had smoked a pipe long before cancer became a fad, but she smoked it for her health and, not counting TB and a few other things she had in her own right, it seemed to work.

George Bowman smelled gasoline. He could be wrong but the wind was right and he thought he smelled gasoline. He put down the saddle.

"No more medicine," George said, cutting the ropes.

"Why really," the medicine man said, "I was right in the middle of an operation."

"You certainly were," George said, taking the rope from around Heinitz' shoulders. Heinitz' face was perfectly white.

"Why really, he is not cured," the medicine man said.

"I promised you he is cured," George said.

"Thank you, Sansi," Paracelsus said. "I do the best I can with the little I have."

"Is there any gas left?" George asked, feeling the clothes of Heinitz soaking with it.

"We had to use it all in the medicine, Sansi. But you didn't think we were going to burn him?"

"It was just a scare," George said.

"That's right, Sansi. Just a scare."

"Well, you scared me," George said.

"Sometimes it is necessary to treat everyone," Paracelsus said. "Evil is that kind of sickness."

Now there was the beginning of the sing. As the strangers sweated to get their cars back across the arroyo, as George Bowman said they must, they could hear the thin, high wail of an alone singer re-echoing off the dark mountains. Then the singer was joined by all of The People and it became a deep low-cadenced chant like a part of the bright-banded cliffs and the mushroomed mesas, the big flat lands and the arroyos enormous with nothing. Perhaps, too, tonight the sing was deep and sad with the now quickened remembrance of things that must always be forgotten—the Navaho Nation was once the greatest of all the Moving People.

"The Navaho Nation was once the greatest of all the

Moving People," George said aloud now, and then he picked up the pen and wrote:

"Dear Alex: All these silly and cruel people that I saw here today made me think that maybe I made the right decision in getting away from the world and living here with The People, for The People and nothing more."

"The Navaho Nation was once the greatest of all the Moving People," George repeated aloud. Where had he heard that? It must have been in one of Alexander's early stories. And what about Alexander's later stories, those he had written in the last fifteen years? He had read none of them, which was exactly as it should be. And yet—? And he began to write now.

"Early this morning I took the trail up on the mesa on the horse and with my binoculars to see if I could see the Moving People coming. I did not see them, they came another way, but I saw the mine shaft—I made myself go there. If it had been dark and I had stumbled in the hole I was all alone, there would have been no one to get help. Are you and Perrette out there all alone now? The people who came here today seemed desperately alone. They have soothed their loneliness in their bright sparkling foreign things. You should have seen them against the hogans. But these things are maybe not enough against the loneliness because they tried to take something out on us. There was a great beating of wings against us here today before they drifted on to a greater loneliness. Alex, what are you doing against the loneliness? Who is the victim of your loneliness? What has the loneliness cost you until now? The Indians are the victims of my loneliness. I'm with them but separate. They must feel it. It has cost me until now the knowledge that I try to

116

protect, help, the Indians—while condemning a brother to another country—and yet the Indians knew what to do against the evil today, I did not. Right now they are—"

The chanting of the Indians rose high now and then lowered abruptly to a steady, endless chanting that would weave far into the morning. Now George felt sleepy. Sleep, he thought, is a better way of avoiding things, of not finishing something, than alcohol. He felt tired and sleepy. He rested his head on his arms on the big roll-top desk. Since the petrified-log house was closed, boarded up, this would be as good a place to sleep, to hide, as any. The small back room of the post was dark. Here, in the back room, at the roll-top desk of his grandfather, would be as good a place as any. Now he thought he heard someone try the door and then the window, but he was very sleepy. Maybe it was someone with a message, someone to help him. And what help could he be? No, sleep was the thing for brothers. Soft sleep.

8

When George awoke the chanting had ceased and the great room was coming to light. The noise of someone breaking in had wakened him, he was certain of that and yet who would want in? He went over and turned on the red plastic battery radio that was on the counter and from his seat over the roll top he listened to the news. Now he rose, shutting off the radio and went back to the letter he had been working on the night before. As he was busy over the desk a young Indian with a gun entered quietly from the rear room and came up in back of George.

George dropped the pen and began to sort the Navaho pawn which was in a large box on the desk, examining each piece carefully until he said finally, and while holding a hunk of turquoise up to the light, "How did you get out?"

The young Indian's name was Four Thumbs. When he was in the army the other soldiers had called him Chief Tom Thumb, but his name was Four Thumbs and he had just escaped, by killing a man, from a psychiatric cell, where he had been placed for killing another.

"You're my prisoner, Captain," the Indian with the gun said.

George repeated, still holding the hunk of turquoise up to the light, "How did you get out?"

"Yesterday about noon I . . ."

"I know when," George said. "The radio is full of it. I expect they're right about that, but how about the other?"

"What other?" the young Indian still holding the gun on the trader said.

"The other man you killed."

"You believe everything you hear on the radio and read in the papers?"

"Most everything," George said. "For example," the trader said, "I believe this."

"You'd believe them before you'd believe a man who served under you, a man, for example, that was in your outfit in France?"

George, who wore a cowhide jacket and a bemused expression beneath his worn, wide Stetson, did not remember who had started this "for example" business but he would try and finish it. "For example, yes," he said.

"You think we got started on the habit of killing people over there and we keep it up here? We got a habit?"

"You have," George Bowman said.

The young Indian grabbed the pistol he was carrying by the wrong end in his wrong hand and walked over to the front door and locked it as he had already locked the back. As he walked back toward George he dropped the gun in his pocket.

"You wouldn't turn me in," he said.

"Can't do anything else," George said. "Unless you leave."

"I got no place to leave to, Captain."

George went back to his letter.

"I came back to this part of the reservation because—" The young Indian hesitated. He had on a white man's blue serge coat that fitted as though it had been taken at the point of a gun. "Listen, he said. "I knew you'd help me. You always have."

"Always have," George repeated and he looked at the young Indian now.

"Yes. That patrol you organized got through just in time. Cut off for six days. Fought off a whole Kraut platoon for six days. But I couldn't have lasted a minute longer. You got through with relief just in time."

"I got through one day too late. I'm sorry," the trader said.

And he thought: When I got there he was all that was left of his outfit. He was the only one alive, if you can call what he was alive. He was giving orders to an outfit, to a platoon of men that did not exist any more. He was giving all the orders and carrying all the orders out. It must have been that, like his forefathers, like the old ones who defended this final mesa above us here in Indian Country against the whites, he did not know how to say "surrender." When his outfit was surrounded in France he too did not know how to say the word. When they were without food and water he did not know how to say it and when all of his comrades were dead he still could not bring himself to say it. He did not know how to say "They shall not pass" or how to say "Nuts" to the Germans either, or any other historically remembered simplicities. He only knew that the mesa—this position somewhere on the flank of Bastogne—must be held. He did not know that his mind must be held also, and, after

the sixth day of the German breakthrough, after six days of bludgeoning artillery fire and no food or water, he did not notice that his mind had deserted the action and left his body all alone defending the position.

"I got through one day, maybe two days too late. I'm sorry," the trader said.

"What? Are you crazy?" Four Thumbs said quickly. "Look, you're not crazy, are you?"

This was a favorite word of Four Thumbs for a long time now. Lots of people were crazy.

"Look, Captain. I'm here. Feel me. You got through just in time."

"One, maybe two days late," George said, but he was not talking to Four Thumbs now. He was looking out the window. There was a big, and seemingly much longer than it actually was, silence with some horse noises coming through the heavy piñon log corral on the south side of the post. The silence made the gentle horse noises very loud.

The young Indian had both hands jammed into some white victim's blue serge coat and he stared at George as though it were George's move, as though George had the gun. The young Indian very much had the gun. It made an awful bulge in the blue serge coat.

"For an Indian a quiet padded cell is no place to die," Four Thumbs said finally.

George continued to look out the window at the endless country of the Navaho. Actually it was less endless even than George's people had promised in the Treaty of 1865 but George thought it had the beauty of endlessness with the sudden violent-colored mesas you could always see beyond. The big blue spaces make the Navaho country a part

of everyone and of everything else. From here you feel you are almost there. It might make a passing safe and easy— almost acceptable.

"A quiet padded cell is no place for anyone to die," George said, still watching the country. "And some foreign castle, some marble tent, is no place for a Bowman to die."

"Then you don't—"

"I don't know yet," George said, turning, looking at the young Indian. "Anyway, give me the gun."

Four Thumbs gave him the gun although he had some trouble locating it. He was used to being armed with an army Garand rifle.

George walked around and put the gun beneath the counter in a case alongside The People's pawn.

Someone tried the door now. The young Indian felt for his gun.

"You better let him in," George said.

The Indian continued to feel in the white man's too big blue coat for his gun. He looked worried.

"You're back in my outfit. You've got to take orders," George said. "I take all the responsibility, give all the orders around here."

The young Indian stiffened. "Yes, Captain."

"Please open the door."

"Yes, Captain," and the young Indian opened the door and let in Rabbit Stockings.

"Why really, have you heard the news?" Rabbit Stockings said to George Bowman.

George was busy.

"That psycho from Window Rock broke out, killed an-

other man, ditched his car in the Chijuilli. They figure he's headed this way."

Rabbit Stockings had begun his talk in Navaho and then switched to English when he noticed the other Indian. There is no damage in impressing another Indian.

"We better be ready."

"We are very ready," George said. "Rabbit Stockings, I want you to meet One-of-Us. One-of-Us, I want you to meet Rabbit Stockings."

The young Indian called Four Thumbs who had just had his name changed to One-of-Us yatayed Rabbit Stockings pleasantly and Rabbit Stockings yatayed One-of-Us pleasantly too.

"If he was headed this way I could begin to put my knowledge into motion," Rabbit Stockings said. Rabbit Stockings was not referring to any mere doctorate degree; Rabbit Stockings had taken a special FBI course by mail. George figured that this was the knowledge Rabbit Stockings was going to put in motion although he had taken a body-building course, a pedicure course, an airplane Diesel engine course and another one the government had stopped coming through the mails. But maybe, George thought, he is going to put the airplane Diesel engine course into motion; a Navaho will fool you.

"One-of-Us," Rabbit Stockings said, "I am about to take my final exams. I think I'll bone up. Would you care to take a look at some of the latest crime-stopper bulletins?"

"No," Four Thumbs said.

George was watching out the window someone in a uniform coming up the trail.

"I think, One-of-Us, you had better go with Rabbit Stockings," George said to Four Thumbs.

"Yes, Captain," Four Thumbs said and he left with Rabbit Stockings for a secret place where all of the FBI and airplane Diesel engine knowledge was hidden from the other Indians.

George was watching Arturo Trujillo, the state trooper, who was responsible for the one hundred and fifty miles between Bernalillo and Aztec, get out of old man Curry's four-wheel-drive Willys pickup. He had been forced to leave his red-flashing, black-and-white, insigniaed Ford, with a radio that was in touch with headquarters in Santa Fe, at the Gallegos' garage in Cuba. The state did not want to buy him a new front end for a red-flashing, black-and-white Ford every time he had to chase an Indian.

Old man Curry stayed outside in the Willys pickup while the state trooper came over to the door of the trading post. The trader let him in.

"George," the state trooper said, walking over where the tobacco was kept, "we got Indian trouble. How about a pack of English Ovals?"

"How about a pack of Camels?" George said, taking them out.

"Okay. And a Milky Way," the trooper said. "And I'm supposed to be watching my figure."

"How's the wife?" George asked.

"Watching her figure," the trooper said.

"And Curry's boy, is he still watching her figure?"

"Not any more, he isn't," the trooper said and he tried to toss the Milky Way wrapper into an Indian basket and missed.

"Where you hiding that Indian?" The trooper put both blue-uniformed elbows on the counter and studied the trader.

"That's why I pay my taxes," George said. "To pay you to find out where they hide."

"In New Mexico they don't collect much taxes," the trooper said, still studying George. "We need your help."

"Don't ask any questions," George said. "Don't ask me any questions, Arturo," George said, taking up a pencil and tapping it on the pawn counter.

"Okay," the trooper said. "But don't make me look bad."

George walked to the window and looked out at the country, still thinking.

"Can you imagine an Indian dying in a quiet padded cell, a billion times removed from everything?"

"I don't like it," the trooper said. "But don't make me look bad. Just promise me you won't make me look bad."

George went back to the counter. "All right," he said. "If you don't want to be a hero."

"I don't want to be a hero," the trooper said. "It's tough enough with the wife."

"You have a very attractive wife," George said. "Take her some of this candy." He put a stack of Powerhouse bars in front of the trooper. The trooper put them in his pocket, looking puzzled at George.

"All this time I never suspected you," the trooper said.

"You should spend more time at home, Arturo," George said.

"I know," the trooper said. "That's where I'm going now. But first I have to take a look around. I got to make a report. A citizen, old man Curry, is outside. I got to take a look around and make a report."

"Just so it's only for a report," George said.

"Listen," the trooper said, standing erect now, his pockets bulging with the Powerhouses. "You got sixty thousand Indians around here. You think I want to be a hero with those kind of odds? You promised me about the boy that I wouldn't look bad."

"All right," George said. "I'll get someone to show you around for the report. Is that citizen still watching?"

"Yes," the trooper said, looking at old man Curry through the window.

"Then I'll get someone to show you around for the report."

"Thank you. Take care of me when I'm gone too," the trooper said and he took out one of his beautiful wife's Powerhouses and began to eat it.

Two Indians entered, Felix Mount Royal and Lord Rundle. They had two bags of turquoise and silver jewelry that they wanted to pawn. They wanted to hang onto their lamb crop a while yet because the present price interested but did not concern them. Try sometime to bargain with a Navaho for his sheep and win something. With his wife's jewelry, George knew, he has a lot of staying power.

The two Indians, Felix Mount Royal and Lord Rundle, did not much like the looks of the policeman so they did not open their bags of jewelry yet. They talked to each other in low Navaho about this unexpected situation, with the trader, George Bowman, listening. Finally, between them, and with no help from the audience, they decided on one answer which took the form of a question. Coming up to George Bowman and planting their bags of jewelry on the counter they asked in classical Navaho, "Sansi, what in the hell is the cop doing here?"

"He's perfectly safe," George said. "He's got to make a report. We don't want to make him look bad."

The two Navahos, still without opening their bags of jewelry, had a short conference in Indian about this before they asked, "Sansi, we don't want to be rude, but what is it he doesn't want to look bad about?"

"That psycho boy, Four Thumbs, who was in my outfit during the war and came back to the States and killed two extra white men during the peace. They think he escaped into this officer's territory. They want to put him back in the padded cell."

The two Navahos thought about this for a while without consulting each other but both tapping their bags of jewelry before Lord Rundle said in Navaho, "Why really, Sansi, what can we do not to help?"

"Why really, not to help," George Bowman answered in their own language, "go find me a boy named One-of-Us, who is with Rabbit Stockings, so he can show this officer around so this officer can make out a report and not look so bad that they will send someone who is thinking in terms of heroic actions, or worse, someone who is sincere."

"Good. As you say, we will find the boy and do our very best not to help and if this young gentleman is not sincere I guess it is safe to leave our jewelry here on the counter."

George told them where Rabbit Stockings' FBI and airplane Diesel secret hiding place was and they left.

"I don't think they trust me," the young Spanish trooper said, between bites on his beautiful wife's Powerhouse.

"They don't trust people who are what they call sincere. They feel their Navaho Nation has been cheated out of almost all it ever owned by those who are sincere."

The trooper looked confused and opened another Power-house, tossing the wrapper at the Indian basket and hitting it this time.

"Just don't make me look bad," he said.

Up the rincon in the Largo Canyon where a big cavity had been caused by the loss of a large tree of petrified wood that had imbedded itself in the sandstone sixty million years ago and had recently departed, Rabbit Stockings and One-of-Us had now more recently arrived. They had to go back to the roots, which had made a large room deep within the Eocene sandstone, through a five-foot-wide, fifty-foot-long tunnel caused by the absence, the weathering out, of the very old and tropic trunk. They had to climb over the silica remains of the actual tree getting up the cliff. George had explained about all this to the Navaho People and the Indians pretended to believe him. "Of course, Sansi. What else, Sansi?" All white men had a few beads missing.

"It's darker in here than a whore's dream," One-of-Us said, speaking army language. He spoke three languages.

"Let's try and keep it clean," Rabbit Stockings said, lighting an FBI bulletin to find his cache of candles. He lit a candle now and set it on one of the fragments of the very old tree.

"Sixty million years old," Rabbit Stocking said.

"Who's crazy now?" One-of-Us said.

"You want to be a dumb Indian all your life? Don't you want to have a white man's diploma in something?"

"No, because I'm not crazy," One-of-Us said.

"I just can't believe that one does not seek to better him-

self," Rabbit Stockings said slowly and as though he had read it someplace.

"Listen, you're being taken in by a bunch of white con artists. Who's crazy now?"

Rabbit Stockings looked hurt and he looked down at the sheaf of correspondence courses he held.

"Well," Rabbit Stockings said, "maybe all of us are a little bit crazy but most of us don't hurt other people."

Four Thumbs began to tense up. He began to work his mouth and a bit of saliva ran down that he did not wipe off. It was cold in the cave but One-of-Us was sweating.

"I could kill you with Sansi's hunk of phony tree. I could smash your crazy head."

One-of-Us lifted a silica-glistening chunk of the lead-heavy wood.

"Hokka-shai." Lord Rundle said thank you in Navaho as he took the chunk that was poised over Rabbit Stockings' head.

"Interesting," Lord Rundle said, examining it in the dim light. "But Sansi's sixty million years—it's difficult even for an Indian to believe."

"Sansi's crazy," One-of-Us said.

"Of course," Lord Rundle said.

"You just saved my life," Rabbit Stockings, who had been too shocked to talk until now, said.

"He's crazy too," One-of-Us said.

"Of course," Lord Rundle said .

Lord Rundle turned the lead-heavy, silica-glistening rock in his jeweled hand, the candle catching all the highlights.

"But you'd better come back to the post. You are One-of-Us, are you not?"

"No. Four Thumbs."

"Come anyway," Lord Rundle said.

Back at the post the state trooper was trying to build a pyramid on the counter with the Powerhouse bars. George was watching and the Navaho women sitting on the floor with their babies stacked along the counter in cradle boards had been sucking Pepsi but now they were holding their breaths while the trooper tried to get the final Powerhouse on the pyramid.

"Don't bother me," the trooper said tensely, without looking up as the Indians entered.

The Navahos from the cave took places along the counter quietly. The leather-strapped Indian babies stacked along the base of the counter in their cradle boards could not see the pyramid that was being built but they could see the tense faces of their fathers who watched.

"Who's crazy now?" One-of-Us said.

The pyramid collapsed just as the final Powerhouse was about to be placed deftly by the state trooper to complete the impossible structure. One-of-Us spoke and everything collapsed.

The trooper turned suddenly on the Navahos along the counter. "Who said that?" he asked tightly.

"I did," One-of-Us said. "I think you're crazy."

The trooper stared at the Navaho hard and One-of-Us stared hard at the trooper. The trooper dropped his eyes.

"Maybe. I don't know. I was just having some fun."

"They tell me I'm the man who is supposed to show you around," One-of-Us said.

"Don't bother," the trooper said, still watching the floor. "I've seen plenty. I been here long enough to make a report," he said over to George. "I think that's old man Curry pressing the horn."

It was old man Curry pressing the horn. The trooper left but not before saying to George from the door, "Don't forget what you promised me."

"One-of-Us, I promised him," George said when the door had closed, "that you would not be caught by somebody else on his territory and that you would always be a good soldier and not cause any more trouble so you would not die in a padded cell—that you would remain here and be a good soldier. I sent for you to show him around so you would not be discovered hiding."

"Yes, Captain." One-of-Us stiffened to attention.

"Rabbit Stockings will take you back to the cave where you will remain until it is safe to take a hogan."

"Yes, Captain."

The door opened again now and One-of-Us grabbed quickly at the trooper's gun that was on the counter next to the candy where the trooper had laid it down and forgotten it. One-of-Us fired two shots quickly at the crazy enemy before George yelled, "Cease fire." The trooper went down on one knee at the door. The Indians picked up the trooper, who was bleeding from the thigh, and carried him out toward Curry's pickup.

"I came back for—" The trooper was shocked and couldn't complete the sentence.

They got him in the front of the pickup and Curry started her up.

"I think you can make it back all right. How do you feel?" old man Curry said. The trooper was feeling better now and felt he could finish his sentence.

"—back for the candy," he said.

George had taken Four Thumbs outside.

"I think you and I had better go up on the mesa," George said.

"Yes, Captain. But I thought I was going back to the cave."

"A new situation has arisen since then. I must give new orders."

"Yes, Captain."

When they had climbed steadily upward for fifteen minutes George remembered that Four Thumbs, who was following, still had the gun. Never mind. Let him take it with him like a good soldier. He heard Four Thumbs come up alongside him now.

"Captain."

"Yes, Chief?"

"I've still got the gun."

"On a patrol you always need a gun."

They were winding up the high sheer mesa, along a path that had been hacked out by Four Thumbs' forefathers one hundred years ago. By rolling down boulders the old Indians had felt they could keep the whites away forever. They almost did, but, defending this final fort, the top of this dry mesa, they ran out of water. No one quit. They were all still up there.

Here, on one side of the narrow rock path, was a slick wall of deep-colored sandstone to the top of the high mesa and a drop-off of almost six hundred feet to the desert rocks

on the other. Soon, on the next switchback, they would be in the clouds and a fall would seem to be into infinity.

George felt the young Indian come up on him again now, as close as he could get, about as close as a small dog will follow on the heels of his master.

"Captain."

"Yes, Chief?"

"You ever hear of an officer being shot in the back by one of his own men?"

The trader wanted to stop and rest now, he was sweating and the sweat was not warm, but he knew he must go on. They had made the switchback and soon they would be in the clouds. The trader was using his handkerchief and now he put it back in the breast pocket of his cowhide leather jacket before he answered.

"Yes, Chief," George said. "We all hear stories like that in back of the lines. Up front—well, I suppose it depends on what kind of a leader a man is."

George steadied himself now. The path was getting very narrow as they entered the white clouds.

"He takes his chances," George said. "And listen," George said. There was a big silence within the clouds as the Indian listened. "When a soldier comes back and begins to kill his own outfit and there is nothing that anyone at all can do to help him, then the soldier himself, in one of those moments when his mind comes back to him, must think of some way of saving the outfit he is destroying. But the command decision is with you," the trader said. "We are cut off from everything and you can do with the rest of us what you will. You got the gun."

Now George felt suddenly that the Indian was no longer

133

with him. And then he heard a voice that was much further to his left than the path say quietly, "Yes, Captain."

George froze, the gray mist swirling around him. There was nothing on all sides except the steady, long shriek of an Indian falling to eternity.

The next day at the post Rabbit Stockings was seated on a high stool alongside the counter. He had all the airplane Diesel engine books on the stool so he could reach the burial prayer stick he was working on. He was looking in the corner now where the trader always kept his Clabrough-Martin rifle.

"That's the first time I never saw your rifle in that corner," Rabbit Stockings said.

"You never will again," the trader said.

"Isn't it kind of primitive," Rabbit Stockings said, "burying a rifle with a man? That was a valuable gun."

"My people believe the man was much more valuable," George said. "And we respect your ancient customs."

"Thank you and thank your people," Rabbit Stockings said. "It must have been quite a climb, carrying that body to the top of the mesa."

"That's the way I figure he would have wanted it—back up there with the other warriors."

"Those old people," Rabbit Stockings said, "cut off up there without water, must have gone crazy before they died."

"Yes," George said. "No one could get through until it was too late."

"But they stuck it out when they could have quit," Rabbit Stockings said.

"Indeed they did," George said. "And he was their son."

Both of them looked out through the adobe-and-log-

rimmed window at the blue mesa that concealed the bones of the very brave Old People—at the bright blue and orange-banded and yellow-lensed mesa that in turn was concealed now within the swirling purple and red refractions of a dying sun—stared up at the long mesa within the mirror cloud which shot the whole sky above the desert with a clear and gaudy light. When you had to go neither George nor Rabbit Stockings could think of a better, a more altogether fitting place to make it across.

George swung around in his oak chair and looked up at the heavy logged ceiling of the room. And where is Alex going to make it across? George thought. In another country, I suppose. And who cares? No one. Well, that's the way he wrote it, wanted it. That's what he asked for.

George let his eyes drift back to the desk and he stared at the piece of paper there a long time.

This soldier who came back . . . I am always, George thought, taking part in something that sounds like an early story of Alexander's. I wonder what the moral would be if Alex were writing it. Alex would probably write it as it happened and let people draw their own moral if any. And my moral would be, George thought, and he wrote:

"Dear Alex: By God, we have got a situation between us we can solve if we would only stop acting like white people. An Indian you must remember by the name of Four Thumbs showed me how like the boy I was twenty-five years ago I have been acting. Four Thumbs became a psycho in the war and when he got back here he continued to kill people. Today in one of his short moments of sanity he killed himself. He came back home to where the brave Old People are, and with courage. I suppose we've all got a dif-

ferent way of killing ourselves. Mine is to retreat and retreat from my life into the life of the Indians. What is your way, Alex? We have got somehow to get around this hardness that stands between us. We have got somehow to stop one of us from killing himself. Hold on, Alex, and I will think of something yet. Hold on and I will write 'Come home.' Until now 'Come home' is too simple and powerful to write but hang on and I will write it, sign it, seal it, stamp it and mail it. Hang on."

"What are you writing?" Rabbit Stockings asked.

"Words," George said. George put down the pen and swung in his chair until he looked out the window. He looked past all the beauty and down to the long scar of dirt road that led to Albuquerque and the world beyond.

"Yes, words," George said. "Words."

9

Yes," Alexander said. "A person could swim to La Paz nicely."

The others around the iron table made no comment at all. Finally Perrette, who was sitting next to Alfred and watching Mimi Jimenez, the owner of the rotted wharf, three tired sports fishing boats and the marlin record, her voice non-committal and playing it safe, said, "You mean, Alex, you're going through with this—?"

"I reject the idea absolutely," Alfred said. "If you're just trying to prove something there must be some other way of proving whatever it is that you want to prove."

"Suppose I want to prove," Alexander said, his voice rising a bit now, "supposing I want to prove that if a man can't go back to Indian Country, if a man can't go home, then he can make things happen he can write about?"

The small smile on Mimi's face had become a big one. They were speaking slowly enough so that he could about follow it. He had been trying to cultivate English but he realized he was making little progress when they spoke rapidly; when they spoke slowly and the subject was of interest to him he understood enough to give this big smile.

Mimi had a huge lizard neck capped by almost no head in which there could have been concealed no brain—a Mexican dinosaur smiling.

"And if he was serious?" Perrette asked, speaking to Mimi Jimenez. "Would they allow it? Would he have a chance?"

Mimi hesitated, feeling for the words, spreading his fat hands in front of him, speaking slowly. "A swimmer no has to be rápido. No es importante ser joven."

"He does not need to be young," Alexander helped.

"In catching the big fish you need to be young," Mimi went on carefully, looking at Alexander, who had helped him. "A sports fisher, yes, he needs to be young. He must have the courage—"

"And stupidity," Alexander helped again.

"Of youth," Mimi went on. "It is muy necesario, but for swimming the presteza of youth no is necesario," Mimi insisted. "A long time ago, before there were automobiles," Mimi said, "on the Day of the Gobernadores, the mayor offered one hundred reales to anyone who could swim to La Paz. On that very day two completed the swim. It was necessary to divide the money between them. Es toda en la resistencia."

"It's all in the endurance," Alexander said.

"Sí. Endurencia," Mimi said, holding up his arms.

A waiter in degrees of dirtiness came from behind a plane tree, examined the fat, small lizard arms that Mimi was holding out and wanted to know what they were going to have.

"Nothing," Alexander said.

The waiter retreated again behind the plane tree.

"Why did you send him away, Alex?" Perrette said. "We

are going to need a drink."

"Drink?" Alfred said, moving forward. "I don't see anything to celebrate in the writer, Alexander Bowman, risking his life."

"Oh," Alexander said dramatically. "Get thee hence, thou cream-faced loon. Those linen cheeks of thine are counsellors to fear. Shak-es-pee-ray," Alex said to Mimi, pronouncing it as a Mexican might.

"Yes. Shakespeeray," Mimi said. And then in Spanish, "I would rather have him make the swim but he's not around."

"You think my making the swim from your old boat harbor would do your ruin some good?" Alexander said.

"Sí. Mucho publicidad. Sí," Mimi said.

"And if we go ahead with the plans and I walk out on you would you kill me, Mimi?"

"Sí. Cómo no? Sí," Mimi said.

"He didn't understand you," Perrette said.

"They tell me you've killed three people, Mimi," Alexander said.

"Sí," Mimi said. "Tres."

"I don't think he understood you," Perrette said.

"Le comprendo perfectamente," Mimi said.

"What was that?" Perrette said.

"Confusion," Alexander said. "But we can have something to eat. I hear there is a cantina, a place called the Del Mar, that is not a bad place. Let's try that."

"When you leave the big hotels," Alfred said, "you run the danger of getting the turistas and spending most of your time in the bathroom. The Cantina Del Mar is a native place and one would certainly get the turistas there."

"Young man," Alexander said, "I am a walking monument

to the fact that in any of the Latin countries you get the turistas wherever you go—at the Del Prado, at the Havana-Madrid, at the Utrillo—anyplace you go. It's a question of time. A few days sooner at the cantinas than at the big tourist hotels."

"The Del Mar has good camarones," Mimi said.

"Well, then," Alexander said, "we will all go down to the Del Mar and have some shrimp. I will arrange for the carriage," Alexander said, standing up.

"Let Mimi order the carriage," Perrette said. "Let Mimi make the deal for the carriage. Speaking the language perfectly well he will arrange a better price."

"I can speak Navaho," Alexander said. "And that should confuse them into giving me a good price. We will take two carriages; that will spread the act and make the war party look big."

Alexander moved toward the edge of the Malecón de las Olas Altas, looking up and down the broad spray-swept street for another carriage. There was one immediately by them at the curb but he could see no other.

"We will give your four pesos to take us to the Cantina Del Mar," Alexander said in Spanish to the defeated and old Mexican driver who stood at the head of his skeletal horse. The cab driver looked at him and said quickly in English, "Okay, boy."

"This is the only carriage," Alexander said back to the others. "If you people want to pile in the back I'll get up in front with the driver."

Alexander hiked into the hard, high, forward seat with the driver and the others came slowly from the table, Alfred remaining to pay the bill.

Alfred could not locate the waiter so he dropped a few pesos on the table and got into the carriage.

"Arre, burro!" Alexander called to the horse.

The driver took the reins and they started slowly down the broad Malecón.

"Do you work this poor horse all day?" Alexander asked the driver.

The old man crouching over the reins did not look up.

"Sí, señor," he said. "My patron owns the bullring. That is, he manages it as he manages all the livestock in town, including the horse that is pulling us today. When the horses get so they cannot pull us then we use them in the ring against the bulls."

"Oh," Alexander said. "And do they bring good bulls here? Bulls that charge straight and are brave?"

"If you substitute the word stupid for brave I might see it," the old man said, still following the horse.

"Oh," Alexander said, smiling faintly. "You have ruined a few paragraphs already. I write books and I was supposed to dominate these early pages. I asked the right questions, I did my part, but you gave all the wrong answers."

"I'm sorry," the old man said, addressing the horse. "But I thought I was being paid to take you to the Cantina Del Mar."

Alexander was silent.

"This book," the driver flopped the reins in annoyance, "will it be mostly about your home country?"

"No," Alexander said. "Not now because I can't go home again. But the people I write about now can but won't because of self-inflicted wounds."

"And people will pay to read about that? About people

who feel sorry for themselves?" The old man was inquiring of the horse again.

"Yes, some will pay for that," Alexander answered. "Because I guess some Americans suffer from self-inflicted wounds."

"You have no relatives?" the old man asked.

"Yes, a brother. Now," Alexander said hopefully, "the conversation in this part is going much better. It is going as it should go."

"Well," the old man said, shifting himself on the hard seat, "you can always cut out the pieces of the story that I ruined. And perhaps I can give you something," the old man said, looking up. "You see that café over there?" He pointed with his stick of a whip. "The one with the red and yellow front marked Tequila y Something? Well, a long time ago, before there were automobiles, the Spanish gobernador was here on the Day of the Gobernadores. The mayor offered one hundred reales to anyone who would swim to La Paz. Sixteen people entered the water and two made it."

"You mean," Alexander said, his voice rising, "that two men who had never swum that distance before, two men with little experience, swam from here to La Paz?"

"Yes," the old man said quietly, going back to his horse. "But the fourteen who drowned had never swum it before either."

At the café they all tumbled out in front of the weather-ravaged shack on the edge of the water. The entrance side was hidden by a thick growth of coconuts and palmettos. Alex bargained the driver into waiting so that he could take them to the wharf after they finished eating. "Or better," he told the old man, "come in with us and have a drink."

Inside there were no lighting and no windows, but the seaward side of the café was without a wall and opened out on a wooden pavilion for dancing, although it would be quite a trick with the heavy boards and wide gaps in between. In the big inside room there was an American jukebox of horrendous size and frightening color. The people in the café were grouped around this, drinking beer out of the heat of Mexico—the four young girls were out of this world.

"They're gone, Jackson!" Perrette hollered to Alexander.

Outside on the pavilion there was a four-piece Mexican orchestra: guitar, accordion, another guitar and another accordion, playing to no one, bravely making a noise against the indifference. The group went out there and quartered themselves around a table that had not yet collapsed.

"Siéntese, señores," a waiter who had followed them said. "You speak English?"

"Of a kind," Alexander said.

The waiter got them some hard extra chairs and they made themselves uncomfortable.

"But we're Indians," Alexander said, "who are still bitter and will not concede defeat to the white man. But let's have camarones all round."

The waiter seized on the word camarones and got back into Spanish quick. "Sí, señor. Pronto," he said, backing off.

The people at the jukebox had stopped their intense interest in the machine and were staring over at Mimi. They had followed him with their eyes as he came in and now were looking over at him and talking it up among themselves. Also another party had come in looking like tourists from the States and they too were interested in the table.

"Pardon me for breaking in on this chapter," Alexander

143

said, "but while we were quietly camping here I think we have been surrounded by our compatriots. They are going to lay siege to us, but it's four of them against five of us. As unprepared as we are I think we can do all right. They've already spotted us so there's no use keeping quiet. I place them as two dentists and their wives. Both of them are joiners. A couple of years ago they were reduced to pulling each other's teeth, but now, since the inflation, they think five thousand dollars will buy them some happiness in Mazatlán. They have had the great sports fisherman Mimi Jimenez pointed out to them, and now they've tracked the inestimable one to his lair where they can watch him from as close as ten feet. But what lies in store for them on this exciting trip? What will happen to their children yet unborn after their encounter with the dashing Mimi Jimenez? Read the next exciting installment of Alfred Marlowe's great novel of tenderness and brutality. You can have that story, Alfred," Alexander told the young man. "You can have it if you have not already used it."

"I think we can tell many stories and have quite a time," Alfred said. "Yes, I think everything could be quite amusing if you would give up your idea of swimming to La Paz."

"Ugh," Alexander grunted. "You tellum story and I swim to La Paz."

"Well, I don't see the humor in it," Alfred said.

"No, you couldn't see the humor in it, Alfred. No, you couldn't be funny," Alexander said. "You couldn't be funny, Alfred. Even when you're stealing something, you couldn't be funny, Alfred."

"Stealing?" Alfred asked. "What am I stealing?"

"It is a good day," Mimi said, trying his English. "Do you

not think, everybody, that it is a good day?"

"Yes," Perrette said. "It is a good day. But what does Alex' wise old scout think about it? Certainly, Alex, you brought him along for his aged wisdom. Will he give us some wise words? Will you translate for us, Alex?"

"A long time ago," the old man began, "before there were automobiles, the Spanish gobernador was here on the Day of the Gobernadores. The mayor offered one hundred reales to anyone who would swim to La—"

"Yes," Perrette said. "But let's not be serious. Let's dance, Alex," she said.

The orchestra began with a high wail.

"You can't even do a war dance on this prairie," Alexander said, looking at the floor.

The Americans had seated themselves at a table near the orchestra and now the two women got up and advanced toward Bowman's table. They were dressed in Jalisco print dresses and a-jangle with tourist silver bracelets.

"You better duck," Perrette said to Mimi Jimenez. "Here come a couple of your aficionados."

Women not quite middle-aged advanced, eager-looking, holding what might have been a bullfight manual for tourists that they sell outside the Plaza de Toros for three pesos.

"Yes," Perrette said. "Now you can explain to them exactly how you catch the big fish and autograph their tourist guides for them."

Mimi blinked nervously and slid in his chair a little, but anxious.

"How old are they?" he said in Spanish. "Quantos años tienen?"

The two women advanced all the way to the table and then

leaned over toward Alexander, extending the books that were novels of Alexander Bowman's that, although good, had become popular enough to get into the paper-backed edition.

"Will you kindly autograph these for us?" the taller one said to Alexander. "We heard that you were in town and went down to the Pan American hoping that we would be lucky enough to catch you."

"Yes, madam," Alexander said. "I will autograph them for you."

She extended the books together with the pen and Alexander autographed both of them quickly.

"We don't know how we can thank you," she said, picking up their books.

"There's no way you can thank me, madam," Alexander said, looking at both of them carefully.

"Just the same it was a thrill to see you," she said, both of them beginning to back off toward their table.

"It was a thrill to see you, madam," Alexander said.

"Oh, I don't see how you could be thrilled by American girls like us." The woman stood hesitating, still standing near the table.

"I am quite thrilled," Alexander said.

"Our husbands sell oil-drilling machinery," the woman said, "and we came down here to join them, but they travel all over Mexico selling oil-drilling machinery."

"That sounds quite thrilling," Alexander said.

"You talk just like you sound in your books." She giggled and the other woman touched her.

"Madam," Alexander said at last, "when I start sounding like that in my books I am finished."

"Oh," she said, still lingering at the table, embarrassed,

the other woman even pulling on her now. "You sound just like the he-man you are in your books. Oh, but you don't want to talk to nobodies like us." She started to giggle again, becoming audible.

"You are somebody who buys my books. That's important to me," Alexander said.

"Oh, go on," she said.

Alexander gave up and stared at Mimi Jimenez.

"Well, good-by now. We're going," the woman said. "Pleased to have met you."

Alexander had given up now and did not acknowledge her, staring across the table at Mimi. The women giggled off back to their table just as a man came over from the same table.

"Is that the way you talk to my wife?" the man said. He was a square, wide man built so that he looked shorter than he actually was. He had been doing quite a lot of drinking and he wiped his face with his hand as he spoke.

"Is that the way you speak to my wife—call her madam? You think she's running a joint down here or something?"

Those at the table remained silent and Perrette winked over at Alfred.

"Don't you say good-by when she says good-by? What's the matter, is she dirt or something?"

"Listen," Alfred said, the only one to look up at the man. "Listen, drop it before something happens."

"Something has already happened," the man said, wiping his face again. "My wife has been insulted. I want satisfaction."

"I should think you would," Perrette said.

"Jesus, that's so funny. Jesus, you people are so funny I'm going to bust a gut. Is that how you people get so famous,

being so funny?" the stocky man said, working his shoulders. "Famous people can go around insulting other men's wives, is that it?"

"You only heard part of the conversation. Nobody insulted her. You better go home now," Alfred said, standing up white-faced and trembling.

"You asked for it. By God, he is asking for it," the man said as he hauled back his big arm and lunged at Alfred. Alex stood up but his movement stopped in midair as the kick that Mimi Jimenez threw at the short man caught him in the groin and dropped him where he had stood. The man now lay quietly on the floor. Two waiters came up and pulled him back to his own table. Alfred sat down, still shaking badly.

"White man never should have crossed river," Alexander said, folding his arms. "White man should never have come to Little Big Horn without better general. White man all dead now so we can eat."

"He never should have done that," Alfred said, clenching and unclenching his hands, his voice high and nervous. "Mimi should never have hit him there," he said. "It isn't fair. It isn't—"

"Oh," Alexander said, "nobody asked white man to come into our prairie looking for fight. When white man do that, anything fair. Anyone fooling with Mimi Jimenez lucky not to get killed."

Alfred continued in his high voice, insistent. "Certainly the man is entitled to an explanation when his wife—"

"White man should keep his squaw home when he comes to our country," Alexander said. "Squaws who can read, very dangerous. Particularly dangerous, squaws who can read.

That's a quotation from a famous Indian named Quicker-Than-You, Alfred."

"But certainly Mimi didn't do it fairly," Alfred said, talking almost intimately now. "It wasn't fair the way he—"

"When white man cross river looking for fight we no ask for everything fair. Particularly when he pick on defenseless poet. That's all, Alfred," Alexander said, going back to his normal voice.

Alfred held his eye for a moment and Alexander looked straight into his and Alfred broke it off and went back to twitching his white fingers between his hands.

The waiters had gotten the other party into an automobile cab that was waiting outside. They laid the short, wide man in gently but then part of him, part of his leg, was still sticking out. One of the waiters pressed the leg in with his own foot and then tried to close the door. Some of his pants leg was still stuck so he opened the door again and pushed the man's leg in heavily with a shove and closed the door and the bright car started off back to the hotel.

"Living abroad," Alexander said, "getting off the reservation, teaches you how the white man lives, makes you able to write about—to see—"

"And feel the whole wide world," Perrette said.

10

I've got to get home," Perrette said, frightened.

"Here. You can go here," Alexander said.

"No. I've got to get home to the Pan American," Perrette said.

Alexander got her out and into the carriage, leaving Alfred and Mimi at the table arguing mayhem.

Soon they were going as fast as they could go and Alexander was leaning far forward and tense and Perrette was much too relaxed and the color of jade.

The high, two-wheeled Mexican horse-drawn carriage, fiery circus red with yellow wheels, tilted into the rutted dirt narrowness of Guillermo Nelson. Now they left the choking Guillermo Nelson for the broader Twenty-First of March, which led into the Fifth of May, which became the Benito Juarez and the openness of the Plaza de la Revolución with its wide-spreading acacia tree, its dedicated stone benches, its ugly marble fountain and its romantic, delicate iron-flowered bandstand of the Díaz regime. Then a short, bone-jolting tilt down the Plaza Hidalgo, which became the Street of the Boy Heroes of Chapultepec with its commerce and its hotels of the later day, the Alcazar and the Central with their lush tropical patios concealing dank, airless rooms.

"Oh dear, oh dear!" Perrette called sharply.

"Here. Right here," Alexander said. "We can stop at the El Central."

"Oh, no," Perrette said, thinking that the romantic façade concealed an antique and rotted bathroom. "No, no, no. We must get to the Pan American."

"A place is a place," the driver said, spreading his hands but starting the horse off on a trot again down the Boy Heroes of Chapultepec.

The carriage careened a little wildly now down to the turn for the Angel Flores. On the left the whole distance was flanked by a grim flat wall of the Barracks of the Revolution with one long scrawl of whitewashed, childish lettering—VIVA GENERAL HENRICO. Then they were on the Malecón de las Olas Altas, a concrete-paved, broad esplanade running past the grand hotels. The street facing the hard, glinting Pacific was suddenly like another country: no press of people, no monuments, vacant lots, streets proclaiming revolution, no one dying in a doorway, no poison colors or desperate music, no garish, shrieking signs. Only an occasional drift of soft, un-inspired foreign music from an unseen room.

"Oh oh oh," Perrette cried softly.

"Here is the Utrillo," Alexander called, looking at a mass of brick on the right. "There's no decomposed plumbing there."

The driver slowed but when he got no encouragement he jerked the horse on again.

It was only a wild minute to the Pan American and then another minute to make the U turn in front of the Escuela Oficial Josepha Ortiz de Dominguez and then they pulled up in front of the fresh, clean, modern shaft of the Hotel Pan

American and the two bright-silk-shirted boys hurried down the steps to assist them.

"Oh, I don't think I should move," Perrette said. "I really don't think I should move."

Alexander reached in with his long body and took her in his arms, lifting her by bracing his stomach against the side of the carriage. He rushed her through the lobby and into the waiting elevator—where they waited.

"Isn't there anyone to run this thing?" Alexander hollered.

A workman stepped in, cement-caked and grizzled, carrying everything of his business in his arms.

"Someone runs this thing?" Alexander asked in Spanish.

"Quién sabe? Who knows?" The workman settled in a comfortable position against the side of the car.

Alexander jumped out of the elevator and started going up the stairs fast, Perrette bouncing. At the top of the first flight was the office with the clerk, facing across from the elevator.

"The elevator boy—where is he?" Alexander asked.

"It's an interesting subject," the clerk said with an air of deep thought.

Alexander turned.

"But have you tried the Bodega of Ortega on the Plaza Madera? His brother—"

But Alexander was already halfway up the second flight, jumping up the stairs in twos and threes, carrying his weight easily. As they turned for the fifth floor Alexander was dragging badly.

"I can't make it," Perrette gasped. Perrette's face was a mild shade of green. "I must go in there," she said, pointing to an open door.

152

The door opened onto a disheveled bedroom and through another door onto the pristine white sanctuary of an American bathroom.

"There," Perrette pointed.

Alexander bolted through the open door, through the stranger's cluttered bedroom on into the bathroom, and deposited her there. Closing the bathroom door after him he went back into the stranger's bedroom and collapsed on the low bed.

"I must be in the wrong room." It was a thick, heavy, dry voice behind Alexander.

Alexander turned and saw an American Negro sitting at the writing desk in a gray-striped, visitor's baseball uniform with the red lettering GUAYMAS written across his shirt. He had a wide, spreading face.

"No, you're in the right room," Alexander said between gasps. "It's that my wife has the sickness and the elevator isn't running and I had to get her in here quickly."

"That your wife you just ran through here with? That young girl your wife?"

"Yes," Alexander said.

"You picks 'em young," the Negro commented slowly, placing his shoeless feet up on the bed.

"I didn't come into your bathroom to be insulted," Alexander said.

"Out of the hundred rooms in the hotel you just happened to pick ours?" the Negro asked carefully.

"Yes," Alexander said. "It happened that this is as far as we got."

"With the hundred rooms in the hotel it happened that this is as far as you got," the Negro repeated.

"Yes," Alexander said. "That's the way it happened and I apologize for the intrusion."

"You apologizes for the intrusion," the Negro continued, speaking with a neutral voice out of a neutral face. "Of the hundred rooms in the hotel you just happened to pick me and Howard's room. It wasn't that you knew that this was me and Howard's room and that anybody can walk in me and Howard's room whenever it's convenient."

"No, I didn't know it was me and Howard's room," Alexander said, his breath coming more slowly now.

"If you choose to mock me," the Negro said, a little lower and a little tenser and dropping his shoeless feet silently on the floor, "if you choose to mock me you can get out until you have gone through the proper amenities of being admitted into the room."

"But I must wait for my wife," Alexander said.

"You can wait for your wife in the hall," the Negro said with formal quietness.

"Very well," Alexander said, getting up and moving toward the door.

"Plan to attend the game?" the Negro asked as Alexander moved across the bedroom.

"No," Alexander said, his hand on the knob. "Will it be interesting?"

"It could be," the Negro said. "Good day."

Alexander stepped out and closed the door after him. A second later the door opened and the broad face of the Negro appeared again.

"Won't you step in and wait in our room?" he said.

Alexander came inside.

"This chair is not too copesetic," the Negro said, pushing

him the one he had been sitting on. "But it is the best we
have. Make yourself comfortable. Your wife should be out
in a moment."

The Negro removed his spiked shoes from under the chair,
brought them around with him and sat on the bed. He was
silent a moment adjusting a pillow under himself.

"It's better now this way. I don't like the idea that people
think they can bust in on me and Howard any time they
want. We paid our money for this room just like anybody
else. That is, the club paid it in our name. Anyway, it's our
room."

"It's your room," Alexander admitted.

"I'm Leroy," the Negro said. "I'm the third baseman.
Howard is the first baseman for Guaymas. He's out now getting a bite but he'll be back shortly. And you're the writer,"
Leroy continued. "Your entrance made quite a commotion
the other day. Howard and I were on the balcony watching
you come in. Howard is a fan of yours." Leroy touched a
worn, paper-bound copy of Alexander's book that was on the
bedside table.

The door opened and a big burnt Negro, broad-shouldered
and with a continuous defensive smile, entered the room,
stood holding the door with his hand, staring at Alexander
Bowman, and then looked over at Leroy.

"Where did you find him?" he asked.

"He brought his wife to use our bathroom," Leroy said
from the bed.

"That's cozy," Howard said, and then he added slowly,
thinking it over, "The elevator's not running and your wife
got the Aztec's Revenge.

"That's right," Alexander said.

"And did he give you a bad time?" Howard asked, closing the door, speaking to Alexander.

"What do you mean, give him a bad time? Of course I didn't give him a bad time," Leroy said.

"Okay, okay," Howard said, watching Alexander Bowman now. "How is the writing going?"

"It ain't," Alexander said.

"It isn't," Howard repeated. "Well, that is disconcerting. Perhaps a change is indicated. We're going fishing, that is if we win today and don't have to practice, we're going fishing. We'll share the boat with you," he said toward Alexander, "if you'll pay half. They want three hundred and fifty pesos. That's pretty steep for Leroy and I."

"How are they running?" Alexander asked.

"Marlin and sail running pretty good," Howard answered with interest. "You pay half and you can use one of the two fishing chairs all of the time."

"Whose boat?" Alexander asked.

"Louis Peron's. Those hulks of Mimi Jimenez' won't float too good. Louis's got a twin universal with beer, Cokes and bait on the boat for three hundred and fifty pesos, you pay half."

"Okay," Alexander said. "But no family. Last time I shared a boat out of La Paz with an Englishman he brought his whole family along—a passel of kids that drank all the beer, ate all the sandwiches before we were out of the harbor, spent the rest of the time playing cowboys and Indians over my body."

"Last time we was on a fisher," Howard said, "we went out with some whores from the Siete Monos. They was down

below with the crew drinking our beer and we went aground on the Tres Marianas."

"I'm topped," Alexander admitted. "Your fishing stories are better than my fishing stories."

Howard got up and paced the floor as though anxious to put on his uniform. He looked over toward the closet and then he walked over to the table beside the bed and picked up the worn paper-bound copy of Alexander Bowman's book and hit it against his hand.

"Good book," he said.

"Thank you," Alexander said. "Did you like the last one?"

The Negro hedged, hesitated a moment and then put the book down.

"Are you ready?" Alexander said, standing up and calling toward the bathroom.

"I think I can make it now."

The slight shade of green in her face had changed to a pale yellowish tinge. Alexander grabbed her around the waist and helped her across the room. Leroy had gotten up and walked across to the door.

"I'm sorry," Leroy said. "But do you think you can make the game today?"

"Thanks for the use of your bathroom," Alexander said and Leroy closed the door.

Alexander helped Perrette up the last flight of stairs, not needing to carry her now, just gripping her under the shoulder of the right arm. In the long white room he helped her undress while she sat on one of the low side-by-side beds. When he got her between the covers he took two of his pillows and put them under her head and then he went into the bathroom

and turned on the shower to see if there was any hot water. There wasn't any hot water and there wasn't any cold water either. He went over to the table that faced the window in the main room and sat down at the typewriter.

He took a clean sheet of yellow paper and put it in the typewriter and looked at it for a while, then he turned around and picked up the Mazatlán paper and looked at that for a while. It was full of today's ball game with pictures. He let it slide to the floor.

"They're awfully bright, those Negro boys downstairs," Alexander said. "Clever."

"It was nice of them," Perrette said, "to let me use their bathroom."

"They're awfully smart," Alexander said.

"Did you get into an argument with them?" Perrette said.

"No. They were just telling me how to write my books," Alexander said.

"That's cute of them," she said. "What did they say?"

"They said an Indian evidently couldn't write about white people, that he should leave the white people alone. They said I was beginning to act and write like an expatriate, that I should get back to the hogan fast."

"They couldn't have said anything as sophisticated as that," she said.

"They said that I knocked myself out on the last book. They said I threw everything at them, they said I tried so hard there wasn't any stuff on the ball and that I didn't have any control, and that it was a very bad performance."

"I don't think they said anything as sophisticated as that," she repeated.

"They said I sounded like a writer who was coming apart,

that I've got to get hold of myself."

A blast of salted air off the bay ballooned the monk's-cloth curtain high against the ceiling. It streamered out now, flapping in mid-room. As the wind slackened it slowly fell down over the typewriter. Alexander did not bother to remove it, just sat watching the spot where the keys should be.

"A child," Perrette said, her voice weak, from the big bed. "Why don't you have a child?"

"Because I'm incorrectly built," Alexander answered.

"I mean you and me," she said, eager.

"You and I," Alexander said.

"You and I," Perrette said, still excited.

"Because we use contraceptives," Alexander said.

"If we had a child then there would be the three of us, that would be a creation more and bigger and more mystifying than any creation," Her voice rang high and clear in the long flat, modern, sanitary room.

"Think of it," she said. "A creation of ours, a warm-blooded, throbbing, full creation of ours. It would be original. It would have a beginning, a beautiful middle and an exciting end."

"Yes," he said. "Maybe you have been reading one of my old books."

"But isn't it exciting?"

"In the first place," Alexander said quietly, folding his hands, "now the idea runs into the reality of the dangerously increasing birthrate factor, and in the second place the idea runs into competition with TV. TV has handled the idea much better, better even than the comic books or the church."

"I am trying to help you," she said. "I am trying to make things different. It could build your interest in life—give you

something to write for."

"Yes," Alexander said, lifting the monk's cloth off the typewriter. "I think you have a touch of genius, Perrette."

"I only wanted to help," she said.

"I only want to write a book," he said in her same tone.

"Yes," she said. "That's what we want to do. That's what we must do—help you write the book. That is the important thing. We must help you to remain great."

"We?" Alexander repeated, going back in the chair. "Who else is in on the act?"

"Well, you know Alfred wants to help you," she said confidently.

"Does he figure in the end of the book too?" Alexander asked.

There was a pause. "I don't know yet," Perrette said finally. Then she said quickly, "But he is a wonderful critic."

"Did he tell you I was an Indian son of a bitch?" Alexander asked.

"No," Perrette said. "No. You know he didn't. Of course he didn't."

"Then maybe he isn't much of a critic," Alexander said.

Perrette pulled the covers tighter toward her small head, her long blond hair spread out over the blue blanket.

"If we left each other then perhaps you could go back home to Indian Country."

Alexander unrolled the yellow sheet out of the typewriter, wadded it into a neat ball in the palms of his hands and then tossed it for the wastebasket and missed it.

"What about a parrot?" he said. "I saw some nice red and blue and green parrots on Gomez Street."

Perrette was quiet and made a pattern of the blanket, fold-

ing and refolding it.

"Sure you wouldn't want a red, green and yellow parrot? Yellow beaks I think they call them."

"No, I don't want a parrot," she said.

"A monkey?"

"I don't think I want a monkey."

"I am in need of a drink," Alexander said, getting up. "What would you like? An aspirin?"

"No," she said. "I don't think I want anything."

Alexander got up and put on his battered jacket.

"You know what I would really like?" she said. "You know what I think would be awful fun?"

"What?" Alexander asked, putting on his coat.

"An airplane," she said, watching him, her mouth big and smiling. "Wouldn't it be fun? You and I—just you and I all alone up there with just the moon and the stars and the big white heavy clouds, with the entire world spread out beneath us."

"Yes," Alexander said, buttoning his coat. "I think it's double peachy. Are you sure you don't want any aspirin?"

"You could get me two before you go," she said, tired, her voice low again.

Alexander went into the bathroom, took down the bottle of aspirin, knocked out two on the palm of his hand, got a glass of water, set it along with the two pills on the small stand beside her bed and then he leaned over and kissed her on the cheek. She smelled of My Sin and Chase Me, but there was always something there that took him back to that first night in the airless motel room outside Albuquerque.

"Kiss me, Alex."

He kissed her and then touched her lightly.

"Later," he said. "White man go now and get firewater."

He waved to her from the door as he closed it. She did not look pathetic there in this last look. She had begun to gather herself up and was preening herself like a young Ute or a young Navaho, Alexander thought as he closed the door.

In the hall Alexander paused and looked at himself in the big mirror alongside the elevator.

The danger is, he thought, that you begin to feel sorry for yourself, that you cease to expect twice as much from yourself as from other writers, that you cease to become hard with your work, cease to become truthful with your work, and that gives other people a chance to be hard and truthful with it. He pointed to the man in the mirror. Fifteen years is such a long time, he said, you should be a grown boy by now. Try to respect yourself and love others. It's important not to love yourself but respect yourself. And loving others at least means not hurting them. If only, he thought, we could cure something by recognizing it. "I don't like that man in the mirror."

He turned away from the man in the mirror.

That man in the mirror, Alexander thought as he pressed the elevator button—back on the reservation I think I could whip him.

11

Alexander stepped into the elevator and Howard and Leroy, the Negro ballplayers, were there and an eager, white-haired man was on the elevator too and he said, "Fellow Americans, eh? Congressman Willborne. I'm down here investigating—"

"Listen," Howard said to Alexander from the corner of the elevator. "I tell you what. You come to the ball game and I'll finish reading your last book."

Alexander continued quiet and Willborne said, "Investigating—"

Howard said, "Still nothing, eh? Well, I tell you what. I think your writing is it. I think it could be very it."

"Listen," Willborne said. "Investigating—"

"So we lost a bunch of ball games," Howard said. "You write a couple of bad books. Is that the end?"

"Let this man speak," Leroy said, touching the eager, white-haired, red-faced man.

"It's not important," the eager man said importantly.

"Say it, man," Leroy said, "and get shut of it."

"Well, I'm actually on vacation," the white-haired man said. "But I'm keeping my eyes and ears well open, you can bet on that."

"Thank you," Leroy said. "Keep everything well open. I

feel safer now."

"Thank you," Willborne said and he drew in a big breath and said, "It has been mÿ now crystallized observation from a former incontrovertible fact that—"

"Yes," Leroy said. "But it ain't your turn."

"Simply that Alexander Bowman," Howard said, "is it and that Alexander Bowman could be very it."

"Listen," Willborne said quietly, "there's a section of town— Only as an official observer, you understand."

"Seven blocks straight right," Leroy said. "Tell them that Reginald—"

"Seven blocks," Willborne whispered.

"I feel safer now," Howard said.

"Thank you," Willborne said stepping out of the elevator. "Thank you very much."

Getting out of the palm-cluttered lobby Howard touched his arm to Alexander's. "Can we give you a lift?"

"No," Alexander said. "I'm just going over and sit on the bench. And I hope you win."

"Thank you," Leroy said to Alexander and then, watching Willborne scurrying, "Thank you very much."

Alexander went over and sat alone on the big stone bench that faced the ocean. He was immediately surrounded by a flight of shoe-shine boys.

"You want a shoe shine, Joe?"

"No."

After Alexander had had his shoes shined twice and paid three times he tucked his feet under the bench and watched the ocean.

"You want to see some pictures, Joe?"

Alexander got rid of that one and went back to watching

the ocean. She was going out still booming but dirty and tired and heavy with foam.

"Where you live, Joe?"

Alexander started to tell him and then realized that the boy didn't care. He lived, he thought, in a land that took in two townships or seventy-two sections with six hundred and forty acres to the section. About one section was deeded, the rest leased, most from the government, some privately. A land where in winter you drove out fifteen miles in the snow and spread cake in a circle. Where you spread the soybean cake pellets, one circle within another circle so that the cattle, flinging themselves out of the low, concealing dwarf piñon and cedar could all get to it. The cake, dung-colored droppings against the very white snow, beginning, as you worked, to form a great rosette in the big draw. The cattle grouped themselves in bold and formal pattern joined soon by elk (the Bowmans allowed no hunting) and then the whole country was a stage full of big dancers neatly arranged against a white world for some wild ballet.

"You want a girl, Joe?"

And Sunday afternoons in town, the men driving their women in to church, the wives' religion having even survived each Sunday's assault by the preacher, the men's not so, as they dawdled, whittling, politicking, in the square, excepting old man Minter, emerging from the church, hand-shaking with the minister. And didn't Minter think in view of the small turnout the preacher had spoke mightily, given it his all? Minter stared at the preacher, coining some answer. Well, Minter answered finally, maybe. But on second thought, when he, Minter, drove out a wagonload of cake to feed, if only three cows showed up he wouldn't pitch out

the whole damn load.

"You want to know a good place, Joe?"

Alexander already knew a fairly good place. It was on top of the Jemez now, in the summertime, where they had government permits for three hundred head. You had to start pushing out the cattle very early to make the drive from the ranch to the mountaintop in one day. It was nice in the years when you had plenty of Indian cowboys who could dive into the brush for a stray and the others could keep the main bunch moving. You had to make it in one day; there was no water on the trail and you risked losing a bunch of water-crazed cattle in the rock and almost impenetrable brush if you had to make camp. Moving them down was easier. The snow was beginning to threaten and the cattle wanted down badly, lowing at the forest gate and bellowing, wanting off the fast-yellowing, aspen gold-turning, autumn-cold, whistling mountain before she closed in. Sometimes there was an animal who would not join the bunch, who would wander alone and higher and stranded, rather than join the others. Sometimes this one they would find alive in the spring, sometimes dead. He took his chances wandering alone and higher but he would not join the others. Alexander lit a cigarette and tossed the match at the foam that retreated down the beach.

"They're all gone, Joe."

Alexander focused on the boy who remained and decided he looked like the others and allowed his eyes to drift over to Mrs. O'Flynn's restaurant (A Home away from Home) and to another tourist trap, Captain Fleet's Oasis (English Spoken, American Understood). The two expatriates had set up their heavens between the only two decent hotels in town so they would catch the Americans coming and going and

falling down. Mrs. O'Flynn was a refugee from Iowa. She had twice been closed by the sanitary authorities, which takes a lot of talent in Mexico. But Mrs. O'Flynn was a genius. The captain was a bore ("Old soldiers trade away") who had come to this small town in Mexico and set up a stand where the Americans could not avoid him. The captain had served under MacArthur in the Rainbow Division and Doug and he and he and Doug. Alexander had not returned after Alexander had told the Captain "I shall return."

Alexander looked on up the spray-swept street where there was no one. The few tables in front of the Belmar were empty and the kiosks were doing business with no one at all. He thought he saw the doorman in general's uniform outside the Siesta but it might have been a flag. Now a gull floated in, lonely and airborne, and lighted on the nose of Cortes leading his bronze troops across the asphalt of the Twenty-first of September toward the concrete boulevard of the Fifth of May.

"Everybody gone, Joe."

Yes, Alexander thought, everyone is gone.

"They tell me you going to swim the ocean, Joe."

Alexander remained silent.

"When Colombus cross the ocean he use three sheeps."

"Yes," Alexander said.

"You no afraid of esharks, Joe?"

Esharks and sheeps. What was the boy talking about?

"I'm wetback, Joe. I swim the Rio Grande all the time. I can give you pretty good tip."

"Yes?"

"Don't."

"Thank you."

"I swim to your country all the time, Joe. You have very good country."

"Thank you."

"When they catch me up there they no give me rough time. They just turn me around and put me on bus. But by that time I got lots of money. It's a good country."

"Yes."

"You know, Joe, this time I make pretty good money, all the money there is in the world. And you look very sad, Joe. I think I give you some for the bus. You want to go home, Joe?"

"Yes."

"How much you want, Joe? Five, six, seven dollars? How much you want, Joe?"

Alexander looked at the boy now. He had a round, dark, smooth peasant face, the kind Goya used in his backgrounds.

"I get this from your people, Joe. I can give a little."

"I too have all the money there is in the world," Alexander said.

"Good, Joe. Then as one millionaire to another we can relax. We can have a talk. We won't have to sell each other anything. We can discuss the future—"

"As equals," Alexander said.

"And our success stories," the boy said. "Mine began one dark night when I was tending the sheep in the fields and I heard a voice say twelve to one, twelve to one."

"Twelve to one?" Alexander said.

"Yes, Joe. This twelve to one, twelve to one meant nothing to anyone in our village. It was when I came to town here, to Mazatlán, that I saw an American exchange, one dollar for twelve pesos, that I saw the great luz. So I sold all my worldly

goods, parted with my family and innumerable relatives and made the journey to the promised land of twelve to one. At the border they tell me I need a passport to get in. Just this side of the border they tell me I can get through the needle's eye if I am rich."

"How rich?"

"One hundred and fifty dollars rich, Joe. For one hundred and fifty dollars a Juarez taxi company would deliver me through all of the immigration traps to Denver, Colorado, for one hundred and fifty dollars. But all my worldly goods in Mexico had amounted to only one dollar. So I swam underneath the camel. Was caught on the other side of the Rio Grande in El Paso the next day and marched back across the bridge. Seven times I tried and seven times el paradiso fué perdido."

"Paradise was lost," Alexander said.

"Yes," the boy said. "One time they put me on a train that did not stop till it got to Guadalajara. Another time they flew me almost to Mexico City, almost dos thousand kilometers de paradiso."

"Two thousand miles from paradise."

"Sí," the boy said. "But the eighth time I got through Texas" (he pronounced it Tay-hass) "and into the promised land. I worked for a month for one hundred and fifty dollars for promised money. The day before payday the man called the immigration and said, 'Come and get him.' There was another man there who had come to buy some cattle and he was standing near the phone and he said, 'Red, you son of a bitch,' and he didn't buy no cattle. Later, outside, he told me where to hide and where to come to him. I did and he paid me one hundred and fifty dollars a month, every month."

"Yes," Alexander said. "And there was a house there that was sealed, a house made of wood that was not wood, that was sealed."

"Yes," the boy said. "Did you work there too?"

"Yes," Alexander said.

"Then we can talk as equals."

"We can talk as equals," Alexander said.

Yes, with the boy, Alexander thought, watching the big green ocean go backward, he could talk as equals. But not with anyone else now. Certainly not with Perrette. To talk as equals you were relaxed, relaxed in such a way you feel you must have known the person well before life began. Perrette's name was Perrette Marin but this knowledge did not help much. He did not even know the name of the boy and yet he felt he had known him even before life began. For example, Perrette knew all there was to know about the fringes of art and the boy did not know what the word meant. Perrette was sexually attractive, came from a family on Long Island with tons of money, had been to all the right schools, which could mean the wrong schools, but the boy had been to nothing, knew nothing about all the things that are supposed to be important, and yet this feeling that he had known him before life began.

The boy snapped his fingers. He was in a crouching position between Alexander and the ocean looking up at Alexander and now he snapped his fingers and said, "Are you thinking of someone you love?"

If he was thinking of the land that was his home then, yes, he had been thinking of something he had openly said he loved. If he had been thinking of Perrette, well then he would have something to tell her. If that was maybe the most impor-

tant thing in the world, perhaps the most important beginning would be to tell her. It had been on his tongue many many times but always something small and hard from way way back someplace would get in the way. He thought he realized now, looking out over the bay at the low, roiling, timeless, dirty sea, that he had neglected people except those that were in his books. This boy and this ocean and all the loneliness of a hundred thousand expatriate nights could bring a person to the fact that the land cannot respond, only people, only Perrette. And the responses must be relaxed, between equals. There had always been this tension that a cliché could cut like a clean knife. Alexander had never used a cliché in his life. Tonight he would use one, but as a clean knife.

"Tonight I could tell her," he said

"Good," the boy said. "You can never tell a woman too much. It is a discovery I have made."

"Perhaps then I would not have to swim that ocean." He looked at the big eyes of the boy now. "Even in three sheeps. Maybe it is a discovery I have just made that between two people nothing should get in the way, not books, not Indian Country, nothing should get in the way of having known a person well, even before life began."

"Yes, Joe."

Alexander thought, she is all I have left, and the boy said. "Yes, Joe."

Now that the boy was even reading his thoughts he would have to break this off. So the boy had gotten a job at the ranch. It was not too coincidental. There were only three big ones in the entire hundred miles north of Bernalillo. A lot of wetbacks had worked there before they were picked up by immigration.

"Did you like the ranch?"

"Very much, Joe,"

"Would you like to go back?"

"No. I've got my home, my own country, Joe."

Now that he has seen it all and has all the money there is in the world, all the experience, he wants to go home to his own country. And he can, too. Me too, I can too. To a hotel room, a bar—climb a mountain, swim an ocean. I can too. A hotel room, a bar. But is it true that Perrette who was slipping away is all that is left? It is about true. It is true.

"I go, Joe. I got to go."

"All right," Alexander said as he watched the boy rise and start down the street. The back of his head, Alexander thought, is Goya too. A friend too. There weren't many. Soon he would be alone.

"Good-bye," Alexander called. "Enjoy."

"Thank you, Joe." And then the boy turned the corner suddenly and disappeared.

Alexander spotted a speck of something way out on the enormous ocean and tried to concentrate on that.

"Your friend said seven blocks. Seven blocks to the right. We went there and there was nothing—nothing but a church. Oh, pardon me, this is a colleague—same committee. We are both investigating—"

"No, no, we're not," the other man said. "We're those congressmen abroad you read about. Kind of a roving assignment, expenses paid, for looking into things. No matter what, we try to keep our eyes and ears well open."

"Right is not the same in every country," Alexander said. "In Mexico you should have gone the other way, and tell them Reginald sent you. But I feel safer now."

"Thank you," the other man said, and they both disappeared.

But I don't feel safer about Alfred, Alexander thought. I should not have left him with that homicidal maniac Mimi, and I should not have left Perrette unhappy and alone. Alexander tried to concentrate on the speck he had spotted before, way out on the enormous ocean, but it was nowhere. We are all alone.

Some young Indios, almost naked, were playing dice in front of Alexander now but he did not see them. The waves were tilting in on him, blowing a fine spray, but he saw them as a series of small avalanches and the fine mist a powdery snow blowing off the long slopes of the Sangre de Cristos above the ranch.

A policeman came up and stopped in front of him. "You need help?"

"What?" Alexander said. Then at last in recognition, "No, I guess not."

The policeman hesitated, still wanting to be helpful until Alexander shook his head slowly and finally in a definite no.

The policeman walked on to the next bench before he looked back at the tall, angular, Norteamericano sitting alone and staring out at the sea.

From his seat at the bar of the Belmar Alfred could see Alexander sitting watching the ocean. He had gotten rid of Mimi Jimenez somewhere two or three bars back and he did not want to see Alexander right now. Not after what I have done, he thought.

"Experiences," Alfred said, watching the bartender through

his green drink. "I will give him the experience of Mimi Jimenez and stop him from making the swim at the same time. I personally called the American Consul and then he called the mayor and had him stop the whole thing. When Mimi finds out, I'm getting out of his way. I hope Alexander gets out of his way. I hope he does not have to have another experience. But when you are cut off from your origins, your roots, you have nothing really important that you know well enough to write about, you have to have experiences. Alexander knows that. We all know that, don't we?"

"Si, señor."

"I'm a poet. I don't need them. And perhaps if he has an experience I can have a little time with Perrette."

"Si, señor."

"It's not that I'm a villain." Alfred moved his green drink. "Those who understand people, the psyche, know that villains outside of books do not exist, so that, unless someone puts me in a book, I'm just a person who happened to be around when things began to fall apart between them."

"Si, señor."

"I don't know how it got started between Alexander and Perrette but I know how it began to fall apart. I don't know for sure but I think it got started between them this way." Alfred took a drink first. "There was a bunch of those Indians sitting around a fire one night on that ranch up there in New Mexico and one of those Indians had a wife. It was Alexander's brother who had the wife, but she got to talking to Alexander about Art. Art can be an enormous item for anyone, let alone a fire-watching Indian, so Alexander gave her her beautiful head and let her talk about Art while he watched. This Perrette comes from a rich family in the East.

Marin. Perrette Marin. Perrette's father manufactures something to cure athlete's foot which doesn't do much harm and comes in three-sized bottles including the large economy fraud. I think she had a normal, healthy, maladjusted childhood and was always beautiful—and she is beautiful."

Alfred pushed his glass for another green drink.

"It is hard to tell where she went wrong, why she married someone she didn't fit, like Alexander, but it must have been that she confused him with Art. Art is most attractive all of the time but few people recognize this until Art is dead. But she recognized Art too early in life which can be very dangerous too."

"Muy, muy interesante," the bartender said, setting down the fresh green drink.

"No, it's not interesting at all," Alfred said. "But it gives you some background, better than my damn symbols. I tell you what, another drink and I could go see Perrette. It's that I respect him as a writer. It's not that I am afraid."

"No, no. Of course not," the bartender said, mopping up in front of Alfred.

"You're not listening. You want your money."

"No, no. Of course not," the bartender said.

"Here," Alfred said, getting up unsteadily. "Ten pesos." He slammed them on the bar. "I go now to do my work."

"No, no. Of course not," the bartender said as Alfred went out through the swinging door.

Alfred came out of the Belmar Café and saw Alexander still sitting there staring out to sea. Oh, he thought, now would be a good time to see Perrette. He had intended to go to another café and work on his poem. But instead now he turned and walked toward the Pan American. Quickly.

175

12

At home, in Indian Country, George wrote down a Navaho's name in the yellowing sheep ledger—Opportunity Knox. George had corrupted this from the boy's given English name, Opportunity Knocks. He had made the change to lend the name some dignity in case the boy went to college. The mission, now defunct, had once promised Knox that opportunity which the Indian had construed as a threat and Knocks had left the checkerboard area for Flag only to return a few months ago. Nevertheless George entered him as Knox—this name and twenty-four dollars in pawn (a concha belt and two turquoise necklaces) against four boxes of eating groceries, a bridle and a paper-bound copy of *Think and Grow Rich*. George Bowman, having finished this business, put the big ledger to one side and began the letter to his brother. Now he would write that letter to his brother and nothing, absolutely nothing, would get in the way.

"Well, he's leaving," Quicker-Than-You said.

That Indian, George thought, is always coming up in back of me and making world-ending pronouncements.

"Don't bother me," he said.

After several lines of writing and rewriting, lines he kept

crossing out, he turned to the Indian with relief.

"Who's leaving?"

"Jack. Diamond Jack. He says an honest rustler can't make a living in this country any more. He's going to Mexico. The State Police are definitely going to pick him up if he's here next week."

"Mexico," George said, swinging in the chair, turning toward the Indian. "Why then he could deliver— He could tell him for me. I wouldn't have to write this impossible—"

"Certainly," Quicker-Than-You said. "But where you'll find him no one has ever been able to find out. Tso's clan has been missing some cattle so he's probably up on the big mountain someplace on his final job. He sent word by Tso's clan that he would shoot anyone on sight who tried to get the cattle back."

"We'll go and find him and get the cattle back too," George said. "Are you with me?"

"No," Quicker-Than-You said.

"You going to let him scare you?"

"Yes."

"Well, somehow it doesn't scare me."

"If I were you trying to write that letter it wouldn't scare me either."

George Bowman left the post alone but he had only got his horse up the far turn of the Penistaja Mesa when Quicker-Than-You pulled up alongside of him.

"Any time more than one white gets together there's bound to be a war. I think I'd better come along to bury the dead. You got a cigarette?"

They smoked and rode in deep silence up through the gradual, gray foothills; sometimes a jack rabbit looked at them

and sometimes a deer watched. Now a buzzard floated close but they rode on in silence.

"What are we doing up here?" the Indian said finally.

"Catching a rustler."

They had to go through a bright narrow pass in the rocks now and when they came out on the other side the Indian said, "That's good because I thought we were avoiding something."

"We're catching a rustler."

"Like in the movies."

"Exactly like in the movies."

They rode now through a wide, gently waving and violent yellow plain of rabbit brush. Interspersed at intervals through the rabbit brush was the quiet, green, deadly milkweed that kills sheep. When the Indian herders hit this patch they drove the sheep hard to keep them from eating and dying, but George and Quicker-Than-You moved through it quietly.

"I haven't much time for pictures," the Indian said.

"Ever see a picture called *The Great Train Robbery?*"

"No."

"A good picture."

"I don't want to play words any more," Quicker-Than-You said. "You should be back at the post writing what you were writing. I'm sorry I interrupted you."

"That was okay," George said, taking off his Stetson and wiping his forehead against the sun. "We should keep our mind on what we're doing."

"You were doing a letter to your brother."

"Not now, I'm not. We're looking for that rustler." George quickened his horse.

"We're doing good works for the Indians," Quicker-Than-

You said, coming up again.

"We're changing the subject," George said quietly. "That's what we're doing."

"Okay," Quicker-Than-You said. "But you're taking the blame for the drought."

"They've got nothing to go on."

"No, but they can see what's happening."

George Bowman could see what was happening too. The Indian was putting on the pressure. Okay, George would get rid of the Indian. He had things to do. He pulled up his horse.

"Okay," he said, pointing. "You try the Chavez Canyon and I'll go up the Baca. Be sure you check all the side rincons and if you need my help fire three quick ones."

"And if you need any help—"

But George's horse was already moving away rapidly.

"If you need any help," the Indian continued to himself. "Jesus, can anyone help him?"

George was happy to get rid of the Indian. Now he could change the subject properly. He would think about the post. Now that Quicker-Than-You was away Tom-Dick-and-Harry would take over. Tom-Dick-and-Harry was brought up at the mission, which kind of lamed him for The People or the whites. That was why George had hired him. The other traders had a theory that you couldn't hire an Indian, based on an observation that they give the store away to the clan. Some of the traders, imitating the traveling salesman who picked a small town to leave his wife in, picked an Indian with a small clan to leave in the store. George picked Tom-Dick-and-Harry because when he got back from the mission school The People didn't think too much of his white ways. There wasn't anybody much who would take the store if

Tom-Dick-and-Harry made the offer.

Now George watched the mountains. George was impressed with the mountains, the heavy endless mass that piled all the way to the snow clouds. They would be his compass. With the wind and the water, a slow, infinite leveling process was reducing the mountains to the plains. In a few billion years, give or take a few millions from the professors, the mountains would be no more. But despite the professors, the mountains would be with us a little while yet. They would not be with us as long as the Diamond Jacks, but give them something. George gave them, not majesty because the word was worn out, he gave them a simplicity and an organization that is understandable to man and called beauty. How about the joy after traveling the low mesa country, the excitement after the monotony of threading up and down the gray arroyos in the badlands, the tingle and awe of an explosion of green and solid mass burgeoning and quick with water and the mountains all alive and all there?

No, beauty is plenty. And you do not have to take from the mesa country to give to the mountains. George lived with the Indians down here in the mesa country and now as the great dark hills came on solid ahead of him he gave the mountains beauty. The mountains gave George a compass.

George thought, I am thirty-seven years old. The horse is not too much younger and the mountains are quite old. The mountain here is named San Pedro. At Diamond Jack's, where I am heading, the mountain is named Sangre de Piedra, but it all belongs to the Jemez, which, of course, is a part of the Nacimiento. This family knowledge can be helpful when you are using it as a compass.

Somewhere, way back in one of the deep folds of the

mountain that was always dark, you could hide things in the inside of the mountain. The old-time bad men knew this, not popular movie boys like Billy the Kid, but unrecorded men who stole cattle—lots of cattle—kept the unheard, bawling longhorns deep near the dark heart of the old mountain until the brand was right, and the righteous indignation had channeled into the log church, and then rode herd over the back trails to Abilene and blew the take at faro before the girlies took them. Diamond Jack had been dipping into books.

George paused now to get his bearings along the mountain. Although he pretended not to, the aged horse appreciated this consideration. Banjo liked to give you the impression, prancing around the post, that he was a four-year-old, but he was older than his master, Silver-Threads-Among-the-Gold, twenty-five. The trader owned three horses of his own but Silver Threads, with the connivance of Opportunity Knox and possibly Tom-Dick-and-Harry, would chase George's horses up the Pierna Canyon each time they knew that he planned a ride. Silver Threads got one dollar in trade every time George used Banjo. Diamond Jack had twice stolen Banjo (the second time accidentally and in the dark) and twice, and in the daylight now, turned him loose. Each time Banjo would drag into the post until spotted and then he would go into his dance of the four-year-olds.

George gentled Banjo out of the wide San Juan into the Baca Canyon. Baca Canyon ran, lonely and heavy with brush, up to the snow on the great mountain. Here the big Baca was gray with chamise. Soon the olive would turn to the dying red of the scrub oak, then the heavy green of the piñon country before you wound into the great and towering ponderosas, fretted with snow, and the ice-cased aspens, scintillant.

Somewhere along the big Baca was Jack's canyon and now George began to track. Sometimes he would slide off Banjo and get down on his haunches and examine something closely before mounting again and spurring his horse.

George was all the way through the red country, part way through the green and approaching the painful white of the Nacimiento. He was not dressed for it. The fine hard sand granules of snow began to beat into his face off the de Piedra haunch. It was below zero and the wind was up and the long shadows were starting to lengthen into the heart of the canyon. Some one of the Indians certainly had logged up here and had a parka. George should have borrowed it. But he had not figured Diamond Jack for the white country; not the gray but probably the red, possibly the green, but never the white. That was George's first mistake; he had underestimated the courage or the stupidity of Jack.

Now George made his second mistake; he dismounted to examine something interesting in the snow and he dropped Banjo's reins ahead of him. You do this to any good cow horse and he will stand stock still till eternity, but Banjo belonged to Silver Threads, a professional tourist Indian, who corrupted everything he owned.

Banjo began to move off to the left away from the blowing cold and into the trees. George was down on his knees and did not see or hear, in the hard blowing snow, Jack move through the trees on horseback and seize the reins of Banjo and lead him down canyon.

Now George, suddenly and without sight of the disaster, became aware that everything had gone wrong and just at that moment too when he had picked up the trail of the Navaho cattle. He rose and retreated from the box canyon and toward

182

the bunching of ice-clad and glaring aspen where his horse had finally wandered, only to see there the tracks of another horse and the series of tracks that were the leading away of his own. George knew there is no more immediate doom than to be stranded up mountain without a horse in a driving snow. The tracks were all gone now and so quickly too. The canyon was in complete shadow and the cross winds beat in, kicking the snow in all directions with tall spumes of it going straight up, and everywhere there was a bitter fog of it blinding any sense of direction. George began to move in what he hoped was a great circle, and at last his feet, not his eyes, stumbled upon what he sought, a huge long U of standstone he had observed before the wind had begun to kick and blind.

George had already made two mistakes and if the third was a blunder too it was to be conscious and of his own plan and making. He crawled now on all fours against the driving snow along the wind-swept sandstone to the end of the U and then went down on his belly and waited.

He was waiting for Diamond Jack to come back and finish him off in Jack's tradition of the Old West, or better, old films, old, thumbed and worn copy of the *Rider of the Silver Sage.* George had no alternative; even if he had known, even if the furies had lifted and he could tell which direction was desert, he could still not make it on foot and without clothing against the burning cold that was already beginning to stiffen him as he lay pressed against the sandstone. George would very much like to see and hear his mesa country once more.

The wind made a dull, high dissonant sound cutting through the deadly cold, but there were no sounds in all the noises of the winds of this last mountain that brought back the drums down there on the desert. George Bowman

183

thought he would very much like to see and hear his mesa country once more.

There was a huge stillness within the noises of the wind and everything was becoming much too soft, much too pleasant, much too dulce—tqidajina, was the impossible Indian word for it—this ecstatic easiness after the first pain of freezing when everything begins to slip away. Oh, most certainly George Bowman would like to see and hear his mesa country once more.

And would he like to see his brother once more? Yes, certainly he would. And Perrette? To hell now with Perrette and to hell with his brother and this cold and the silly mountain and the crazy Indian Quicker-Than-You who kept interfering.

Things were even quieter now and softer and he wondered if there was any use struggling. Maybe he would write that letter. It was the only thing to do. He would be well again. He could see the letter written all signed and sealed and ready to put in the mail bag. Then he could walk in beauty.

Now for a split second and then gone again in a sudden kick of the wind, George saw Jack, a wraith figure within a dervish of swirling white, leaning into each new direction of wind, slack-jawed head down, and clutching a readied Winchester at port, still able to make out the quick-dissolving tracks of the trader. George waited for Diamond Jack to reach the center of the U before he made his dive for the horses. Diamond Jack had tracked him to the sandstone now and was coming out on the U. Soon the distance between Jack and the horses would be greater than the trader's on the other end of the U.

Suddenly George made a quick lunge to where he knew

the horses must be and felt as though something within his body had frozen and two shots went off in the time it takes to work the big lever beneath a Winchester 30-30 carbine. George tried again, this time not to run but to spring and fall forward, successfully now, and then again and again within the jerking bursts of the Winchester. He fell against something now—a horse—Banjo. He pulled himself up into the saddle, not having to use that part of his body that was dead with the cold. He turned Banjo in a quick circle, in the same motion picking up the reins of Jack's horse.

George spurred Banjo and dropped the reins and the old horse began to move in the direction that George hoped was the corral where Banjo did his dance. The Winchester somewhere around him was still snapping but wildly, directionless, a protest but impotent now against the blinding curtain of white darkness closing in around Jack.

Two days later and at the post George watched, interested, as Rabbit Stockings helped Tom-Dick-and-Harry stack the trade goods along the back counter. There had been an inventory and very little had been stolen—"taken" would be a better word. George hesitated, putting down the bridle he had been assembling. The Indians had taken, absconded, raided, any way you want to put it, and every chance they got, from every trader between here and Star Lake. Some of the traders were bitter; one of them at Rico had taken to beating the Indians until he himself was killed and the post burned down. All the traders had a defense. Some had bitterness, all had a system. The man at Rico had called his a system too.

George Bowman's system began in the mind and it was to

recognize that the Indians had a system and that their system had a priority over the itinerant whites. At length and in detail, the Indian system was to rob the traders blind. It was an old old system with all sorts of equities and legal tenures and had precedent way way back to the time when the first white man with a gun poked his first bald head over the first mesa. But the Indians were not ready to become extinct. They swam alongside the current, the long winding current of covered wagons. They picked them off one by one and divided the take. It amounted to kind of a tithe, a tax for the use of the land that was theirs. Sometimes they had had to follow the Moving People all the way to Needles, where the difficult crossing of the Colorado made it easier for the Navahos. Sometimes they collected scalps too, but this, George thought, was a reciprocal tariff for what that first white bald head, with a gun, over the first blue mesa, had begun long since. Then came the cavalry alongside the winding wagon trains of the whites and it became difficult and expensive for the Indians to collect. Then came the U.S. Army and it became impossible. But the Indians had within them the same stuff the whites were made of and they thought and they prayed, but mostly they had the instinct to wait, to survive. And it was not a very long long time before the whites, the Bowmans, came and laid everything right out on the counter without the cavalry or the United States Army anywhere in sight. The traders, the Bowmans, were a complete and unequivocal answer to their thoughts, their prayers, their instincts, their survival, their wildest peyote dreams. It was too good to be true and to this day George Bowman knew the Navaho People practiced fantastic and unbelievable restraint in their taxation. Then, too, after all, The

People knew that not even a white man can be made to work for absolutely nothing.

All this stealing business was in George's mind because he had been thinking about Diamond Jack. What would happen to Diamond Jack now—now that Jack no longer had a system? Would he too, like the profession he had chosen, become extinct as the Indians had failed to do? Was he already a victim of his Old West, his box canyon, his frozen mountains, his dreams?

George heard a commotion in the back of the store and then he heard a voice, Lord Acton's, who spoke no English, say in Navaho, "Why really, the Jack of Diamonds is dead."

George made his way back into the warehouse among the hanging and stinking hides. Lord Acton was talking with Silver Threads.

"Why really, what do you mean, dead?" George asked in Navaho as he came up. "You mean they found his body on the mountain?"

Lord Acton waved a dark weathered hand along the red sweatband across his forehead.

"No. I saw his body walking around Cuba but he told me Diamond Jack is dead."

"Why really," George said, "where is he now?"

"Now he is back of the corral. He asked for you yesterday and the day before but of course I told him you would not see him."

"I will see him," George said.

George went back to his office, to his grandfather's old roll top in the back of the warehouse, surrounded, almost buried, by hides.

He motioned Diamond Jack to a seat on a bale of raw

wool. Diamond Jack moved as though he had been hit in the back with a board, or as though he had been deep frozen.

"Listen," Diamond Jack said, "when I came back to that sandstone U I was looking for you—wanted to give you back your horse that had wandered. I fired only in the air to stop you running."

"Maybe. I don't know," George said. "But I couldn't take that chance. I didn't know what Wild West book— what moving picture you had just seen."

"You know I wouldn't shoot at you, George. But some of those cows you took off the mountain were mine," Diamond Jack said.

"They're in the corral in back of Rabbit Stockings' hogan. Take them," George said.

"Don't want them," Diamond Jack said. Jack spoke out of an uptilted face, petulant, inquiring, delicate. "I'm moving now," Diamond Jack said. "You see, you've got to move with the times, the frontiers."

"Yes," George said. "Especially when the police are after you. What business—?"

"Frontiers, that's the only thing that's certain, definite, the only thing that changes."

"Yes," George said. "This business is in Mexico?" He leaned forward. "Then you can take a message. No, never mind. As long as your business is nothing that will bring you back here," he said finally, lightly hesitating, swaying in the chair.

Diamond Jack advanced to the roll top and laid three halves of walnut shells on the oak surface along with a pea.

"This is my new business. I'm going to give up rustling. Doesn't pay."

"Get out," George said.

"Then you don't want me to—?"

"I want you to get out," George said. "But if it will help you to quit this idiot business too, the pea is under that shell," he said, pointing to the shell he had not seen it go under, knowing Jack, through conjuring, must have put it there.

"For the six cows," Diamond Jack said.

"Anything if you will go. The six cows," George agreed.

Diamond Jack swept the shells into his pocket. "Take my word for it, it wasn't there, it wasn't under any of them, it was between my fingers."

George thought now, staring at the ceiling.

"I'll take your word for it that you're just getting a start, that you're new at the business but that you'll always stay away from here, you'll always leave my Navahos alone."

"Agreed," Diamond Jack said with the sobriety and solemnity that would have served to conclude all the oil rights. "As a matter of fact the police will see to that. But how do we stand now on those six cows?"

This was getting too complicated for George and staring at the ceiling didn't help much this time.

"They're yours," Diamond Jack said. "For old time's sake." Diamond Jack got up. "I'm a busy man. I'm off for Mexico."

"Wait," George said. "I want you to tell something to my brother. He's staying at the Pan American in Mazatlán."

"Yes?" Jack hesitated, his hand on the door.

"Tell him to come— Tell him he— Tell him all is—"

"Yes," Diamond Jack said. "Yes."

"Tell him I—"

"Yes, yes," Jack said. "What language is this?"

"He's my brother. You tell him that I feel now after all these years—" George broke it off staring at the desk and looked at Jack. "You and I know the drought will break when it breaks. And the mine shaft—you know the truth about that."

"You all right in the head?" Jack said.

"Tell him," George said. "Tell him—"

"I got to go," Jack said. "People are after me."

"Tell him I will try to write a letter."

"Good. I'll tell him. And good-by," Jack said and he slammed the door.

"But tell him," George said to no one except his reflection in an Indian trade mirror he did not see, "tell him things keep getting in the way."

13

Approximately in the middle of that enormous stretch of emptiness that separated Alexander and George Bowman there were two young gentlemen in a large yellow car with THE WHEEL OF FORTUNE URANIUM COMPANY gold-lettered on the side, entering El Paso, Texas. There was a leather flap that could be dropped from the inside to conceal the sign. It doubled as an arm rest and obliterated the sign when there was a situation that the two gentlemen did not want to bring the Wheel of Fortune into.

The two young gentlemen in the Cadillac coupe de ville, Leland Hepburn III, who carried a letter addressed to George Bowman, and his friend Garry de Grasppe, were on their way to an almost non-existent place called Tonatai, near Cuba, New Mexico.

You could maybe say, to all purposes and intents, legally— anyway as far as uranium, which is do re mi, which is what makes the world go round (or are you one of those people who want to stop it and get off?)—you could safely say the Wheel of Fortune had discovered Tonatai. Perhaps New Mexico when all was said and done. No one at the Wheel of Fortune, not even these two young gentlemen from the

public relations department, claimed that the Wheel of Fortune had discovered the United States; but then again, where would the country be, would it truly be the United States, without their élan vital?

The traffic was heavy as they entered El Paso, as it had been heavy since they left Houston. They would have to go across the border to Juarez to get themselves in the right frame of mind to deal with the Indians. The Indians were backward around Cuba, and primitive, and did not know what was good for their own selves. So you might say that the two young gentlemen were going across to Juarez to help the Indians.

They paid their bridge fare and drove the coupe de ville across the border and then decided that this was no proper place to leave the Caddy so they drove back across the international bridge and left the coupe de ville in a parking lot in the United States, paid their fare again and walked back across the bridge to Mexico. They were going to a lot of trouble, you might say, to help those Indians who did not know what was good for their own selves.

Garry de Grasppe had regular, beautiful, clear-cut features, vacuous and emasculated. When he had completed his rise to stardom at the Dairy Dell Little Theater in Houston, Texas, Oveta Culp Hobby's newspaper's theatrical critic had promised "Garry de Grasppe will take Hollywood by thunderstorm." But he went into uranium instead because that's what all the smart boys were getting into. The future belongs to those who sense nuclear possibilities. Blow everything up. Leland Hepburn III had had an identical short and immature career except that the columnist had chosen him for television.

"No girlies," Garry said.

"On the way back then, after a successful venture," Leland said.

"After a successful venture, who knows," Garry said, "we may buy the town."

The two blond gentlemen from the public relations department of the Wheel of Fortune who had left their coupe de ville in the United States walked around Juarez, Mexico, to see, you might say, what they would get.

"No more either," Garry said, "than one or two drinks. You might say we are the spearhead of an expedition. There should be almost no drinking in the field."

"Almost none," Leland agreed. He always agreed with Garry de Grasppe because Garry de Grasppe had been with the company one month longer than he had. He did not think of himself as a sycophant in continuously agreeing because the company had already been in existence six months and if they continued to get a raise each month, even by the salary route alone, they woud soon each and all have a Caddy of their own and what man could ask for more? Uranium's got a wilder future than your dreams are made of. And whatever might be said by weird types against the young gentlemen from Houston, they knew their Horatio Alger.

"You got that letter you were asked to deliver to someone at Tonatai?" Garry asked.

"Right here," Leland said, touching his coat. "It goes to George Bowman. He's somewhere near where we're going. He's the brother of the writer, Alexander Bowman."

"Alexander Bowman," Garry de Grasppe said. "I liked his last book very much but the critics didn't. They don't like books you can't understand. If we don't have things we

193

can't understand then there is no place for God. You got to have faith in the un-understandable."

"That's right," Leland Hepburn said seriously.

"They're a bunch of frightened Philistines."

"That's a good phrase, frightened Philistines."

"It's the title of a book by James Farrell."

"I bet it's a swell book."

"Show me a book that's un-understandable and you'll see me beneath it reaching for it with star mud in my eyes."

"Star mud is a good switch on star dust. I like it."

"Thank you," Garry said.

"But supposing that Alexander Bowman's book has no meaning?"

"All the better. Then you're striving for the unattainable, hearing the unutterable."

"Hearing the unutterable is a good phrase," Leland said. "I like it. You should be a writer yourself."

"Thank you," Garry said. "And this man who wrote the letter, is he a writer too? I never heard of him."

"No one has. Alfred's stuff is much too good. He writes a word here and a word there and no word bears a relation to the other words. It makes you think."

"I like it if it's well done," Garry de Grasppe said.

"Oh, Alfred does it very well," Leland Hepburn said, carefully. "He does it swell."

They were on a street now just off the international bridge. It was jammed with peep shows, missions, prostitutes, beggars, priests, Texas millionaires, a revivalist road show, burros, Cadillacs, weeping and laughing mujeres, Mexican gentlemen sleeping in the street and against decomposing stone walls that did not a building make.

"Those savages out there on the reservation," Leland said in the confusion, "they must really want to take their place in our civilization. It's the romantics among us that do all the damage."

"No, it's the Indian who's his own worst enemy."

"They've got to be protected from themselves."

"Check. But don't call them savages."

"Did I call them savages?"

"You did."

"Then I apologize."

They both felt tolerant and generous now and in need of a drink. But now they were being swept down the street by the flow of animals, people and things. They were wedged in between a woman and an old man trying to sell them something and a boy standing on a burro and holding a dog and trying to show them pictures. They were also being pushed along toward the river by a giant smell and tons of things that were being thrown out of windows and shoved out of doorways.

"Your letter," Garry de Grasppe said, picking it up out of the mud. Leland Hepburn shoved the letter back in his pocket. A piece of tin roof fell near them and a radio drifted close, advertising, in rapid machine-gun Spanish, a machine-gun. The tin roof sank. A long-boned man in a silk hat who said he was God drifted by announcing in a clear impartial voice the end of the world, followed by an English type who said he was left over from the revivalist road show and that the man in front of him, who must already be in the Rio Grande, was an imposter.

The two young gentlemen from the public relations department of the Wheel of Fortune Uranium Corporation of

Houston, Texas, made one final surge to free themselves from the swarming tangle and smell of six generations of the North American continent and they were assisted by a console TV set, seven reels of a recent spectacular and a pile of paperbacks that gave them a push so that they shot head first into the Amigos de los Americanos liquor store. There was an international brass band playing outside.

Inside the liquor store they demanded and got a straw, wicker-bound gallon bottle of Jamaica rum with a counterfeit label for almost no money at all plus no tax.

"It hits the spot," Garry said, drinking and then passing the bottle to his accomplice.

"It does, you know," Leland said after he took a drink.

"Please, thank you very much," the Mexican liquor-store owner, who was not running a funeral parlor, said. "It's against the law to drink in here."

The two young gentlemen took the wicker-bound gallon of rum with an interesting label back across the bridge and put it between them on the front seat of the Caddy. By taking drinks of it along the way it would help them to face the Indians at Tonatai.

By the time they got just outside Truth or Consequences, through no fault of the young gentlemen, it was impossible to tell which side of the road was which, and the blond driver was singing above the radio that was going too, "City gals they may be fine, but give me that squaw of mine, roll along, covered wagon, roll along."

It was now also impossible for either of the two blond gentlemen to remember the name of the tribe the Wheel of Fortune Uranium Company was going to emancipate. The Apaches? The Navahos? The New York Yankees?

"We got to get hold of ourselves, boy," Garry said as he took down a sign entitled "The Rotarians of Truth or Consequences Welcome You."

"You got zeal," Leland said. "Getting the Indians to sign will be pigeon soup."

The sky over the Indian country at Tonatai was black. The Indians had taken their accustomed place for the meeting and they were convinced that George Bowman was going to spoil everything. The women were seated on the floor in all their jewelry with their babies stacked in cradle boards along the flour sacks. The women too were concerned that the white trader might ruin their day. The babies, leather bound into the cradle boards, did not care much one way or the other but their serious, same faces looked up at their fathers' faces at the counter and mirrored their worry.

"Look, Sansi," one of their fathers said carefully to the trader. "Why do you want to ruin everything?"

George put down his pencil and looked up at More-Wives-Than-Anyone. (He only had two. He did not have more wives than anyone. He did not, for example, have more wives than A-Cover-for-All, who had four and his eye on another.)

"I don't want to spoil anything," George said quietly and for the seventh time to the dark and powerfully square-built Indian with the hair bun on the back of his neck called More-Wives-Than-Anyone. "I don't want to ruin anything. I just don't want you to sign something away that you would regret later."

"But put yourself in their hogan, Sansi. You come all the way from Houston, Texas, to see the miserable Indians. Can we be rude? Would that be nice?"

George had been over this many times this afternoon so he did not look up from the marks he was making in the sheep ledger to say anything.

"They come all the way from Houston, Texas, and you wouldn't cross the trail to give us hello."

"Maybe not." George was annoyed now and went ahead with his marking in the ledger seriously.

"I withdraw that, Sansi. You come with your bottled magic when we're sick and credit when we're hungry. But all the way from Houston, Texas, is quite a thing even if they are dishonest. It's a long way to come even to steal something."

"It is," George said without looking up.

"Then they think highly of us."

"Of what you've got," George said.

More-Wives-Than-Anyone turned now to the ladies seated on the floor. He had made the trader concede something and he felt entitled to some small applause. The Indian women gave it to him with their eyes and the jiggle of their heads and they looked over to the Coca-Cola box for their hero to buy them Pepsis all round. More-Wives-Than-Anyone nodded his head to George's flunkey, Tom-Dick-and-Harry, that he would pick up the tab and Tom-Dick-and-Harry began opening the bottles.

"One more victory and I'll be ruined," More-Wives-Than-Anyone said.

Paracelsus came in now. He was dressed in a finely tanned leather jacket and matching moccasins. He must have divined that the Indians were baiting George because he gave More-Wives-Than-Anyone an annoyed look before he sat on a pile of sheep hides in the corner where he could speak to everyone.

"Why really, I hate to say this but this section of The

People is so smart."

The others looked down on the floor.

"I hate to say this, but you think nobody has a culture but yourselves."

The People shuffled their feet.

"Why really, I hate to say this but you think everybody on the big reservation is crazy. You think their religion gives them no togetherness with nature, has nothing to do with medicine and is for the ignorant and the superstitious. You think their work is to go around in circles rapidly. You think their gods are the dollar, the big car and inspirational books. You think they think what is good for the big car is good for the country and what is bad for the big car is good for the enemy. Why really, I hate to say this—" The medicine man hesitated now, began again and hesitated and then said in a weak voice, "Why really, it is only in part true."

More-Wives-Than-Anyone was feeling set up. He half turned at the counter. He had won a great victory without even opening his mouth. The medicine man had come in to do battle with him and the medicine man had knocked himself out. The victory was so complete, enormous and sudden that More-Wives-Than-Anyone did not trust it; it might be pyrrhic. The medicine man might have laid an ambush. More-Wives-Than-Anyone said nothing, just rolled his body in the corner of the counter in front of the women on the floor and the babies at his feet and hoped the medicine man would hit himself again.

"Oh, you're so smart, oh so smart, making me do that to myself," the medicine man said. "And I hate to say this but it is true that The People feel themselves so superior to the white man. You make no allowances for the fact that the

white man never had an opportunity to become civilized, no allowance for the fact that he has spent all his time learning and studying without any opportunity to think. To you a white man is just an animal with just enough brains—" the medicine man looked out toward the mountain that held Los Alamos—"to build something complicated to kill himself with."

The medicine man got off the stack of sheep hides. "But that's not the terrible thing," he said, pacing the floor in front of the brown and stiff-boarded babies. "The terrible thing is that you've got me believing it. But there is a salvation," the medicine man said carefully.

George dropped his pencil. The word, any word that dealt with absolutes, always scared him.

"Our salvation lies," the medicine man said, thinking carefully and in a low voice on which everyone hung. "Our salvation, our loss of arrogance" (he used the Indian word "asidisah") "lies in helping these two white men from Houston. If they want the uranium, give them the uranium. If they want to get rich rich rich, let them."

"You could use a few dollars yourselves," George said. All the Indians nodded in agreement.

"But, Sansi," the medicine man said with confidence, "we could all use a few hundred dollars but those people from Texas talk only of billions. What would a civilized Indian do with billions except perhaps become uncivilized." All of the Indians nodded in agreement.

"But those particular people,". George said slowly to the medicine man, "are dishonest."

"Evil," Paracelsus said. "But I'm not their medicine man."

"But how do you know the whites will not put our uranium

to peaceful things?" More-Wives said.

"They never have," the medicine man said.

"They could change."

"But evil does not change. Sin changes; it is a way of looking at things. They punish sin. They allow evil to grow great."

The other Indians did not agree this time; they did not want to rub anything in, and Paracelsus too went back quietly and sat on the hides.

George Bowman thought: we live and we change big or we do not live, and maybe that is why, for the past fifteen years, I have been only half living. George let go of it with this and went back to his ledger, consoling himself with the knowledge that the Navahos in this allotment area, although it was not a true part of the reservation, could not lease the mineral rights to anyone without a tribal council okay, and the government Indian agency would not allow them to sign anything before a battery of Philadelphia lawyers looked at it. Nevertheless, if his Indians signed something it would tie the rights up in court for a long time with the Indians getting nothing.

"Look what I got." Silver Threads had come in the door with a piece of yellow something. He had been to town playing professional Indian for the tourists in a costume that amused the Indians and on his way back he must have discovered this. He placed it on the counter.

"I found it in the Puerco Wash," he said. It was a beautiful object, yellow and chrome and all sparkling.

The medicine man touched it gingerly with his brown, turquoise-ringed finger.

"It must have something to do with the white man's religion but perhaps I can use it at our next yebechai."

George had been examining the chrome and yellow object with the care of an archeologist. Now he stepped away from it and the Indians waited for him to identify it correctly.

"It is," George said slowly, with a scientific caution for the truth, "a left rear gas cap top, stop light and combination design treatment for the fender fishtail section of a late '55 or early '56 Cadillac Eldorado or coupe de ville."

The Indians were impressed by this careful classification of an unknown culture.

"Then I was wrong about it being something to do with their worship?" Paracelsus said.

George thought about this awhile and said, "You could be wrong."

The Indians were impressed by the scientific lack of certainty while George looked out at the dark, lowering sky.

"You say you found this in the Puerco Wash?" George questioned Silver Threads.

"Yes. Enormous wheel tracks going up the wash."

George looked out carefully at the sky now and with the same movement reached blindly for his large Stetson.

"We got to get going fast," he said. "Some white strangers are up the wash. They can't turn around in the Puerco and won't have enough knowledge to run before it's too late. The way the rain just broke on the mountain the water will come down in a flash flood with a fifteen-foot head."

George was already through the door with the Indians following. Outside, the sky above the Navaho country was very low, weighted down, black within a heavy dimension of black.

They got the taut, quick-dancing, wild-eyed horses pinned

along the corral and threw on bridle and saddle. Rabbit Stockings got off first, pulling his wild, paint horse within a tight circle outside the corral. George came out now and pulled his lashing horse into another small circle alongside, then they both broke toward the cloud-shrouded mountain where the water had collapsed.

Lord Acton, Paracelsus, Silver Threads and More-Wives-Than-Anyone shot out of the corral all at once, causing a storm of dust that enveloped them and the post and any sense of direction so that it was minutes before they caught Rabbit Stockings and George, long horsetails flowing, and leveled out, running easily and fast beneath the gay-striped flag rock of the Penistaja Mesa. Silver-Threads-Among-the-Gold flowed up in back of George, deepened his spur until he pulled up alongside, leaned out and over and shouted in perfect Hollywood English, "Ride 'em, Cowboy!"

At the Puerco Wash there was another tangle of gaudy, flashing horses within an explosion of dust before Rabbit Stockings picked up the trail and fled up the wash followed by all. The canyon rose, sudden bright and towering on both sides, the horses were diminutive, antlike and scurrying toward the wall of water they could all hear now, the horses panicked and charging toward the equally charging wall of death, bearing down with all speed on each other with the gentlemen from Houston, Texas, somewhere in between.

"This is a nice place," Garry de Grasppe said from his seat down on the running-board section of the yellow coupe de ville. "But I don't think it's the main highway." He passed the gallon of rum to the other.

"I don't think so myself," Leland Hepburn said, taking the bottle.

"Let me read that letter," Garry said. "I want to read everything Alfred ever wrote."

Leland passed him the letter.

"Can't read it," Garry said. "The type keeps moving." He tossed the letter on the ground. "It looks like there's a storm up ahead of us."

Leland picked up the letter and put it in his pocket. "It might be an important message. Anyway if Alfred wrote it it's important."

He paused now, the giant jug frozen in mid-air. "You hear something?"

"Yes! Yes! Yes! Look!"

Now they saw the wall of water like a sudden miracle in front of them as their extended, horror-risen arms were yanked almost from their sockets and their bodies flew behind the mad horses up the cliff. Everything was a giant roar and flashing of bright hoofs in their cut faces before they were deposited or thrown high on a pile of greasewood.

The horses, sobered now and thick-lathered, paced deliberately in 8's above the heavy flood, the riders still helpless yet to talk. The two gentlemen from Houston, thrown on the greasewood, were too shocked seemingly to talk ever.

They all had a furtive glance at the yellow-and-chromed coupe de ville poised at the top of a crested, pig-and-chicken-house-foaming mountain before it collapsed, the yellow-and-chromed monster sucked within the great curling lip of water and smashed down somewhere deep into the banded iron red earth from which it had so recently arisen.

"Sho'h. Sho'h. Sho'h," the medicine man said, dismounting and beginning a circle around the two whites which the others joined. They all seated themselves, none speaking, all

still insensible from the sudden happenings. They all waited, deadened, for the medicine man to speak, to explain the happenings.

"You bring contract?"

"Yes, but after what happened we'll tear it up. We bring peace. Peace," the white man moaned low. "Peace. Oh yes, and this letter for a man named George Bowman."

George took the wadded letter that Leland extended. He noticed that it was from someone called Alfred Marlowe. He put it in his pocket. He would read it when he got home.

"Sho'h," the medicine man said to the Navahos. Sho'h, George knew, meant listen. He walked to the outside of the circle while the medicine man repeated again, "Sho'h."

"The gods have taken away the white man's magic and cast it into the earth again. Sho'h. Listen."

The Navahos leaned forward.

"It could be a sign to all the earth-surface people that we are responsible for the world."

"Sho'h. Sho'h," all the Navahos repeated.

"A sign that all the earth-surface people are responsible for the world, but soon the world will go back into the world and bright objects will be no more and earth will become earth again like it was when The People came."

"Like it was when The People came," the Navahos chanted.

And the Navahos continued to chant, "Like it was when The People came," weird, rich chanting that became a polyphonic sing above the heavy flood.

Even after George Bowman left and was working his horse back slowly and alone beside the bright-banded cliffs he could still hear their high sing above the steady, deep movement of the flood. They might have a sing far into the night, certainly

until the loud, quick flood receded and the white men made their way back across the arroyo, back to the seething city, and all this quiet, sprawling land, shot with a fiery sky and empty with the weird, strange-shaped emptiness of the beginning, was again filled with the huge, awful silence—like it was when The People came.

George gentled his horse across a flat world of rock and sage, sharp and pungent with its perfume, alone, and the whole broad spread of the infinite land, still virgin from the oily chrome paw and smoke of civilization, still blessed—like it was when The People came. George was home now and he dismounted.

14

George dropped his horse at the corral and as he moved toward the post he noticed a purple convertible making its way over toward the buildings beneath the mesa. Ten minutes earlier and he would have been caught in the flash flood, George thought. But he dismissed the arriving car from his mind and went inside and over to the roll top desk to read the letter that simply had GEORGE BOWMAN on it, that the tall blond gentleman had handed him. He straightened it out and read.

My dear George Bowman:

As a friend of your brother's I write this because nothing he has written to you seems to get through. Perhaps when you suspected the source you tore them up. Perhaps you had good reason. I only write this to say that if Alexander does not get home he will die. That last obstacle to your allowing Alexander to come home again will removed when you get this. I am leaving with Perrette. I meant Alexander will die not only literarily but literally too.

Sincerely,
ALFRED MARLOWE

P.S. After much thought and discussion with Perrette we have decided that the best way to leave a person like Alexander that she does not want to hurt would be to do it quickly.

"Well?" Quicker-Than-You said. He had come in silently and was standing over George Bowman's shoulder.

"I thought you were at the sing," George said.

"I left," the Indian said. "The medicine man is getting orthodox. What about the letter?"

"I will answer it."

"When?"

"As soon as I have some time. I have things to do for The People."

"He is one of The People."

George Bowman looked sadly around the post then up to Quicker-Than-You and then back to the letter on the desk.

"He is my brother," he said.

"That should make it easier."

"Supposing someone ran off with your wife."

"Which one?"

There wasn't any use talking about it to an Indian, George thought, fingering the letter, or a white. You couldn't talk about it to anyone. You couldn't talk about it to yourself. This is one of the things you bury. You forget it. You do good works for the Indians. Other people do good works for the Lord. You do good works for the Indians. You bury things in good works.

Some of the other Indians had come back from the sing now, probably to buy something. Then George Bowman noticed a white stranger coming through the door. He was probably out of that odd car George had seen when he was coming home. George got up from the desk and went behind the counter. There was something about the white man that set him apart from even white men. It was not the careful carelessness of his expensive clothes nor the shock of red hair

above the typical wide, simple, open, honest face of a confidence man; the white stranger was set apart by some strong inner, spurious dedication that was scored in money or names and pictures in the papers and gossip columns and called success. He was, in all probability from Mars, and if George had reckoned incorrectly on his first guess, then it must certainly be Venus, New York City or Saturn.

"Hollywood," the man said, stopping in front of George Bowman. "I'm from Hollywood. Tell me," the man said, stroking his violent red hair and leaning forward on a pile of blankets toward the trader. "Did they even bother to deliver the letter up here that you did not answer?"

"Yes," George said and he began to make a geometric design out of the boxes of wool dyes that were scattered on the counter.

"And you did not bother to answer a personal inquiry from the director John Dykeman?"

"No," George said. He was stacking all the turkey-red dyes in a separate pile.

"John will get a big charge out of that," the Hollywood man said. "John Dykeman is outside now."

"Who is John Dykeman?" George asked.

The Hollywood man turned to the seated squaws who had arranged themselves in a line on the floor against the counter facing the babies who were thonged into private boards and stacked against the flour sacks.

"He asked who John Dykeman is," the Hollywood man said, smiling toward the squaws.

The squaws sympathized with something the turkey-red man was telling them, with an understanding nod of their heads toward him, and then they all looked at the trader with

a stare that said he was impossibly dense. They spoke and understood no English.

"John will certainly get a charge out of this," the Hollywood man said, studying the trader. "Look, maybe you can see him out there. We're serious up here all by ourselves. No women. All the rest of the studios are around the world someplace making *War and Peace*. They'll shoot a million feet of film and five million dollars in Yugoslavia or someplace, then they'll come back to Hollywood, burn what they took and make the picture for a hundred thousand—all that's left in the budget. Not John. John will make *War and Peace* when he's in the mood to make *War and Peace* and he'll film it all in Russia. Look, you can see him through the window now. No women. I'm not kidding about the no women bit. We actually came all the way up here without any women at all. John will be in as soon as the notion strikes him."

The group of male Indians that had drifted in from the sing were watching the scene, leaning against the adobe-log wall alongside a stack of hides. One of the braves, More Wives, was mounted on his own saddle on a wooden sawhorse. He had pawned the saddle with the trader but he used it when he felt like it which was now. He was practicing leaning far out dangerously on the saddle and picking things off the ground. More Wives was upright in the saddle now after a swipe that pleased him. "Who in the hell is John Dykeman?" More Wives said.

"I like this. I like this. I like this very much," the Hollywood man said. "But I suppose we can carry it too far. The gag, the bit is good but don't milk it."

George went back to his business of arranging the rug dyes, More Wives went back to practicing (he was roping

cattle now from the saddle), the babies went back to staring at the women and the women went back to staring at the men.

"I've got it! By God, I've got it!" the red-haired man said. He took out a beautiful handkerchief and wiped his face. "The bit is good, so good that it fooled me. The bit is that you never heard of John Dykeman. Let's play it that way."

"That should be easy," George said.

"That's a good line," the Hollywood man said. "But don't try to fool me any more. Remember I'm in on the bit now too. I'll go find John. John will get a charge out of this."

When the turkey-red-haired man with the very white skin had left More Wives got off his saddle, coiled his rope and came over and sat on the counter in front of George.

"I think maybe we go too far, Sansi," he said to George. "You were a genius not to answer the letter. It worked perfectly. It brought them down here on the double. But I do not think John Dykeman will get this charge out of not being famous here that Turkey Red thinks he will. I think he'll charge right back to Hollywood and we won't get a chance to wear feathers and holler, shoot white men and get overpaid for it."

The Indians in the shadows along the adobe back wall chanted an Indian word in agreement.

"Maybe," George said. "But if we want to build him up we won't recognize which one he is even."

"He'll be dressed in some clown costume," More Wives said. "And he'll act like God."

"All right," George said. "But what pictures did he make? You won't know what to tell him he is great about."

"Hollywood God is not interested in the particulars, Sansi. You worship with words like 'spectacular,' 'the greatest.'

211

Words like 'More-Wives-Than-Anyone,' " More Wives said.

"That's an Indian important word," George said.

"But you get the idea, Sansi."

"I get the idea," George said. "And I agree to try it. But don't overdo. Don't ham it up."

Outside the Hollywood man did not find the other Hollywood man for a time, then he saw the purple car parked on the edge of the yellow mesa. He was a while climbing and when he got there such a long minute had gone by that he couldn't hold it in any longer.

"John," the red-haired man said, "they've got a wonderful bit going on down there. I'm in on it now too. The bit is that they never heard of you, don't know who you are. To them you're just another white man."

"It's not bad," the other Hollywood man said thoughtfully. "As long as they don't overdo, as long as they don't ham it up."

The Hollywood white man, the director John Dykeman, who did not have red hair but a plaid cap, also wore a suede jacket with a fringe line along the chest, a black string tie and squaw boots.

"I cased the tip," the red-haired man, who was the assistant to the assistant producer and who was named Wiles Baedecker, said. "Like you thought, it's the real thing, John. A picture here would lose tons of money."

"Listen, Wiles," John Dykeman said, relaxing from his poetic pose, moving his suede squaw boots under him. "I don't want to lose tons of money."

"John, John," the other said.

"No, I mean it, Wiles," John Dykeman said. "No, Wiles. Just because the studio said I could do one of my own after

the last smash I did for them, that doesn't mean necessarily that the thing I do now will lose tons of money."

"Oh?" Baedecker said.

"I simply want to make an honest Western picture of Alexander Bowman's first book right here where he wrote it."

"A sincere picture."

"That's right, Wiles."

"A germane picture."

"That's right, Wiles."

"Bust the studio."

"I don't follow your humor, Wiles."

"You won't get to shoot *War and Peace*." Baedecker's voice was edged hard now. "Remember they said no *War and Peace* for you if you lost a bundle on this one."

"I've got to have *War and Peace*, Wiles. And I've got to make this Alexander Bowman Indian picture honest, sincere and germane."

"You're getting me in the heart, John."

"I must say I don't follow your humor, Wiles," John Dykeman said.

Inside the log-and-adobe post the Indians were practicing a war dance. They had never done or seen a war dance before but Tom-Dick-and-Harry and Silver Threads had seen many movies and the other braves had seen some and they were all going up and down in a conga line and making war whoops when the director and Baedecker entered.

"Oh no," John Dykeman said. "Oh no."

"Aren't you John Dykeman?" George Bowman said.

"Oh no," John Dykeman said. "Oh no."

George took a long pipe and offered it to the director.

"They switched the bit on me, John," Baedecker said. "They're playing me for a patsy."

"Stop them," John Dykeman said.

"Cut!" Baedecker hollered.

The Indians halted the war dance, More Wives stopped shooting and the dead Indians were risen from the dead. When all the noise of the shooting ceased the babies and the squaws seemed disappointed.

"You people are not with it," Baedecker pronounced in a loud voice. "We're up here to get a story line on an honest, sincere, germane script on the contemporary Indian. Let's not have any more war dance."

"But they thought this was going to be fun," George said.

"No, let's get this straight, sir," Baedecker said carefully, but his voice still low. "John Dykeman is an artist, sir. Anyplace else in the world except right here they would recognize John for the artist he is."

"Don't overdo, Wiles," John Dykeman said, examining the beaded belts.

"No, I've got to say this," Wiles Baedecker said. "It's got to be said wherever false values threaten integrity. John Dykeman is the type of man that what Louella Parsons and Hedda Hopper and all the other movie columnists say in praise of him means nothing. He doesn't even read them. You know what he was reading on the way up here? Spinoza. Bennett Cerf and Leonard Lyons mention him every day."

"He knows they're just columnists," John said.

"See what I mean?" Baedecker said. "The *Saturday Review*, the best newspapers, to John they're nothing. He's in a class with George Bernard Shaw."

"Shaw is dead," John Dykeman said.

"You see?" Baedecker said. "To John even George Bernard Shaw is dead."

"I mean Shaw is really dead," John Dykeman said, putting down the belt.

"You see what I mean," Baedecker said. "With John Shaw is really dead."

"I think we've established the point, Wiles," John Dykeman said. "Let's get down to the business."

"Okay. Everyone line up along the wall."

The Indians had already resumed their former positions along the wall and were ready for anything.

"Okay," Baedecker said, going to the head of the line. "Now, after each of you answer the first thing that comes into your head I will place in your hand this crisp new five-dollar bill."

Baedecker removed a sheaf of new money from his inside coat pocket. "I guess we're ready to roll," Baedecker said. "Remember this has got to be spontaneous, we've got to find out what you Indians are really like. We can work better with you if we know what you're really like. No help from the audience. Say the first thing that comes into your head."

He stepped in front of Rabbit Stockings. "Okay," he said.

"Okay," Rabbit Stockings said.

Baedecker placed a five-dollar bill in his hand and stepped in front of More Wives. "Okay," he said.

"Okay," More Wives said.

Baedecker placed a five-dollar bill in his hand and stepped in front of the next Indian. "Okay," he said.

"Wait a minute. Wait a minute please," John Dykeman said. "Wiles, they only repeat what you say."

"Please, John, let me do this."

"I won't let you give them each five dollars to mimic you."

"It worked with the Esquimos, John."

"It didn't work with the Esquimos. They said okay too."

"They're both primitive people, John, so they both happen to say the same thing. Is that so strange? To me cogs are beginning to mesh. It traces the primitive pattern right down to here."

"I think they know we are the primitives by now," John Dykeman said.

"John," Baedecker said, running his hand hopelessly through his red hair and relaxing the sheaf of money to his side. "John, I don't think you meant to say that. I don't think you want to lose face this early."

"Okay, roll it," John Dykeman said.

Baedecker stepped in front of and got an okay from each of the Indians and when he had finished John Dykeman asked how much it had cost.

"Seventy-five dollars," Baedecker said.

"And we call the picture *Okay, Baedecker*," John Dykeman said.

"Please don't fight me, John."

"Gentlemen, gentlemen," George said, sliding over the counter. "What are the Indians going to think?"

"Young man," Baedecker said, rising up in all his small majesty. "We might spend one million dollars right here if John Dykeman is pleased. Now, after your speech, do you think John Dykeman is pleased?"

"Don't overdo, Wiles," John Dykeman said.

"But," George said, "do you have to act like a tribe from Hollywood? Can't you act like human beings at least?"

"No," Baedecker said, his voice rising. "Because we're not

from Hollywood and we're not human beings."

"We are human beings," John Dykeman's voice was insistent now. "And our residence *is* in Hollywood. That's true, Wiles. That's true."

"All right, it's true, John," Baedecker said. "But it's not true, John. You're not a human being. You're a great artist. There's a difference, John. You're not Hollywood, John. You happen to live there but you're not Hollywood. How many times has the *New Republic* said that? How many times has the *Nation* said that?"

"How many times?" George asked.

"You never heard of the *Nation* or the *New Republic*?" Baedecker said.

"No," George said.

"Then your inquiry was an attempt at levity."

"And humor too," George said.

"Well, we don't think it is funny, do we, John?"

"It wasn't a bad line, Wiles. But I think we're all hamming too much. Let's get back to the business."

"All right," George said. "The way I understand it you want to make a Wild West cowboy and Indian picture here and my Indians think it would be a big time, a lot of fun."

"I'm sorry, sir," Baedecker said. "But art is serious. There's nothing better that John would like to do than make the picture you describe."

"Oh, I would not. I would not," John Dykeman said.

"Will you wait for my punch line, John? Will you please wait for the punch line?" Baedecker turned back to George. "John would like to be human. He'd like to relax too and make Hollywood pictures but he's an artist. Can you understand that? Am I getting through?"

"No," George said.

"Then we're wasting our time with these feebs, John."

Quicker-Than-You pushed himself off the wall now and made his way through the squaws and babies and saddles. He was tall and broad-shouldered and he stopped annoyed in front of the talking people.

"Our trader, here," he said, touching George Bowman and looking down on the Hollywood people, "I don't like you strange people trying to—" The Indian hesitated and began again. "I don't like you people—"

"Patronizing him," George said. "But they're not, Quicker-Than-You."

"I think we were," John Dykeman said.

"I still don't think we were," Baedecker said.

"I think you'd better go out and wait for me outside, Wiles," John Dykeman said.

"No. I want to—"

"I said to get the hell out."

Baedecker crept out.

"I want to try now to make this clear," John Dykeman said.

"I think you've made it very clear," George said. "But we've all got to make a living."

"Yes, but we shouldn't fool ourselves," Dykeman said. "I'm beginning to believe what the columnists say about me. I think I've been believing it for a long time now."

"You've got to make a living," George said.

"But how low can you get?" Dykeman said.

"You don't hurt anybody," George said. "And I understand you have made some pictures that are better than most.

That must be difficult with the pressure and I respect you for it."

"Thanks," John Dykeman said. "We make one sometimes that I think might stand up. But I think this one is off."

"The Indians could use the money," George said. "Why is it off?"

"I've been looking around," Dykeman said, "at the country outside and the Indians here and I think it's too real. I think the landscape looks too real and the Indians too real. It's not convincing. I think it would lose money and, as Baedecker says, I can't afford to lose money on this one, not if I'm going to make *War and Peace*. True, the book was about this country but *Oklahoma!* was about Oklahoma and we made that in Arizona. *The Texan* we made in Utah and this one, I guess, we'll make in Hollywood."

"Well, I hope the red-haired man recovers all right," George said.

"Their feelings recuperate quickly when their swimming pool is at stake," Dykeman said. "I tell you, I would like to buy these Indians a drink."

George nodded to Tom-Dick-and-Harry to serve Pepsis all around, which he did.

Baedecker thought it might be safe now to creep back in again but he stayed well on the periphery of the room until he was absolutely certain.

"What's the picture now, John?" he called from a distance and from the protection of a row of saddles.

"The picture is we don't make this picture here," John Dykeman called back.

"Great. You mean we're going to make *War and Peace*?"

"Yes. We're going to make *War and Peace*," John Dykeman said.

"And we'll make it in the Ukraine, John?"

"Where else would one make *War and Peace?*" John Dykeman said.

"What about the Russians, John?"

"I think you can take care of the Russians, Wiles."

Baedecker was across the room now and had his arms around John Dykeman.

"Baby, baby. John, doll!"

"Don't overdo, Wiles."

"No, baby. I mean, I'm serious, doll," Wiles Baedecker said, pointing up to where the Indians could see the hanging hides. "I can see your name up there now in red neon half the length of Broadway. *War and Peace*, produced, directed and written by John Dykeman."

"Well, good-bye," John Dykeman said. "If he ever writes another book we'll be back."

"Who?" George said.

"Your brother," John Dykeman said. "You didn't think we came here by accident? We were here considering a re-make of an old book of his, *The Big Rider*. We own the rights."

"It wouldn't cost us anything for the rights," Baedecker said.

"Why don't you buy his last book," George said, "and make that?"

Dykeman looked around the room and toward the door.

"Because it was terrible," Baedecker said.

"Well," John Dykeman said, "it wasn't that—"

"It was terrible," Baedecker said. "Terrible."

"We'll make the next one," Dykeman said.

"He's finished," Baedecker said. "Alexander Bowman is dead." Baedecker walked out the door and stopped under the log overhang, his small voice resolute now with satisfaction. "Alexander Bowman is not really dead. It's worse, much worse. Alexander Bowman is simply dead."

John Dykeman closed the door and faced George. "Don't believe him," John Dykeman said. "A man, as long as he's alive—"

"I know," George said.

"And don't judge us by people like Baedecker. This Baedecker is a clown, a hunker," John Dykeman said. "A Hollywood name for those who get our coffee, know the baseball scores and we strike matches on."

"Yes," George said.

"You'll see," Dykeman said. "Soon Alexander will be back here and in a position to see things as clearly—"

"Yes," George said. "Certainly."

"God," John Dykeman said. "You look awful."

George followed the visitors out and when they got in their car and drove away George kept right on walking. He walked for several hours, and he thought—I write you this to tell you that if he does not come home Alexander will die. I mean this not only literarily but literally too. Alexander Bowman is dead, the red-haired man had said. Not really dead but worse, simply dead. Dead and dying. Dead—

George walked until he was on top of the mesa and until his foot struck something. It was the old mine shaft.

"This," he said, touching the top of the mine shaft with his foot, "was my first attempt to win something or to get even with a person who always won, to become a person my-

221

self, to exist. And after he won the last one, after he won Perrette, then I did not want to play any more. Since then it has been a steady retreat, a withdrawal into the Indians in the guise of protecting the Indians from the Moving People and all the rest of it, including the drought and the uranium people and all the rest of it. But all along it was the Indians who were protecting me from life. Getting back into life again is not easy. Alexander had to lose everything. And does that make me win something?" He kicked the mine shaft. "Not a damn thing. Fifteen years trying to win. Not a damn thing. Fifteen years is a long time but it will never be more. You can't win because the other guy loses. It will never be fifteen years and one day more. You can't back into victory. You can't win because a brother loses."

George turned and, moving fast, stumbled down the mesa. He ran through the desert, the moon edging up now and the sage cutting him as he ran toward the boarded-up petrified-wood house. He made a big jump that landed him on the porch. He reached up and ripped off the two by six that was nailed across the door and then heaved all his weight into the door against the rusted lock whose key had been thrown down the mine shaft fifteen years ago. He heaved his weight again and the door splintered and George found himself in an enormous space. He went around lifting dry and dusty window shades, letting in some pale moonlight. The pallid light lit up the great fireplace, the oval rotogravure pictures of the Bowmans around the wall, the wide bear and Indian rugs along the floor; it lit up too a candle placed upon an oak desk above a drawer from which George extracted pencil and paper.

He sat down and wrote and when he had written it all he

signed it, sealed it and stamped it and wrote his brother's name and address on the envelope and got up and breathed easily and deeply and well for the first time since God knows when.

"Since eternity," he said, moving toward the window.

I tell you I seen her—Perrette," Jack said. "Or somebody who looked exactly like her. And there was a man there too, in the same place, with a book."

"And the man with the book, could it have been Alfred?" Alexander said. "Could it have been a poet?"

"Poet? I wouldn't say anything about a man that I wouldn't say to his face," Jack said.

The Mexican village was quiet and dark and the noise of the horses was very clear in the narrow street. The houses were joined together and made a wall so that it was like going down a dirt lane banded on both sides by the same dirt. Each house in the wall was marked by a piece of burlap door that was lighter colored in the darkness than the wall. On horseback you were higher than the low mud barricade and you could breathe and feel the cleanness of the quiet night. There wasn't any moon.

Alexander and Jack rode into the big square now, which had a fountain where the washing was done. At the far corner of the square, on the leaning mud wall, there was a green globe with the numerals 504. It was supposed to light up the sign *Casa de las Santas* but it didn't quite make it. On the street of the café were abandoned several tired cars in junk attitudes

dangling Mexican license plates. Guarding the cars that, years before, had had everything stolen, was a sharp and yellow-faced man who might have done it. When they rode into the square the car watcher ignored them with the thoroughness of a used-car salesman during a war. The car watcher was stationed under the green 504 globe with a piece of somebody's sweat-rotted underwear in his hand. He was stationed also in front of the only car that looked as though it might run. It was a sparkling chrome-and-pink, bucket-seated, disk-wheeled sports MG with California plates. Along the fountain was a rusted iron rail where two wisely stupid-looking burros were hitched. The two men dismounted near the burros and tied up.

The sharp-faced car watcher abandoned his MG and scuttled over to them, only a dim shape now away from the light.

"Guardo los caballos para un peso," the car watcher chanted.

"No," Jack said.

"Cincuenta centavos?"

"No," Jack repeated.

Inside it all went very dim. There was a good-sized oval dance floor with orange and blue Chinese lanterns strung across it. It must have been intermission when they walked in because the orchestra wasn't making any noise at all. It sagged on a platform in the rear, all pomade and teeth and once red jackets. When it spotted them it made a noise, dismal and without hope. It became a loud inertia; a wild chrome trumpet went off alone, blown by a fat man and muted with rags.

They had to make their way along the edge of the dance

floor to get to the bar that ran the long length of the other side. The girls pulled in their legs for their passage. They had made their faces into the universal female mask of Hollywood so that they could not be separated from the *New York Times* society page or the girls working the Via Veneto. Their dresses ran from white, hand-sewn cambric with lace such as children wear for their first communion, to the latest J. C. Penney imitation of Dior and Mainbocher thrown out by some desperate drummer from San Diego.

When they got to the bar Jack said, "There he is, the man with the book."

"Hello, Alexander," the man with the book said. "I've been looking for you." It was Bentley.

Alexander and Jack sat down at the bar.

"Where's the girl?" Jack said.

"Oh, the girl," Bentley said. "I sent her back to Hasbrouck Heights. It wasn't Perrette," Bentley said to Alexander. "I was sorry to hear about it."

"Yes," Alexander said.

"I figured you'd be low," Bentley said, "with your last books and now this happening. Here, let's have a drink."

They had a drink.

"I have a proposition," Bentley said.

"Oh?"

"Yes," Bentley said. "I guess we never figured there in Europe when you were somebody and I was nobody that old Bentley would make it to the top and be able to help you the way you helped me. Top?" Bentley repeated. "Well, I guess some people would call it that. I got a big job at the studios. Top?" Bentley said again. "Well, let's call it that. Anyway I can help you."

226

"Help me?" Alexander took a sip of the drink.

"Yes," Bentley said. "I'm story editor and the studio wants big names. If it's a has-been it doesn't make any difference. Even though you haven't had anything good for five years I've convinced them that you still have a name."

Alexander looked around the room and then at himself in the back bar mirror.

"You've convinced them that I have a name," Alexander said.

"Yes," Bentley said. "It took a little doing."

"And if it's a has-been it doesn't make any difference," Alexander said.

"No," Bentley said. "You kind of coast. At the moment we have in mind an Indian Country story. We got a couple of young whiz boys at the studio. We've already cracked the story. All you have to do is leap-frog these boys, do every third scene. Then on the credits you get all the credit. The studio wants a name."

"In the credits I get all the credit," Alexander said. "All I have to do is leap-frog the boys and I get all the credit."

"And all the money too," Bentley said.

"All the money too," Alexander agreed. "And all the credit. Credit for what?"

"It hasn't got a name," Bentley said. "We'll think of something on the plane."

"Certainly," Alexander said. "How stupid of me. Why didn't I think of that? We can do the whole thing on the plane."

"Almost," Bentley said.

"And then when the plane lands I can leap-frog the boys," Alexander said.

"You mean you don't want it?" Bentley said.

"That's right."

"Think a bit," Bentley said.

A man came up and put his hand on Alexander's shoulder. It was the congressman who had been asking for directions back at the hotel, long days before.

"Well, I found it," Willborne said. "It took me a long time. I had been by it four or five times. If only I'd stopped to think a bit the first time I wouldn't have wasted so much time. All the time I thought it was a church, nothing but a church. But inside it's the real thing. How's about a drink?"

"No, but thanks," Alexander said.

"Oh, there's a man looks like an American," Willborne said, marching toward Jack.

"Who was he?" Bentley asked.

"The world is in his hands," Alexander said.

"Yes," Bentley said, "but let's get back to this important thing. It could be that you have had it. I'm not saying you've had it, but I want you to think about this offer for a while."

"It's no," Alexander said.

"I think you should think about it awhile," Bentley said.

"I've thought about it all my life."

"All right," Bentley said. "I'll tell you the way I see it. You people see a few writers like Fitzgerald get pushed around out there and defeated, but don't forget Scott was a rummy." There was a silence and Bentley ordered another drink. "That's the way I see it," he said.

"It's the way you see it," Alexander agreed.

"I'm offering you your last chance," Bentley said. "All right, so you go along with some box-office pictures, but if

you make good you'll get a decent assignment, the chance to adapt something of your own."

"If I make good," Alexander said.

"Oh, this art bit," Bentley said. "This art kick. We all go through it. God knows I have more than anyone, but we grow out of it. We face reality."

"Do we?" Alexander said.

"If we're going to survive," Bentley said. "Where's the bartender? Yes, I can't quite follow you, Alex. You're the one writer I know, including those who are taking from them, who never panned the movies. And now they offer you what may be your last offer on a silver platter—and nothing?"

"Nothing," Alexander agreed.

"Well, I give up."

"Thank you," Alexander said.

"You just keep repeating," Bentley said, "everything I say."

"You say it so well."

"I was just trying to help you," Bentley said. "You know you helped me. God, back there in my naïve days I printed a lot of junk. If it wasn't for your stuff we would have collapsed long before we collapsed."

"Let's go," Jack said, attempting to escape Willborne.

"All right," Alexander said.

"Before you go, Alex," Bentley said, "how about a loan? I could let you have a thousand."

"No. No thanks," Alexander said.

"And don't worry about Perrette. She can take care of herself."

"I wish you were right," Alexander said, moving toward the door now.

"We must keep in touch," Bentley called.

"Yes," Alexander said as he closed the gold-leafed door for himself and Jack.

"Well, I guess we looked for her about every place that's likely," Jack said.

"Yes," Alexander said. "She's gone back to the States."

"With that fellow you spoke about. The poet."

Alexander sat down on the curb in the dimly lit street. "Yes," he said.

"Well, neither of us could follow her there," Jack said, still standing and commencing the business of a cigarette.

"True," Alexander agreed.

Alexander lit a cigarette and passed the light up to Jack, who had completed making his.

"Not until I hear from George," Alexander said. "But I should be hearing from him one of these days, especially now that Perrette has—"

"I've got to tell you something," Jack said. Jack sat down on the curb next to Alexander. "You know," Jack said, "back in Indian Country they call me a rustler but you people always got back what I took accidental."

"Yes," Alexander agreed.

"You remember as a kid," Jack said, "whenever some of your cattle was missing you two boys used to ride out to my place, used to carry a wooden gun to ambush me, launch attacks at me from the bushes, until I got off my horse and laid down and died for you. Then you'd go home and tell your father you couldn't find the cattle but you'd killed Jack the Rustler again. But your cattle always did show up cause we got along. Remember all those Wild West stories I told you?"

"Yes," Alexander said, "but what's that got to do with what you want to tell me?"

"Nothing," Jack said, "except I got to tell you a Wild West story this time that's true." Jack paused and went down on his haunches next to Alexander. "You've got to get back to Indian Country and you're waiting for a letter from George. And I got to tell you something."

"Yes."

"It's not coming," Jack said.

"There must be something more."

"Yes. He said he would try to write a letter."

"Nothing more?"

"No," Jack said. Jack's cigarette flared brightly. "You weren't thinking you'd hear from him because—?" Jack blew out a puff of smoke that Alexander waved away. "Well, because he got you out once before—the mine shaft?"

"Maybe," Alexander said.

"Well, there's nothing wrong about that. It adds up all right," Jack said. "Except—"

"Excepting what?"

"Except nothing," Jack said. "It adds up all right."

Alexander got up now. "Excepting what?"

Jack's hand-rolled cigarette had flamed briefly then collapsed. Now he thought he would roll another.

"The facts," Jack said. Jack mothered the makings of the cigarette into his chest.

"He got me out. That's enough," Alexander said.

"I didn't want to tell you this, but there's no use you wasting your life waiting for a stubborn brother. No, he got you in," Jack said. "Anyway he saw you fall in. I got it from an Indian that George swore to secrecy. George knew where

you were the whole three days."

"Then why didn't he, the first day—?"

"Maybe it was because he was at last in the position of your not being the hero. Maybe for the first time he was the brother who was somebody, the brother, the somebody who was going to rescue you."

"Then why didn't he the first day?"

"Maybe because he enjoyed being important, enjoyed being a person for the first time without your shadow big over him." Jack paused and went back to his cigarette, then said, quietly, "He is gentle but he is stubborn. So maybe he will make you wait forever."

"But he did finally. It was him—"

"No it wasn't," Jack said. "It was Tom-Dick-and-Harry who was walking straight toward your hole—couldn't have missed it. It was only then that George decided he must find you."

Jack noticed the expression on Alexander's face and said quickly, "But I think he was about to do it, about to find you. Anyway just about to pull you back like he is now," Jack said.

"Now?"

"Yes," Jack said. "Something could happen back there to make him change. Time could make him change. Back there when I talked to him he almost got it out—almost said you could come home. You've got to hold on."

"But there's nothing now to hold on to," Alexander said, beginning to walk away.

Bentley came out of the café and walked toward them.

"You boys want to join me?" Alexander said, making toward another yellow café door. Jack and Bentley paused.

"This could be the final chapter," Alexander said, turning. "I'm not too bad at last chapters. Why don't you join me?"

"I—I guess not," Jack said as they both turned and moved off, leaving Alexander alone. They had seen his face beneath the dim café lamp. They were both frightened.

16

Alexander entered the café that was mirrored all round. He sat down at a mirrored table on a mirror-backed chair and had several drinks. Then he began carefully explaining to himself what a great old Indian fighter Kit Carson was. No one disagreed but he felt he should concede the point anyway that Kit Carson, the old Indian fighter finally had difficulty locating old Indians. Alexander broke away from his profound thoughts now and looked up from his drink.

"O Captain, my Captain!" Alexander called to a dim figure who had just entered the house of mirrors through the yellow door and now seemed to be trying to go through one of the walls. It was Captain Fleet, the bore that Alexander had been avoiding with all of his craft since his arrival, the one who owned the tourist mecca next to the hotel.

"O Captain, my Captain!" Alexander called. "The ship is in, the prize is won, oh come and have a drink."

The captain moved over to the table, seeming in the mirrors to be coming from all directions. His many heads were covered with a stiff crew hair cut that was gray and a stubble of beard the same shade so that his whole head seemed to be one bristle. His small dark eyes, almost no nose and weak mouth were the only alien matter in a perfect brush.

"Oddly enough I have news," the captain said with a British cut to his voice. "It's rather important too. I think you better leave and get back to the foreign quarter. Mimi Jimenez is looking for you."

"Sit down, O Captain," Alexander said, patting the mirrored chair back. "If there is a war party coming we may have to take to the hills. The captain must not be found sober. Now what is all this talk about getting back to the foreign quarter? You sound as if you spent too much time reading my lesser works. Where did you ever pick up dialogue like that? I've been bad but never that bad. Tell me, O Captain, have you been reading the opposition?"

"You are underestimating the situation," the captain said, taking the chair. "This chap can become very awkward." The captain had acquired British mannerisms of speech to, in the expatriate tradition, isolate himself more completely from himself.

"It seems," the captain said, "that you chaps arranged a do and now it's been called off and he's very drunk and he's got this machete and he's looking for you. It seems as though he holds you responsible for the whole mess."

"I didn't call it off," Alexander said drinking his tequila. "Alexander Bowman never call it off. Government call it off. Alexander Bowman is annoyed with Jimenez for co-operating so abruptly with government."

"Well, it's gotten most complicated," the captain said, fishing his eye around for a drink. "He's down in Louis' bar now, or he was a few minutes ago, explaining it to everyone who would listen. It isn't logical any more. You know it never is with a Mexican-Indian chap when he gets drunk. It seems as though it's boiled down now to the fact that he thinks you

235

want to get yourself killed and he's going to oblige."

"Never should sell these Indians firewater," Alex said. "It's against the law in my country. Keeps them off the warpath."

"I don't think we should make a joke of it," the captain said, with thirsty seriousness, still casting his eye. "That old wharf of his you know, it's been in desperate circumstances for the last years. Since the tourist fishermen won't use his boats any more he's been up against it. What with the city condemning his firetrap and the local people not using his boats now he counted quite heavily on your name for the tourist publicity. It seems now that this thing has been called off the poor chap is ruined."

"That's too bad."

"After all it isn't his fault, old man, exactly, is it? After all if the government—" The captain interrupted himself to help himself to one of the drinks. "And don't forget that machete he's got," the captain pronounced, squeezing the lime directly into his tequila.

"Ever hear of Geronimo?" Alexander asked, finishing his drink and motioning an order for the captain too this time.

The captain shook his head as though he had never heard of any kind of an Indian.

"There are only supposed to be three great Indian warriors," Alexander said. "Unless you call that wild flurry of Sitting Bull's important. But there is another fighter, my boy Geronimo."

"Does your son actually fight?" the captain asked.

Alexander quit. The captain was not sharp today. The captain was never sharp. It was impossible to write lines for the captain and if you changed the captain's dialogue as much as it needed to be changed it ended up not being the captain,

not being any captain, not being anybody at all but some fig-
ment of some anoymous typewriter's imagination with all the
credibility of my last book.

"But why should you, Mon Capitaine, why would you not,
Mon Capitaine, make a decent last book?" Alexander asked
aloud through the brain fog of his ten tequilas, through all
of the cheroot soot and perfume stink, through all the whore-
dom and boredom of the Tres Bolitas. "Why would you not,
O Captain, make an admirable admiral, O Captain."

"You don't seem to realize this machete business is bloody
serious." The captain's voice was excited without any of the
inquisitorial dignity of Alexander Bowman's booze. "You
don't seem to realize, old man, that Mimi Jimenez is out to
give you what for, right here, tonight. You see," the captain
was intimate, sliding his glass forward for emphasis and hint,
"he's figured it all out. He's figured that only a man who's
reached the end, only a man who wants to commit suicide,
would swim to La Paz. So he's figured his last charitable act
in Mazatlán before he leaves this ingrate town for a brighter
land will be to oblige you. To kill you. This last auto-da-fé
will be made somewhat easier for him he claims by the suspicion that he does not love you."

"Does not love me," Alexander repeated, stroking his face
as though hand and face were frozen with alcohol. "I do not
believe it. I conclude," he said with his inquisitorial alcohol
voice, "that it is a plot to get back on the plot and I want to
live my life. I do not want to be a story book, I do not want
to become an adaptation for the movies, I do not want to
become another book club selection. I only want to get drunk
—that means irrelevant dialogue, that means no story line.
Can't you understand that people have a right to live, a right

237

to write, to be real, alive, irrelevant, irreverent and impossible?"

"Yes," the captain interrupted. "But you'd best get back to the quarter. You can get drunk, do what you like there, but it's bloody dangerous here."

And now Alexander noticed that the mirrored walls had twisted his face, distorted his whole body; all the objects in the room became rubberized. Things distended and then all crammed together in a ball. Mouths as wide as caves and feet on stilts as though they were all in some childish fun house of mirrors.

Perhaps I have been given a Michael Finn, Alexander thought. Why don't they get some air in this place. His body was turning all hot and then suddenly cold with the same rhythm that the multi-faces in the mirror switched from crouching gargoyles to giants. The thing to do, Alexander told himself, was to maintain his freedom of movement, not to fall down sideways into a lump under the table and become the prey of every cutthroat in the quarter. Alexander heaved onto his feet, not feeling his legs under him but feeling the higher altitude, feeling the change of air, the increased thickness of the swirling smoke, but still not focusing absolutely on anything. The strategy would be to work his way back to the bartender, to anchor his flank at the bar so that they would have to come at him frontally. Then too, the bartender would be directing the enemy and there at the corner of the bar, Alexander thought, he might be able to get in on their staff conferences. He floundered now, hitting a glass-top table, and listened to the crash, but always maintaining his mobility. He was going well; one more good step and it would be an orderly retreat. He made one last final lunge at

the corner of the bar and made it, clutching, dangling there. And now I can regroup my forces, Alexander whispered to himself and wiped a sheet of cold sweat off his forehead with his numbed hand.

"Usted," Alex commanded the bartender in a gravel voice, "usted, bring me the bottle of tequila. Tráigame la botella de tequila, por favor. Put down the bottle in front of me so I can pour it myself. And a glass of water."

The bartender did as he was commanded and Alexander congratulated himself that he had put the enemy to work bringing up his supplies.

Alexander observed now the squashed bulk of Bentley surrounded by Leroy and Howard with Guaymas still written across their chests, spearheading a flanking operation against his right wing. The mirrors multiplied them into a small army, elongating their foreheads into a hundred gleaming helmets. Don't fire until you see the whites of their ties, Alexander told himself. Bentley halted now to reconnoiter the position.

"Lay on," Alexander baited him.

Bentley and the same army of Bentleys leaned against the bar. "I want to buy you a drink," the spokesman for the Bentleys said.

"Yes, you want to poison the command. Are you afraid to fight it out in the open?"

"I want to buy you a drink," Bentley said. "I'm with you."

"With me? Then you should know what it's like to be me, to lose everything, your home and your work and everything that was close. But I'm just resting now. I'm planning a way back. I'm going to try and find where I did it wrong and try to do it right another time."

"Splendid," Bentley said. "I will help you."

"Yes," Alexander said, stalling, adjusting at the place at his neck where his tie should have been. "Yes," he said, and thinking now—the thing to do is to plunk him with an arrow as soon as he comes out. And if that doesn't work try not to fall for his peace offerings.

"Do you want a treaty of peace?" Alexander asked.

"I simply said that I wanted to buy you a drink," Bentley said, getting up on the green stool.

"Do you know who I was?" Alexander asked, turning the white bottle of tequila on its axis and studying the lettering.

"Yes," Bentley said, "you were The Writer."

"No. I was That Indian," Alexander said, but he mumbled "that writer" to himself a couple of times to figure if Bentley meant well or ill, then he suddenly progressed several jumps ahead in his thinking and decided that Bentley was trying to sell him something and he slammed the glass down upon the counter just as a man came up at his elbow and confided in a bartender voice, "Let the kid alone," glancing at the corpulent Bentley. "The kid's all right," the voice continued in a hushed whisper. "Let the kid perform. Let the kid ride. Don't rope his animal."

"I was just walking along minding my business when out of a Mexican sky this man—but that's all right, Jack," Alexander interrupted himself. "Just stop this place from going up and down, if you've got any interest in it at all. Stop these mirrors from squeezing everybody, stop my legs from going rubber so I can withdraw from this position in good order."

So Jack and Bentley had not deserted him and neither had Leroy and Howard, so there are good whites, including the blacks.

Alexander felt now for Jack along the bar as far as he could

reach but he was gone and Bentley was gone and Leroy and Howard were gone too; the only thing that was still there was the recurrent waves of heat and cold, and all that was there was an awful mob of whores and bores squashed into one big blob spreading and contracting on the mirrors.

Alexander mopped his numbed hand across his forehead. Everything was icy and desolate and the cause was lost. Terry was all for turning back, Reno and Colonel Benteen were all for crossing the Little Big Horn. (Face the arrows, Custer, the beer people want to paint the picture.) But Reno was a fool and Benteen was ambitious and now Custer was forced to lean heavily on his Indian scout for advice. Under the weight of the leaning Custer Alexander slipped on the ice that darkened the swamp down to the Little Big Horn. The Indian scout sprawled heavily on the rubber ice. Reno and Custer reached down and grabbed the Indian scout and Jack whispered into Alexander's ear, "Steady, old man."

"The ice," Alexander mumbled.

"No ice in it at all," Jack told him. "You're drinking straight tequila."

Alexander got up into a position where he could hold onto the bar.

"Now get those Indians under cover and feed them properly. I'll address them in the morning. But as for now, let's have rum all around," he told the bartender.

"You've been drinking tequila, sir," the bartender said.

Alexander could see that the bartender was oily but a mere white boy, a mere white boy who had never played Indian.

"I said rum," Alexander said. "You pretend to speak English. Rum. Ron. Aguardiente. I know where I am and what I'm doing. I'm in Mexico and in a little town outside of

Mazatlán. Although I appear to be here alone on a scouting expedition there is more than meets the eye. I am actually reinforced by a visiting cattle rustler, a literary chap—and two friends. Now let's have rum all around."

"Yes, sir."

"And don't sir me," Alexander said. "I'm an egalitarian. I left General Custer there on the floor."

But Alexander was not thinking about that. He was thinking very much about how he was feeling, and he was feeling very much the way the people in his stories felt after they had been given a Mickey Finn. For certainly, Alexander thought, he had only had nine or ten drinks and he had always been able to go nine or ten drinks with the best of them without falling on the floor and fighting the war. Soon, he knew, if it continued to go like this he would be on the floor fighting the Civil War, assisting General Grant, or maybe on the floor with Georgie Patton, advising against a frontal attack on Metz, or on the floor with General MacArthur at the Republican Convention. Anyway soon, in here in this heat and with that knockout wallop in him, he knew he would be on the floor. Right now he knew he must get back to the Indian Country. But he must not, he thought, go out the front, he must not go any place or anywhere that anyone who might have had anything to do with harassing him could be. Even Bentley, who was obviously innocent, must be avoided. Certainly the bartender and even O Captain and quite decidedly Jack, who on the surface seemed decent enough but who, after all, was a white man. That left only Leroy and Howard. No, somehow he must back out the rear, covering his retreat with remarks about the arrival of the cavalry. Somewhere back there among the pileage of bottles, garbage, boxes and broken

crockery there must be an exit, an escape to the Indian Country.

"Hold it," Alexander announced, holding his long arms over the heads of the others. "Everyone keep their seats and no one retreat until I get back."

When Alexander was safely away from their eyes, behind three stacks of Carta Blanca, he came to a sign marked CABALLEROS. He knew that to go in there, in the stink and airlessness of the small room, was to invite an immediate knockout plus a small session on the floor at Wounded Knee, and then to be searched and macheted and thrown in an arroyo to die with the dogs. Maybe that was building it up but he could not take any chances. He felt his way back now in the semi-darkness, past more cartons of cerveza, piles of broken chairs and shattered mirrors until he saw a piece of neon light falling through a busted door. Alexander got out the decomposed door, and even the hot tropical air, thick and humid, smelling of rotted flesh, iron roofs and alcohol—even this felt refreshing and sharp and gave him enough lift to be able to sit down on a nearby beer barrel without falling.

A harsh electric sign blared out now across the street—TOME PACIFICO—and somewhere a radio was going at incredible speed advertising sex hormones. The lights began going on down the alley, yellow electric weaknesses that lit the religious signs over fallen doorways. There was a faded bunting of purple and once-white over each hovel signifying the day of St. Teresa. A weak-kneed drunk trotted bandy-legged from a camouflaged and decomposed bodega and collapsed triumphant. Some parchment-old mestizos were making their way gently down the intersecting alleys toward the church, and above him and to the left angry flocks of birds were be-

ginning to fight for the right to a night's refuge in an over-hanging jacaranda tree.

Alexander managed to get to his feet. It was not an easy thing to do. Although the dry retching had left him he was seized now with vertigo. The sign across the alley—TOME PACIFICO—bleared in a weird whir of color. The birds above seemed to dart with insanity and the obscene world about him tipped at an odd angle. Alexander leaned back heavily against the wall and grabbed at a molding of rotten brick. He would hang on here at the corral until his head cleared, until the awful belt he had received in the stomach was no longer trying to turn him inside out. If he could hang onto the corral long enough it would clear up.

Just when he had the plan all figured out, just when things were going to pan out all right if only he had the time, just when he was pulling out of his disgusting and abject helpless-ness—then Alexander saw him.

He came around the broken corner of the alley, the machete first, red and blue in the Tome Pacifico glare. Then the greasy and protruding belly, beneath a conical-shaped head, long Asiatic eyes and no neck. It was Mimi Jimenez come to see if Alexander had tried to beat it out the rear. Alexander could do nothing, his body still numbed and racked. His only sense of feeling was where his fingers dug into the rotted brick, his long form impaled against the decomposing and iron-shot wall. The only thing that could help him was that the Indian was borracho too. He seemed to be balancing himself with the silvery machete.

"Har you wanting to play, har you wanting to run away?" Mimi had a long silky mustache that would never need cut-ting; it seemed the only place on his face that hair would

grow. He used a soft musical, almost gentle voice. He said, "Har you going to make goddamn fool of Mexican by not keeping word?"

"I keep word," Alexander said almost as though he were trying to reassure himself, not speaking aloud.

"Makes no difference anyway. Lose everything anyway. Goddamn writer sonabitches talk against my wharf. Now everybody go watch American bazaball. Condemn my wharf for firetrap."

So that was it, Alexander thought. Mimi was going to blame him for everything that had ever happened to the poor wreck.

Mimi sidled up to Alexander now with an arrogance born out of Alexander's helplessness. The top of his conical head did not come up to Alexander's shoulder. As he rubbed closely Alexander could smell the reek of cheap mescal and perfume. Mimi raised the machete with a gliding motion and then lowering it slowly ticked off the buttons of Alexander's jacket with the razor-sharp edge. "You will never more need these," Mimi whispered.

Alexander knew he had no strength left, not even enough to hold himself up without grabbing the wall. But he could drop all his weight on him—Mimi Jimenez was directly under him now, slithering the machete down his side slowly as though measuring Alexander and at the same time planning a quick insane run down the alley while Alexander bled away in the gutter.

Abruptly Alexander dropped all his tall hulk on Mimi and felt him beneath his body like a gigantic inner tube. Alexander tried to grab and hold him but his arms were useless, still numbed. Alexander got up with an effort of violence and

with the same momentum began to run crazily down the narrow passage, careening from one hard wall to the other, feeling his hands and head scrape against the aged brick. And now he reached an intersection where there was no wall to careen off and he fell face down on the cobblestones, where he could hear the scrape of the retrieved machete, and he knew that Mimi was close again.

Alexander made it up once more, not feeling his legs under him as he made another long drunken dash. This time it ended falling through an open doorway, smashing into some wooden benches. His head was against another wall beneath the flickering light of two candles. The noise following had ceased now as though this particular doorway afforded some invisible bar to the pursuer, as though the doorway he had fallen through were some taboo, some sanctuary.

Some church, Alexander thought and glanced up past waving candles to the waxen face of a carved saint. He tilted his head toward the five-and-dime festooned altar, garish with tinsel, paper flowers, bloody saints and varicolored votive candles. There was no service at the altar, no movement in the church save around the confessional booths that stood like sentry boxes down the aisle.

Despite his noisy entrance Alexander seemed to be going unnoticed. Not that this happened every day but their ignoring it seemed to be their technique of discouraging it. A young woman in rags dropped a coin in the box above Alexander and exited with the weightlessness of the starved.

Alexander's head was commencing to ache, a long throbbing steady beat, and he could hear above the pain a low, low murmur from the confessional boxes. Cuántos veces? The voice of the priest repeated quickly. The priest was confess-

ing two people at once and Alexander noticed that there were
cubicle holes for three so that the priest was only working at
two thirds of his efficiency. Alexander wondered, watching
the somber aquiline face, if the young Jesuit was not up to
confessing the entire world—the universe. And if God Himself had walked up to the third cubicle, would not that
unassailable face murmur, Cuántos veces?—How many times?

Just when things were clearing up again, just when he
felt he had some control over his limbs, at this point he had
a relapse and he could no longer make sense out of anything
in the church. He could no longer see the things around him
properly or think about them at all. He could think of
Perrette and then he thought of Alfred and wondered what
Perrette and Alfred were doing. What would become of
George and his Indians? That would certainly be worth writing about and living about and that he would never know if
this insane Mexican had some luck when he stepped outside
the church.

Now he got back to Perrette, and Alexander was very very
unhappy that he had said such unkind things about her in his
last book, and no one could mistake who she was. He had
done everything but mention her name. Yes, one of his big
regrets, if the machete had any luck, would be that he had
talked too much in his books about the things that he knew
a great deal about, and although that was the way they told
you at the universities, why had he been fool enough to do
that? Why had he cheapened every experience in his last book
by telling the whole world about something that was none of
their business? He had not done it for money or fame because
he had both of these things when he started telling the truth.
No. He did it because he wanted to confound all those who

admired him, to be alone and the big cock of the walk. Instead of that, near death now— Near death now. The thought hit hard even into his numbed, insensitive brain and there was a surge through him to regroup himself, to organize some sort of resistance back here in the rear and make some attempt to break through to the reality of the reservation. Near death on the steps of a small Mexican church in a red-light district was not the way he had written it in any of his books. His last book did not count. Expatriates always die of self-inflicted wounds. He was repeating himself, he had already told the cab driver that. But he had not told the cab driver that they were administered by a gentleman named Boredom. But in his books that counted his heroes met their death for other people. On the surface it was something else that was mixed up with war paint and banners and fate and circumstances but beneath it all they were in control, they were not victims, they were not men that things happened to. They were men who had a healthy respect and fear of death but preferred it to watching human beings become not human beings.

No, this kind of gutter death here would not read well. It would make a lousy ending. It would give too much satisfaction to too many writers that Alexander thought had sold themselves cheaply. The fact that his friend Tolstoy had died in a railway shack didn't help any. After all, a railway shack could be associated with the working man but a gutter is associated with dead dogs and drunks.

And what can I be associated with now, Alexander wondered. His head was spinning and diving, huge colors tearing all over, with no sight. He felt the church tilt under him and he thought he saw the black, moldering Pieta above him

oozing blood and all of the altar seemed on fire, and before the blaze small men in black were struggling with a catafalque marked CIVILIZATION which in reality was only a horrendous emptiness that they were offering on the pyre. And their strugglings were a mere simulation of great effort to confuse the new arrivals that clustered around the now empty three cubicles of the Jesuit priest's inlaid sentry box for confessional. Now they all marched inside the box, first a man with his brother's wife, then they came two by two. Two wise men and two fools, two of everything and still they came. The inside of the box was neon lined and on the ceiling were the scalps of those that had been there before. Now they all began to dance around a hole in the floor that might have been a mine shaft. There was someone way down there at the bottom of the hole; they could hear him calling but they knew it was only a human being down there so they continued to dance. They did not seem to realize the scalps on the ceiling might be the scalps of the dancers who had been there before so they continued to dance. People dance. What's wrong with dancing? Let's all dance. Those scalps on the ceiling might be artificial and the people below us are different from you and me. Let's dance.

The priest had pulled Alexander now onto a hard wooden bench, had an altar cushion under his head and was administering convenient holy water.

"Usted está muy borracho," the young Jesuit said in a low voice.

"Cómo no en este país?" Alexander tried to answer to the dim voice that was coming through. "Why not drunk?" he said in English.

"It's a small matter," the priest said, following Alexander

into the new language.

"You turn a confessor out?" Alexander wanted to know, his heavy lips moving, his eyes still not open.

"We'll get you to a hotel," the priest said, ignoring the other's drunkenness.

"But I have come to confess," Alexander insisted with some roughness.

"We will get you some coffee and we will get you to a hotel." The young Jesuit continued to wipe Alexander's forehead with holy water.

"I want to confess that I never should have tried to live among the whites, be tough. It must be that I am really a gentle Indian."

"But you're white. You're white."

"You grow up with the Esquimos and you're an Esquimo. You grow up with the Indians and—" Alexander broke it off and then said, "His wife."

"Whose wife?"

"My brother's."

"Then you have something to confess."

"It's too late," Alexander said.

"There is one God," the young priest said.

Alexander got up, stumbled. "I got to see a medicine man," he said. "I need the whole treatment."

"But someone is pursuing," the priest said. "I saw someone with a machete."

"I can take him," Alexander said, standing up deliberately. "I feel good enough to take him."

"I'll call a taxi and get you to a hotel," the young priest insisted.

"I tell you I can take him," Alexander said. "Anyway it's

not whether I can take him or I can't take him. You just don't run away from things, that's all."

"You are being—what is the word?—silly," the young priest said.

"No. It used to be courage. I don't know what it is called now. In my youth in the Indian Country it went for courage. Maybe they use 'silly' now but I guess I just never grew up. I mean by that, that when people grow up they lose everything that it's convenient for them to lose when the going gets rough."

"Black coffee," the priest pronounced.

"No, I'm this way most of the time," Alexander said, leaning against the big wooden door now. Then he turned heavily away from the young priest and started going down the long low steps. He could hear the high voice of the implacable Jesuit call down, "Black coffee. Many times."

The soft night air across Alexander's face cleared the fuzz off his vision to the extent that he almost did not miss the step that he did miss, that sent him crashing down on the hard stone. He worked himself quickly into a sitting position on the standstone and wondered why he had been fool enough to trust his rubbery legs at this stage. He would need a little more of the night air before he tried it again. Perhaps the priest had a point with his black coffee.

"Har you tired, my fran? My goddamn sonabitch writer fran." It was the low intimate voice of the assassin, mi amigo Jimenez.

It wasn't fair, Alexander thought, that after he had built up characters in his books so carefully, so that everything they did and thought was well motivated and inevitable, he should have it out finally with a weakly drawn insane.

251

"Sit down and build yourself up," Alexander said, touching the still sun-warm, rough stone alongside him.

Alexander listened but heard no reply from behind him, no noise of movement or even sense of presence of his very good friend.

Alexander was feeling set up. This was the way to handle them—to ignore them or treat them with extreme lightness. Yes, he thought, Mimi would not even be worth a line in the book; he would reduce him to the myriad background; he would relegate him to one of those same anonymous faces that stared out at his war-painted hero from some continuous neon, burro alley saloon or bright banana patch. Why did I run from him at all? It was in the manner in which you would run from a bad odor, the reek wind of humanity, when all a person in my profession would have to do is slam the door with a few chosen words.

Yes, Alexander was feeling better. He even straightened himself a little on the hard steps in front of the cathedral. Alexander Bowman felt that soon he would be back in Indian Country. Then the full, heavy blow of the wide quick blade, going all the way, entered his back just to the side of his right shoulder and above his heart.

"Brother!" he whispered heavily into his big clenched wet hands.

There was an awful quiet in front of the dark cathedral as Mimi Jimenez stood straight a moment and took it all into his small, unsteady eyes before adjusting himself and then trotting softly across the alley to get on the winding street marked Boy Heroes of Chapultepec.

17

Indian country. That's what the train whistle blew, blasting out the syllables as clear as flame. When the train got going the big drivers picked up the rhythm—Indian Country—Indian Country—Indian Country. Now it stopped. It might never get going again. It was a very old train.

"It will get here any day now," Jack said, placing a nugget-studded watch back in his pants. "Like I said, I'm wanted back in Indian Country under the improbable name of Diamond Jack." Jack touched the long pine box. "He wasn't wanted back there under any name at all."

The six Americans were crowded in a bar, huddled around a box, waiting for the tired train, somewhere near the station in Mazatlán, Mexico. The man in the cowboy outfit, Jack, sat on the box. The two Americans closest to the box, Alfred Marlowe and Charles Bentley, asked the questions. Alfred's face was drained and poetic too, if he would remove the eagerness, which he never did, and Bentley was in tweeds and had graying hair above a too youthful face that was listening now.

"Yes," Jack said. "Man has bred hisself out of room and man is done finished. Indian Country's the only place left

where a man can stretch his arms without breaking another's radiator."

"Yes," Charles Bentley said. "The Indian Country is even more, I suppose, then you presume it to be. But we want to know— Some of us, have come all this way—" He pointed to the others.

Jack looked at the others, then back to his drink, shifted his weight importantly on the box and then looked back to the others. It must be that they had all been Alexander Bowman's friends, Jack thought, except Perrette. She had at least been married to him. Perrette drank slowly and steadily, lifting her drinks with a regular rhythm to a superbly composed face, poised and invulnerable, all-wise and absolutely certain. Insane, Jack thought. Ready for the bughouse. Either that or the rest of us are. The others, Jack thought, were in some way connected with Alexander's business, or profession I guess they call it when you write. But not those two Negro ball players who were drifting with self-consciousness on the fringe of the group in the dim bar in Mazatlán, Mexico.

"A long way back to Indian Country," Jack said importantly and aloud and probably to annoy Charles Bentley and Alfred Marlowe. Jack shifted again on the long pine box, possessively and with a vanity as though he occupied a stage and the others were an audience.

"What do you two Negroes want?" Jack said.

"It's a public place," one of the Negroes said from the darkness he matched. "We don't have to want anything. Me and Leroy got the same rights as anybody else to be here or anyplace else. No one's goin' to push us—"

"Did you know him?" Jack said.

"Yes," Leroy said, the voice coming from back there

somewhere in the darkness he was mated to, the light as he spoke catching a gold highlight.

"Then I'm sorry," Jack said. "Perhaps one of these gentlemen will buy you a drink."

Alfred ordered more drinks and the Negro ball players pressed closer to the pine box. They still had their bright jackets on with GUAYMAS written across their chests.

Jack, Alfred thought, was maybe fifty-five, sixty or seventy years old. His age was hard to come by, concealed in a long and lank and wind-burnt and finely wrinkled face and a figure that had been horse-bent at nineteen. The Bull Durham string and label that dangled from his striped shirt pocket was impossible to come by in this part of Mexico so it was a badge, a kind of campaign ribbon, of the Indian Country, along with the boots and spurs too.

"So," Jack said, "first I'll fill you in on the—what do you call it?"

"Background," Charles Bentley said.

"That's correct," Jack said. "If you stand at one point in the Indian Country, say near Window Rock—well, I don't know. Say near—"

"Brooklyn." It was Perrette who spoke between the rhythm of raising the glass of straight American whiskey toward her youthful face. Youth—an age you grew out of except Perrette. She grew more into it. More into youth, excitement and new things. Youth, and finally now into this triumphant childishness, alone and absolutely dependent, sipping her whiskey like milk.

"Like I was saying," Jack said, "standing near Nargeezi." Jack rolled a cigarette with one hand as though a conjuring trick to pull them all closer, but the audience was listening

anyway. Even Perrette paused now to get her bearings in this darkening Mexico.

"Of course this Indian Country's in New Mexico," Jack said. "All sage and mesquite, greasewood and dry, very dry. There is the Colorado mountains off to the north and east and that peak to the south and east is Sandia. After they concentrated the Indians in a camp and died off half of them they give them this plateau, dry, very dry, that was up for grabs with no takers. Alkali and such. No water. Kit Carson," Jack said.

"But we didn't come here for a historical—"

"No. To get the story," Jack said. "But there's no story without—what's the word you use?"

"Background," Charles Bentley said.

"Correct," Jack said. "Well, maybe Kit Carson wasn't the hero."

"I quit," Charles Bentley said. "But there is a story someplace in these woods and I will settle for your part in it."

"That's what he did—quit," Jack said. Jack had worked the cigarette up to his mouth finally and lit it with the same hand like a one-armed man. "Quit and took to trading with the Indians. Just traveling around trading without a gun among the brutal, warlike savages who must be killed or concentrated in a camp."

"That was in Alexander's book," Bentley said.

"Yes. Well, he finally settled down with a post and ranch in the Cuba country."

"All right," Alfred said. "That was in the book too. But how about the brothers now?"

"Now?" Jack said and he tapped the box.

"I mean," Alfred said, "did Georgo and Alex get along all

right as brothers will? Did this thing happen quickly?"

"Nothing happens quickly," Jack said. "It never does. That's just the word they use out of laziness to explain what happened. When you're going to steal some fine cows you don't do it quickly. You study them a long time to figure if they're worth it. Maybe you are taken quickly by their beauty when you first see them, but after that the act itself takes a long time. Between the day you spot the animal you want and the day you cut the fence takes a long time."

"But how long did it take with them?" Bentley looked at the box and then over at Perrette. "She's not much help to us," Bentley said.

"You need a drink, Ole Hoss," Perrette said dully.

"But first you got to see it, how it was before she came there," Jack said. "Corn as high as an old shoe where people try to grow the stuff that don't belong there. Nothing belongs there that grows well anyplace else. Indian Country's the place for everything that the rest of the world's trying to get shut of—Russian thistle, chamise, grama grass, the Bowmans, myself."

"You don't think there was a place for them then on the outside?" Bentley nodded toward the box. "Among us?"

"No," Jack said. "They was Christians. I guess no place for them anywhere in the world. Leastwise not in any Christian country."

"But you knew his father," Alfred said.

"Yes. I used to steal quite a bit from him. A fine man," Jack said.

"But there was nothing in him that could have led to this?"

"Yes. He used to read," Jack said. The others waited patiently for him to begin again, studying over their drinks.

"By reading I mean that it got his sons in the habit of reading. It did no harm to him. He had lived long enough on the outside to be able to allow ample for the lies and prettifying of the men who wrote about the outside. And the stuff they wrote about Indian Country didn't confuse him either of course. But his son Alexander here," he tapped the box, "was ready to believe most anything he read about the outside. George, the other son, he went off to a war. That's where he found out. But Alexander never went anyplace except to a university before she came." He nodded toward Perrette. "I guess there's nothing more to unfit a man for life on the outside than a university."

"I used to teach in one," Bentley said.

"I figgered so," Jack said.

The two Negroes crowded toward the center now to where the others were grouped around the man who sat on the long pine box. The Negro named Leroy went down on his haunches alongside the box, then reached out and touched it.

"I knew him well enough," the Negro said. "He is titled to his privacy. If he wanted people on the outside to know about his life he would have written it. That's what he was, a writer, wasn't he?"

The big Negro still standing, said, "We didn't come for the story. We came for the funeral—the funeral of an artist."

"There ain't goin' to be one," Jack said.

The assembly moved over to the bar as the waiter set out the new drinks. They leaned over the drinks in an attitude of prayer.

"We just set it down in here awhile out of the sun," Jack said. "We're taking it to the train."

"No," Bentley said. "There couldn't be a funeral. I guess

258

all you would want the preacher to say would be. 'The poor son of a bitch.' I guess you couldn't hire one to say that and nothing more—not even that."

Bentley paused and someone went on. "How did he become a writer? I mean there must have been something honest—I mean plenty of opportunities—"

"He figured," Bentley said, "there had been so much dishonest sentimentality written about his country, the Southwest, by people all the way from dying Englishmen to those who gather in Santa Fe to read their gems to each other that he— Anyway he wanted to right wrongs."

"Oh, the poor son of a bitch!"

"No matter," Bentley said, "what original justification or cause he had for beginning writing, later on it can't be stopped. It becomes a habit, a disease."

"Like rustling," Jack said.

"Yes," Bentley said, not listening. "But about the Bowmans, I don't want to extrapolate—"

"Not near this box," Jack said.

"I mean," Bentley continued, "I don't want to put words in your mouth but was there something different—?"

"They was human," Jack said.

"Not really?" Bentley said.

"They was Bowmans," Jack tried again.

"But what was different about Bowmans?"

"Well, for one thing they had this peetrified-wood house."

"Then what happened to this one, Alexander? Did your damn petrified-wood house burn down?"

"Nope," Jack said.

"Then bring us up to date, to the brothers."

"This one's dead," Jack said.

"You're a big help, Jack," Bentley said, walking up to the bar with the others. Bentley took Jack to one side. "I'd like to get all the information I can on him. I'm planning a book—"

"He's gone," Jack said. "Someone's done made off with him."

"What?" Bentley said.

"The box," Jack said. "When we come up here to the bar I left the box back there. Now it's gone."

"No need to alarm the others," Bentley said. "Some fool Mexican saw you guarding it, thought it was something valuable, waited for his chance and made off with it. No need to alarm the others. We'll slip out the back here and have a look around. They'll abandon it when they pry it open and see it's worthless."

"Worthless?" Jack said.

"Yes," Bentley said. "Now we go right through this opening."

They stepped into an alley.

"Now here," Bentley said. They stepped into another bar.

"We'll wait them out," Bentley said. "Give them a chance to take it to their hideout, den, whatever word they use. Give them time to pry it open and discover it's worthless."

"Worthless?" Jack said.

"Yes," Bentley said. "Two beers, please."

"Por favor?"

"Two beers," Bentley said louder.

Bentley looked around the adobe, cool room, clean and empty, white-washed pink, then out into the hot street.

"Nothing doing now," Bentley said. "We'll keep our eye on the alley." Bentley watched Jack examine his watch with

style and then begin a cigarette. He doesn't tell time or make cigarettes, he performs, Bentley thought, and then he said, "That Alfred, I guess he wants material too. Material for a story. And those two Negro ball player friends of his, they want—"

"A funeral," Jack said.

"Now, Perrette," Bentley said. "When I first saw her in Europe she was painting a picture. It was very bad and she was quite pleased with it. I was editing a small magazine in Paris. I was embarassed about asking Alexander for anything because the magazine paid very little for stories."

"How little?" Jack asked.

"Well, we didn't pay anything," Bentley said.

"That's little enough. Two more beers," Jack said.

"I scout around now," Bentley said, "for a movie company that pays plenty."

"Make that two whiskeys," Jack said.

"You want the beer or the whiskeys?" the bartender said.

Jack stared at the man, who wore a big mustache on a round red face with a conservative, gray Homburg hat that had had the brim torn off.

"Both," Jack said.

"Well, I guess I'm not going to get very far with my story," Bentley said.

"I apologize," Jack said and he drank the whiskey. "A movie company. I apologize. I take off my hat. A movie company." Jack tipped his hat and the bartender touched his too.

"Well, now," Bentley said, "about the book. There should be a market for memoirs by people who knew him, now that there's been this trouble."

"Trouble?" Jack said.

"Well, death," Bentley said.

"That's trouble enough," Jack said. "Go ahead."

"I first ran into them on the boat, then again in Europe—"

"But where is he now?" Jack asked.

Bentley watched Jack take out his nugget-studded watch again, examine it and return it to his pants.

"I don't know," Bentley said, without humor. "I'm not a religious man."

"But we're supposed to be looking for him," Jack said. "I've set myself to see that this box gets on the train and back to—" Jack waved away some of the smoke to find his position in relation to the brimless gray Homburg of the bartender.

"From here," Bentley said, "we can cover the alley and beyond that you can see the plaza. From a well-stocked, well-located bar one good man might cover the whole country."

"Yes," Jack said, "if the whiskey held out. You said you met him again in Europe."

"Hello, Alfred," Bentley said.

Alfred Marlowe had entered, taken a seat at the bar and ordered a crème de menthe.

"Oh, no," Jack said.

"It seems," Bentley said to Alfred, "it seems that Alexander here—"

"Where?" Jack said.

"Oh, incidentally," Alfred said. "We have found him."

"Where?" Jack said.

"Those two Negroes, the ones advertising Guaymas on their chests, they have taken him to a church."

"Church?" Jack said. "Come on," he said, touching Alfred. "We've got to rescue him, bring him back here, wait

for the train, take him back home and save his damn soul."

"Soul?" Bentley said to the bartender when they were alone. "Words are my business, yet I never knew quite what that one meant."

"In Spanish, alma," the bartender said. He pushed down on his brimless gray Homburg and then gestured emptily in the air. "It means nothing."

"Exactly," Bentley said. "Won't you join me?" The bartender poured himself a tequila.

Bentley looked out into the alley and back to the bartender.

"He got back to Mexico. That's as far as he got."

Bentley looked around the clean adobe room, out into the hot alley and over to the plane-tree-shadowed plaza. He could see too the corner of the gold-striped brothel and beyond and above that the slightly leaning tower of the church.

"Yes," Bentley said. "But now he will go all the way."

Outside Alfred paused. "No, I can't face him again," he said.

"He's dead," Jack said.

"He has passed over to the ages."

"Well, I reckon we'll still have to do something about him," Jack said.

Alfred leaned against the adobe wall of the cantina.

"How about a funeral pyre on the beach? That's what Byron did for Shelley."

"That's what who did for what?" Jack said.

"They were men without a home," Alfred said.

"Well, Alexander's got one and I'm fixin' to get ready to take him back. Back to Indian Country," Jack said.

"Yes. Then take him home," Alfred said. "That would be nice. A home would be nice. I was brought up under the influence of oil myself. We had about five houses located any place in Texas that was close to a very large bank. But no matter. I will found another magazine and Perrette can do the art work. People who have four or five houses apiece should stay together I guess and found polo teams or magazines against homelessness. Your taking Alexander home would be nice. He has luck to have a home. Your taking him back would be very decent. I cannot face him again myself but tell him this for me. Tell him I'm damn sorry. Tell him I'm awfully, awfully sorry. But tell him he made it. Tell him he will last."

Alfred looked up. Jack was gone.

Yes, Alfred thought. Yes. Yes.

Jack walked toward the falling-down railway station that backed up on the plaza. The two huge black Negro ball players were carrying the coffin easily toward the tired, long train that had finally arrived.

"They wouldn't do any good at the church," the leading Negro, Leroy, said as Jack came up. "They said he did not have the right religion."

"That's what they all say," Jack said. "Slide it in here."

They slid the box through the car entranceway until it rested between the seats.

"I don't know what religion you two fine gentlemen have got," Jack said. "But more people ought to get it." Jack sat down on the old velvet car chair next to the box. "Yes," Jack said, "if we had more Americans like you scattered around the world we could get shut of our ambassadors."

"Thank you," the Negroes said, leaving.

Jack tapped some of the Bull Durham into the clean white paper and arranged himself for a long trip. "And a right smart idea," Jack said.

Jack leaned over and raised the worn green window shade as the the train began to jerk, trying to get off. Outside Jack could see no one at all across the bare plaza. No one at all had come to see the train leave. Finally a figure, a woman, emerged from a bar on the far side of the plaza and began running now obliquely across the square. The train was slow and soon she was running alongside the train. She raised her arm when the train picked up speed, and as she began to fall back now she cried, "Good-by, Ole Hoss."

18

The slow black train that was working its way up the aged, worn track that writhed like a pair of shaken steel ropes along the Gulf of Baja California paused each mealtime so that those riding and hanging on to the train could eat. They built fires alongside the train in the morning and at noon, with vendors carrying things on their heads and women with great baskets selling things and putting things on the train. At Mazatlán they put something big on the train and when the train paused that dark evening at Culiacán they lit the long string of miniature dancing fires; they reflected against the aquiline, slanting Indio faces and the glittering machetes. The glare lay somber now, then leapt up in sharp pennants and, like small fires of hell, they silhouetted everything in grotesque. It was raining.

At Mazatlán a long box had been put on the very slow old train with coaches that had been discarded a long time ago from the fast, bright trains in the United States. Some of the coaches still had the frosted glass light globes in the shape of tulips. One of the Victorian tulip light globes shone on the long box the two days it took to make the trip to the border at Nogales.

Jack sat on the outside aisle in a velveted, old-fashioned chair next to the long box. When the train was jammed with people, animals and fowl at Huatabampo, some of the lady Mexicans, carrying wicker baskets crowded with gay-plumaged roosters, sat on the long box and Jack fed them cigarettes and candy and Wild West stories to pass the time of day. At Guaymas Jack explained to them about the long box and no one would sit on it now. One Mexican lady had three red-headed Muscovy ducks tied together with cactus fiber inside her coat with their three bright heads sticking out watching the world go by between her breasts, also watching while the Mexican lady put a flower on the long box.

The border at Nogales was as far as Jack dared to go but he stood quietly with his enormous hat in his hand while they transferred the long box to the bright United States train and then he went quickly and got himself the drink he needed.

At the Nogales side there were some people who watched the transfer too. They had come from the Arizona towns of Twin Buttes, Tubac and Pomerene. There were not many of them but they were there and they all had a small bunch of flowers they placed on the long box. The same thing happened when the Super Chief pulled into Flagstaff and at every town where the Super Chief stopped. It was still raining.

There were some New York and Hollywood people on the train going back and forth, back and forth to New York and Hollywood and Hollywood and New York. When they discovered who the other passenger was some cried and some told reminiscences but they all got drunk. When the train approached Albuquerque a whisper ran through the long,

gliding train that the passenger was getting off and no one seemed to have much more to say. There was a deep, still hush now above the clickety click, clickety click, clickety click of the Super Chief.

"A man steals his wife and he goes to all this trouble to take care of him after a man steals his wife."

"Sansi tells me that Alexander wanted to see the whole world."

"But he took the wife of Sansi and left Sansi all alone and lonely with nothing to provide for except us miserable Indians. He stole the wife of his brother."

"We cannot take without taking from our brother," the medicine man said.

Paracelsus, the medicine man, was talking to Coyotes-Love-Me, but there were as many Indians as could get in the trader's blue pickup waiting on the railway platform in Albuquerque—waiting for the Super Chief that was bringing the long box. The long box would make a seat for the Indians that had to sit on the floor of the pickup on the long trip down from the checkerboard.

"A man steals his wife and he writes the man a letter telling him it's all right now, it does not hurt as much as it used to hurt, anyway it does not hurt as much as your not coming home hurts, as much as it hurts you and hurts me and hurts The People, your having no home to come to. It must hurt until something breaks. . . ."

"He was a lot of years writing a letter like your letter."

"Yes, he was a lot of years but he finished it, his writing of the letter. He finished it three days ago. He must have finished it about the same time something broke in the other

country. And these last days he has been carrying it, switching it from one hand to the other, looking for a place to mail it, wanting to mail it but knowing there was no place to mail it to. He could have written it, finished it, mailed it maybe, a long time ago, when there was someplace, someone, a brother, to mail it to, but he was a Bowman, a white man, a human too. Things keep getting in the way," Quicker-Than-You said.

A group of the Indians were huddled in the corner near the ticket office because the wind, cutting with rain, was blowing across the platform. George Bowman was standing alone with a small white envelope in his big hand, in the middle of the platform, upright against the rain, waiting for his brother, Alexander Bowman, and the Indians were letting him alone.

"A man steals his wife and the other man spends all night digging a grave on top of an impossible mountain."

"A brother steals from a brother and the brother spends all night digging on the impossible mountain," Paracelsus said.

"It sounds worse the way you put it," Quicker-Than-You said.

"No, you can't steal another person. You can only make a chance they were waiting for. It's hard to get a white woman to live among the miserable Indians. If Alexander had not stolen Sansi's wife the miserable Indians might have lost Sansi."

"Isn't that kind of selfish of the miserable Indians?" the Marquis of Steyne said.

"It may have been," the medicine man said. "The all-knowing whites might have been able to use one like him."

The band of Navahos watched while the trader, standing

alone on the big platform, faced into the blowing rain as they could all make out the growing hum of the distant Super Chief.

"I rode down in front with Sansi," the medicine man said. "I rode down in front with Sansi and he didn't say much. But he said his brother was an artist. I said yes but even an artist cannot smash things and he said that was not too important. The important thing was the work. I said yes but you don't let people smash things. Not if they can't make something better you don't, he said."

As the Super Chief wound into the station it could not seem to make up its mind exactly where it wanted to stop. It went forward and backward twice with the bunch of Indians chasing the baggage car back and forth, back and forth. There was the danger of something becoming a comedy.

The Hollywood and New York people had their faces pressed against the glass of the club car watching to see their passenger get off. There was enough curve to the track and with the long make-up of the Super Chief they could watch the Indians chasing the baggage car.

"It would make a good shot," someone in the club car, holding a very dry martini, said.

The Indians had caught the baggage car now and they banged on the side of the train with a stick and waited for the great door to slide open. The tall white man with a huge black Stetson who was alone on the platfrom held onto his hat and leaned into the rain-heavy wind as he made his way to the freight window to clear the long pine box.

The Indians had made the door of the Super Chief open now and they all crowded forward as the whites inside pushed the long pine box to the edge of the car with their feet. The

Indians reached in and slid the long box until it pointed toward them. Then as they pulled it out a pair of Indians, one from either side, put their shoulders under it. Quicker-Than-You and Rabbit Stockings were first, then More Wives and Lord Acton, then the Marquis of Steyne and Coyotes-Love-Me, then Tom-Dick-and-Harry and Silver Threads. Paracelsus, the medicine man, led the way with Lord Rundle holding on and guiding the end of the box. When the white dispatcher tried to stop them, demanding a piece of paper, Tom-Dick-and-Harry hollered from beneath the coffin, "Go to hell, man, and get out of the way!"

When they got to the blue pickup the white dispatcher was still trying to hold up the parade and he kept interfering until the trader, the tall, lank man in the big black hat who had been standing alone on the platform, came up and handed him a piece of paper for the box.

Paracelsus dropped the tail gate and they slid the long box into the blue pickup, each pair of Indians letting go with their shoulders as their portion of the box reached the deck. When the long box was safely in, the Indians climbed aboard and took seats on either edge of the box so none faced each other and they could all see everything that happened.

The Super Chief began to blow a high message now that she was going to leave. The people in the club car still had their faces pressed against the glass of the window as she began to move.

"A damn good show," the man still holding the very dry martini said.

On the long trip back to the Indian Country Paracelsus and Rabbit Stockings sat in the front cab with the trader. There was a Montgomery Ward car radio beneath the dash

and Paracelsus turned on the Indian station in Gallup.

"What does an Indian want most?" the announcer said. He let the audience think about that for a while as he played a chant on the turntable.

"Money!" The announcer was back on again now. "Money. And you can get all you want from the Indian's white friend, Lending Sam Sepowsky, 999 Welter Street, Gallup. 999 Welter Street, Gallup."

The announcer played another chant but first he gave the Indians something more to think about. "How would all you forward-looking Indians like a used Lincoln to make you feel like you belonged? The Indian's friend, T. Texas Taylor, has permitted me to say that this car will be given to the first Indian who arrives on the lot with nine hundred ninety nine dollars and ninety-five cents. Never forget the Indian's friend who makes this offer possible, T. Texas Taylor. I repeat, the Indian's friend, T. Texas Taylor."

"You going to stop at the Casino de Paree for some gas?" Rabbit Stockings said.

"I filled her up at the Gulf in Cuba this morning. I should have plenty," George said, watching the road and thinking about something else.

"The boys all gave me a little to pay for the gas. They'd like to pay for this trip. So if you'll stop at the Casino de Paree."

"Okay," George said.

It was a long way to the Casino de Paree and the announcer from the Indian station in Gallup did not help much. In the back of the pickup the boys were getting a taste of weather their wives had on every trip.

"I hope he stops at the Casino de Paree," Tom-Dick-and-Harry said.

The road from Albuquerque to the checkerboard area swings gradually but steadily up and up. You leave the flat country of the Pueblo people not long after you cross the Rio Grande at Bernalillo but you do not get to the country of The People for a long time. There is not much in between. First there is the ranch country where you can run one head to thirty acres, then there is the country where you can run one head to forty acres and then the country where you run one cow to sixty acres. Anyway, by the time you get to the checkerboard area you've got to cut way down on everything. But all the way up is beautiful. It is the country where those who are called paleontologists find fossils that prove things about the whole world, where the uranium hunters are certain they will find something to change that world. And here there is mostly beauty; beauty in the long, high, ever-running-alongside-you cliffs; beauty even in the deadly erosions that are killing the earth; and beauty in the pure blue distant spaces with the Brahma-bull-shaped, cloud-hung mountains rising like other countries in another land; beauty that the blue Chevvy pickup was chasing through with quickness up to the top of the blue mesa. Up to the high, sighting-clearly-everywhere top of the blue mesa to a grave a brother had dug.

Between every Navaho chant he played the announcer would never let the people in the blue pickup alone.

"How would all you Indians like a conservative drape-shape to show that you belong? When you go some place you want them to say, 'There goes somebody.' Be somebody. Show them that you belong. See Dress Up Sam, the Indian's

273

Indian. They will say, 'There goes somebody who belongs.' The secret medicine is Dress Up Sam, the Indian's Indian. Sam, spelled S.A.M. Sam remembers you. Remember Dress Up Sam, the Indian's Indian."

This went on for another hour between chants and then they were pulling into the Casino de Paree. The Casino de Paree was a two-story hogan that appeared to be strapped together, lashed tightly to keep it from falling down, with neon tubing. Their first and last floor show was given by a medicine man who lost so much face he left the reservation and tried acting in wrestling but was last heard from making a comeback leading an evangelist rally in Stockholm. The neon tubing had never lighted up since its construction a lot of moons ago but there had always been plans to replace the gasoline Colemans any day now. When they entered the place Liquor Joe was seated in back of the bar with his hair properly tied in a bun on the back of his neck. When they had all yatayed each other More-Wives-Than-Anyone asked what the floor show was going to be tonight.

"Greta Garbo," Liquor Joe said.

"Every night Greta Garbo," Lord Acton said.

"Popular acclaim," Liquor Joe said. "Anyway she's all we can afford."

The Indians went around the place examining and looking under things until Liquor Joe set a bottle of Old Moccasin on the bar in a spot where it had long since burned a ring.

"What you boys drinking?" Liquor Joe said.

"Pepsi-Colas all around," Silver Threads said, letting a picture slide back that he was looking under.

"Big-time Indians," Liquor Joe said, getting the Pepsis. "Did you strike oil on the checkerboard?"

"Uranium," Quicker-Than-You said. "Soon as you get lights in here we're going to make a big bang."

"Big-time comedian," Liquor Joe said, opening up the Pepsis. "You give the Indians a nice place like on the outside and they run it down with bad talk."

"Haven't you heard," Quicker-Than-You said, "we Indians are victims of a one-way stream of acculturization. The whites are forcing the worst of what they got off on us and accepting nothing of our culture in return. So we are both becoming poorer. What I am trying to tell you is your whiskey is lousy."

"Planning a book or are you going to run for something?" Liquor Joe said, stroking his bottle.

The Indians continued to drink their Pepsis and look under things at the same time.

Liquor Joe stared out of the window and then suddenly his head gave a little jerk.

"What's that you got on the pickup?" No one answered him and he said, "Indians shouldn't get too close to something like that."

"You better fill her up with gas," Tom-Dick-and-Harry said.

Liquor Joe put down his bottle and moved toward the door as George came in.

"I filled her up," George said. "Ten and a half gallons."

"You probably could use a drink," Tom-Dick-and-Harry said.

"Yes."

Liquor Joe made a movement toward a shot glass with his favorite bottle but the trader shook his head and Liquor Joe got out another bottle and filled the glass. George dropped a small white envelope into his pocket and drank the drink

down with haste and allowed Rabbit Stockings to pay for it from the fund. This was their day.

When they got the Chevvy pickup going good again they were hitting her along at sixty miles an hour, which is about all the Aztec-Bernalillo road will take; with the highway right-angling through the Chinle purple formations and sharp twisting through the red of the Wingate you have to be able to cut her down quickly. Signs like SLOW TO 40 and SLOW TO 35 went by. Signs like SLOW CURVE and signs like DANGEROUS WINDING ROAD went by.

"He did not know when to cut her down," Rabbit Stockings said.

George Bowman pulled down his hat. "He was going someplace," he said.

"Fast."

"Fast."

"He had to see the whole world," Rabbit Stockings said.

'But things keep getting in the way," Paracelsus said.

The blue Chevvy pickup was going through the old Spanish grant of Ojo del Espiritu Santo. It ran flat on both sides of them forever; way back up there someplace it ran into the Jemez Mountains. The elk and the deer and the bear and the mountain lions came down when no one could see them and took what they could from Cass Goodner, who leased part of the grant. Cass Goodner's cattle came down to where everyone could see them if it was not branding time or herding time. Now as the Chevvy approached it was time for them to stand exactly in the middle of the road. Several older bulls seemed to have thought the idea up and stood in front of the four hundred head, their front legs planted apart, heads down, defiant, waiting for the Chevvy pickup to make the next move.

The Chevvy pickup crept up to them slowly, cautiously, and then began to feel its way between the forward bulls; one of the bulls pawed, tried to plant his feet within the asphalt as the blue fender touched him gently and shoved him to one side. As the rear of the pickup went by Silver Threads reached out and patted his great head. He let out an enormous bellow. The game was up now and the rest of the cattle drifted slowly to both sides of the black pavement.

"Cass Goodner should have made steer out of those bulls. They'll cause him a lot of trouble."

"You can't make them all into steers," George said.

"Certain ones you can."

"Let's drop it," George said.

"I didn't mean to be rough, Sansi."

"I know you didn't, boy. It's all right."

In the rear of the pickup all the Indians were perched forward watching everything go by. They were in the Indian Country now and they felt better except Tom-Dick-and-Harry, who did not know where he was.

Tom-Dick-and-Harry was sucking a bottle. He had borrowed some of the fund and bought a fifth from Liquor Joe when no one was watching. He did not know where he was now or what he had done now, but all the Indian Country and all the white country, no matter what, looked rosy; everything looked fine. He set down the bottle on the long box when they left the pavement for the checkerboard area. As they began to climb and twist up the final mesa that looked down upon their hogans, the bottle fell over and before he could retrieve it a lot of the precious stuff had bled down between the cracks in the coffin.

After much twisting and turning and shifting down into

277

compound low they were on top of the long high mesa finally and the pickup stopped. The Indians piled out of the pickup and slid the coffin out, each pair taking it on the shoulder as it came off; Silver Threads and Paracelsus were a pair; Coyotes-Love-Me and the Marquis of Steyne were a pair; Rabbit Stockings and Lord Acton were a pair; More Wives and Quicker-Than-You were a pair. Tom-Dick-and-Harry just sat alone on the tail gate of the pickup examining the bottle in which there was nothing more.

The Navahos walked the coffin with measured, synchronized step to the edge of the grave, then they lowered it gently to the ground, where they tied a leather thong and then they lowered it, still gently, beneath the ground until it touched.

As George had left the pickup something—a letter—dropped out of his pocket. He recovered it and now, as he stood alone above the grave, he kept switching the letter from one big, dry, hot hand to the other. There did not seem to be any place for it at all. He felt someone, the medicine man, take the letter gently from him and then he saw it flutter quietly into the grave of Alexander Bowman, his brother. It made no sound when it finally touched.

All of the Navahos stood in peace above the grave for a long minute before they turned and made their way on foot down the high, blue mesa. Now, and for the last time, they would leave the brothers alone.

When the Navahos reached the bottom of the mesa and started along the long flat prairie of the Indian Country, by turning and looking far far up they could see a spade working, brightly signaling in the rain that soon something would be all over. The Navahos knew that, from way up there

with the wide clear sky of the Indian Country, Alexander could see and feel the whole world.

One of the Indians, before he entered his hogan, looked up one final time to the long blue mesa. Now he raised his turquoise-ringed arm to the sky and shouted into the deep, pure distance above, "Go in beauty."